All the Signs

"*All the Signs* is a charming story about love, family, and fate. Jessie Rosen has written delightful and entertaining characters that draw you in and immediately and steal your heart. Once you pick up this book you won't want to put it down!"

—Jennifer Close, bestselling author of *Marrying the Ketchups*

"Jessie has crafted another charming and dreamy journey whisking readers around the world as we follow our heroine's heartfelt and relatable search for purpose."

—Nikki Erlick, *New York Times* bestselling author of *The Measure*

"*All the Signs* is a quirky journey of self-discovery, as a woman wrestles with and ultimately embraces astrology's power—not to dictate who we are, but to reveal who we're meant to be."

—KJ Dell'Antonia, *New York Times* bestselling author of *The Chicken Sisters*

"An immersive, relatable story about eventually finding your way and living life more authentically. Readers will be swept away by Rosen's descriptive prose as Leah travels city by city in search of answers. An enjoyable read from start to finish!"

—Suzanne Park, author of *One Last Word*

Praise for

The Heirloom

"Dazzling . . . [with] a colorful cast of characters and vivid imagery that'll take you on a mental vacation, you'll fall in love with Shea as she investigates the truth about her ring. The most appropriate book to bring with you on a European holiday."
—The Knot

"Marvelous . . . *The Heirloom* is an impressive debut with a gorgeous, heartfelt ending."
—*Shelf Awareness*

"An earnest exploration of the trauma that can follow the children of divorce into adulthood . . . that emphasizes female autonomy and independence."
—*Kirkus Reviews*

"Snappy and compelling."
—*Library Journal*

"Rosen's captivating debut features strong family ties, tons of superstition, and romance. Rebecca Serle fans will enjoy this novel."
—*Booklist*

"Heartfelt and beautifully told, *The Heirloom* is mystery wrapped in a love story that calls into question the very subjective meaning we attach to family stories. Five stars for sure."
—Annabel Monaghan, author of *Nora Goes Off Script* and *Same Time Next Summer*

"A sparkling globe-trotting adventure that is both heartfelt and hilarious. This novel is a must-read for anyone who has ever dared to shape their own destiny."
—Jo Piazza, author of *The Sicilian Inheritance*

"Jessie Rosen has created a charming and propulsive international trip, with wanderlust balanced by a grounded truth: there's no place like the home we find in ourselves and with the people we love."
—Avery Carpenter Forrey, author of *Social Engagement*

Also by Jessie Rosen

The Heirloom

All the
Signs

A Novel

Jessie Rosen

G. P. Putnam's Sons
New York

PUTNAM
— EST. 1838 —
G. P. PUTNAM'S SONS
Publishers Since 1838
an imprint of Penguin Random House LLC
1745 Broadway, New York, NY 10019
penguinrandomhouse.com

Book design by Alison Cnockaert

Library of Congress Cataloging-in-Publication Data

Names: Rosen, Jessie, author.
Title: All the signs: a novel / Jessie Rosen.
Description: New York: G. P. Putnam's Sons, 2025.
Identifiers: LCCN 2024044526 (print) | LCCN 2024044527 (ebook) |
ISBN 9780593716076 (trade paperback) | ISBN 9780593716083 (epub)
Subjects: LCGFT: Novels.
Classification: LCC PS3618.O831455 A78 2025 (print) |
LCC PS3618.O831455 (ebook) | DDC 813/.6—dc23/eng/20240924
LC record available at https://lccn.loc.gov/2024044526
LC ebook record available at https://lccn.loc.gov/2024044527
p.   cm.

Printed in the United States of America
1st Printing

The authorized representative in the EU for product safety and compliance is
Penguin Random House Ireland, Morrison Chambers, 32 Nassau Street,
Dublin D02 YH68, Ireland, https://eu-contact.penguin.ie.

For my parents, who gave me everything,
including the time, date, and place I was born.

No one's gonna drag you up to get into the light
    where you belong.
But where do you belong?

—Ace of Base

All the
Signs

Prologue

THE DJ LOWERED the music as I shifted in my too-high heels and clinked a fork to my champagne glass.

"Hello, hello!" I called out. "Can I have everyone's attention? I know it's probably a sin to cut off Springsteen, but I'd like to make a toast."

"A cardinal sin!" Father Dan yelled from the dance floor. The crowd cheered in agreement, then found their seats. Front and center among them was my dad. His proud smile served as my deep breath, though if I knew this room as well as I should have, this speech would go off with three laugh lines, one surprised reaction, and plenty of tears at the big finish. Well prepped as I was, I still couldn't believe we were finally here.

"As you all know, we're gathered tonight to celebrate an incredible man at the end of an incredible era," I started, trying to find the perfect spot at the mic. "And while it's my greatest honor to be the one to make this speech, I have to be honest, I've been struggling with what to say. First, because seventy-five percent of my former English teachers are here tonight." That got the first hearty laugh. "Second, because I need to do at least as good a job as my dad did when he gave this same speech for *his* father. But mostly because you already know everything I could say about the one and only Dr. Peter Lockhart. You know he's the most generous brother in the world because he gave you lifelong carving rights over the Thanksgiving turkey." My uncle Ted cackled. "You know he's the best neighbor because he walks your trash cans up your driveway before he even does his own." Mrs. Nevins clutched her chest. "Over at table ten is the jogging club he's been leading with a fair and even pace for forty years, even though you all know he can run double your speed."

"Then we wouldn't be the Shore Shufflers!" someone from that set cried. That made me smile and relax just a bit more.

"And you know he somehow found time throughout his career to serve on the town council, run the beach cleanup committee, volunteer as a track coach for every team I ever ran with, and become the most winning chef at the Highlands annual clam Bake-Off, thanks to his absolutely killer Clams Johnny Cash." The crowd went rightly wild. I had to clink the glass for quiet again.

"But finally, there's the reason we're all here tonight," I continued with a look over to the group directly surrounding Dad, our team. "You know that he is the brilliant, attentive, caring doctor who delivered—*drumroll, please*—one thousand one hundred and twenty-two babies in his forty-year career."

Mouths dropped open as that rightly set a new cheer-level record.

"Okay, so that *number* was a surprise, but nothing else, right? Because Peter Lockhart has made himself so incredibly easy to know, love, and respect. But as I sat down to write these remarks last week—on his final day as the head of Lockhart Women's Medical—I realized there is something that absolutely no one knows about my dad, and it's especially relevant on this very special night." The room went extra quiet. I tightened my center, not used to having all eyes on me, but this was the part I'd rehearsed the most.

"Every time Dad dropped me off somewhere throughout my entire life—whether it was school, a friend's house, a track meet, or a party—he'd turn to me and say, 'Have fun and remember your name.' We all know he didn't mean Leah. He meant Lockhart. He was telling me to remember who we are—and have always been—as a family: people who put our loved ones and community first. He was saying be proud of that heritage as you walk about this world, but also make us proud in how you carry it."

Tears fell from my cousin Charlotte's eyes at that line, just as they had during every single rehearsal. But mine were clear and focused as they looked straight at the man of the hour; my final words were for him.

"Dad, you've been my favorite teammate for my entire life—from three-legged races at the county fair to Sunday-night pizza-making in your kitchen—but it's been my greatest honor to work beside you at the practice our family built, and I promise I'll remember our name as you leave me to continue its great legacy."

I raised my glass toward his beaming face as the room burst into applause. "To Dr. Peter Lockhart!" I said, then every voice in the room echoed it.

Dad stood and started walking in my direction, arm already outstretched for our shake.

"She's your daughter, not your accountant, Pete," my mom had said when he instituted the special greeting somewhere around my fifth birthday. But I'd always loved it. *Kiddo*, he'd said with the clasp, until I graduated from medical school. From then on it was always *Doctor*.

"Thank you, Doctor," he said now, his hand still dwarfing mine. "That was—" He shook his head, searching for the right word.

"You're welcome, Doctor," I jumped in. Then I let my grip linger just a second longer than usual. "You deserve it."

Charlotte raced to our sides, eyes puffy. "How did neither of you cry?" She was trailed closely by her mother, my aunt Kath.

"I know! My god, I was a mess from the turkey-carving line!" Kath said.

"Trick of the trade," said Dad, giving their shoulders matching pats as he headed off to greet the long line of people that had formed to offer congrats.

Aunt Kath shoved her phone screen to my face. "I recorded you from start to finish. I'm going to send it to every woman I know with an eligible-bachelor son!"

"Mom, *no*," Charlotte tried on my behalf, for the thousandth time, but my aunt flitted off with a mischievous grin. "You did look incredible up there," she said, handing over black flats for the shoe change we'd planned. "Very glad we went with the black jumpsuit. It wouldn't be the worst idea to snag a fresh profile pic in it . . ."

My younger cousin had been gracefully bossing me around since before she could say my name, especially in things right-brain related. But she'd left me in charge of left-brain tasks for our duo. We were the only girls in our generation of Lockharts, and I believed we made two halves of one formidable future matriarch.

"Thank you. I am surprisingly comfortable in this thing," I said, peering down at the rare view of myself wearing something other than scrubs or running clothes. "TBD on the photos until I have a drink, or more likely two."

"Deal," Charlotte said as she grabbed my hand and whisked me toward the bar.

The rest of the night was a beautiful blur. Tequila shots with the labor and delivery nurses from Riverview Medical Center. A group photo with Dad and every baby he'd delivered in the room. My aunt Kath convinced the venue to allow thirty-five full-sized sparklers on the custom doctor's-coat cake she'd baked. I danced my heart out to "Born to Run" with the Shore Shufflers. And at some point, Charlotte took more than a few photos of me on the restaurant's sunset-view deck. It was after midnight when the small group of us still standing took our last drinks down to the beach a block away. Most people ran ahead for a toe dip in the icy-cold ocean, but I stopped, struck by the full moon above. It looked like a surgical light lodged in the sky, pure white and glowing. The dozens of stars surrounding it—sparkling against the inky backdrop—were so crystal clear I felt like I was inside a planetarium show. *Was the view always like this here?* I felt the odd urge to stop following the others and lie down on the sand for a better view. Then I heard Charlotte's voice ahead.

"Leah, where are you?!"

That dropped my gaze back down to the scene below. All that mattered to me was right here at eye level.

Chapter
One

I SNAPPED MY laptop shut, prepared to call this a 4.5-star week. My team had delivered two sets of twins with zero NICU needs, my running club had made the thrilling annual transition out of long pants and into shorts, and Dad and I had found the time to change every wall of my new condo from nineties pastels to a tranquil Sea Mist. I tucked a strand of hair behind my ear, then remembered that my brand-new lob took 50 percent less time to blow-dry. Five stars it was.

With one precise kick against the second drawer of my desk, my rolling chair and I were perfectly positioned to see out the left dormer window of my office. And there she was: beautiful Sandy Hook Bay. It was late May, making six thirty p.m. Magic Hour. A fried-egg sun shot its rays across the water, turning the streaky clouds above into pink cotton candy. And if I squinted, I could see the Manhattan skyline straight ahead.

Thanks, Grandad, I thought, part two of the daily ritual.

Dr. Peter Lockhart Sr. had bought this gingerbread Victorian as the offices of LWM because of this very view, planting himself in this second-floor office for all forty years of his career. I moved in once he retired and had no plans of taking over Dad's larger space downstairs. He'd always needed closed shades to focus. My requirement was sun streaming through a window. I took one more glance before heading down to find another precious detail that had remained consistent since Dad retired: our office manager, Edie. She was restocking snacks in the kitchen.

"That's still way too many Werther's Originals . . . ," I teased.

"No such thing," Edie replied, dumping a full bag of the gold-foiled candies into the bin. She reserved two, popping one in her mouth with little-kid delight and handing the other to me like the surrogate grandma she'd become.

"Ready for the Friday Dot-and-Cross?" I asked, unwrapping my candy. This was our term for the sessions Grandad instituted at the very start of Lockhart Women's Medical: five-minute meetings to ensure every *i* was dotted and *t* crossed before the weekend.

"Clipboard at the ready," Edie said, grabbing her wooden relic off the table and lowering her massive glasses down her nose.

"Great. For scheduling: I'm watching Becca Alton closely. If there's no movement by next Wednesday, she'll likely want to induce. Jeanie Lands's glucose came back high but borderline, so I want to run it again Tuesday. Just schedule her for a tech appointment." Edie scribbled furiously: seventy years old, but still the high school class secretary at heart. "For the office: I'm worried about the A/C holding up this summer."

"And the roof, if we get the kind of storms we had last year," Edie added.

I held in a sigh. This was the downside of a century-old property. "Right. Which means also the front porch. Let's get my uncle in to give us an estimate on replacing both, and let's hope the family discount is steep. But to end on good news: I need to place an order with you for two more blues. It's twins for Hallie and Jon." Newborn hats handcrafted by Edie were the LWM signature gift-with-delivery.

Her eyes went extra wide. "*Ohdeargod* . . . Two boy babies become two boy toddlers lickety-split. Those two church mice are not ready for that."

I shook my head. "I know, but please don't tell them that when they come in next week."

Edie pursed her always-mauve lips to say she'd try but probably fail. "Okay. My list is just to check in with the hospital board on Monday about our equipment order and the rest of the staff about staggering summer vacation schedules. I'll give you those two days before and after your birthday for the Cape May trip with Charlotte. Need more?"

"Not until we hire the second doctor."

"About that . . ." Her eyes went from class secretary to school principal.

"I promise I'm reviewing résumés."

The clipboard lowered with Edie's gaze. "I want you to promise you're not secretly waiting for some fourth-generation Lockhart to get through med school."

"Ruby will be ten this year and shows signs of excellent bedside manner," I joked, sort of.

Now Edie shook her head at me. "All right then, there's one more thing I want to raise," she said. "We've had a few more requests for patients to bring their *doulas* to their appointments." She pronounced the word as if it were a controlled substance. "Are we still allowing that?"

"You know we allow patients to bring doulas or any supportive birth partner into their experience here, Edie."

She leaned in close even though we were the only two people left in the office. "Well, then the least they could do is wear a bra, Leah."

I tried hard not to encourage her with a laugh. I failed. Sometimes Edie was seventy on the inside, too.

Thanks to the prime location of my new home, I had time for a quick run before girls' night at Charlotte's. I'd spent years renting a little bungalow closer to the hospital, watching for one among a very prized row of bay-side condos to come on the market. Again. I'd missed my chance and a *way* better price almost a decade ago. Shane and I had just celebrated six months together when Mrs. Biddle put hers up for sale. That was five months longer than any relationship I'd had since med school, but I wasn't sure if he was *the one*, and it didn't seem wise to buy myself a condo that he didn't like while I waited to decide. Shane grew up in Pennsylvania with a family that preferred giant lawns over water views. I should not have been surprised when he announced he wanted us to move there four months later. My "no" was instant. My devastation over missing out on that condo lasted until one finally came on the market again. This time I made an offer without having to consult anyone but my accountant, a silver lining of still being single. One perk of the wait: I ended up with a unit steps from the head of the Henry Hudson Trail. Tonight I was out and back from the picturesque, three-mile loop to Conover Light Beacon in thirty minutes. The actual five-star end to the week.

I cooled down at the kitchen table and gave my work email one final check. Friday evenings tended to bring last-minute questions, like *Can I paddleboard at twenty weeks? Do I have to put more sunscreen than usual on my belly?* And *Will the green curry from Kunya Siam make me go into labor?* Answers: yes, no, and it hasn't made anyone yet. But I found a very surprising subject line tonight: Hi from David Remy. A little gasp escaped me. *My David Remy?*

> Hey Leah—Hope you've been well. I regret to inform you that I'm writing to officially call off our pen pal arrangement. You've owed me a return letter for twenty-six years and three months. I'm sorry, but I have my standards.

I laughed out loud. It was him. That sense of humor was one reason I'd developed a crush on David soon after the Remys moved into the house behind ours the summer before fourth grade. Another was the pitch-perfect dimples I could picture now as if he were reading to me through the screen. Why had I stopped writing after he moved back down to New Orleans?

Still, I'm willing to bury the hatchet. I'm living in
Manhattan for the next few months to do some
specialty work at a PT clinic in North Jersey. (I'm
a physical therapist. Those sprained wrists and
ankles from our tumbles on the jetty really
inspired me.) I've been thinking about coming
down to visit the old stomping grounds. Would
love to see you if you're around. Bonus if our
creek hasn't succumbed to global warming. Let
me know. —David

I'd sat down on a kitchen stool to read, but David's last line
lifted me to my feet. *Our creek.* There had always been a little
stream of water running through the ravine between our two
houses, but I barely knew it was there until David moved in.
We'd begged our dads to build a bridge across. In the end,
they—a doctor and an engineer—supervised while my con-
tractor uncle handled the job. How many hours had David
Remy and I spent talking on that bridge? How many times had
we maybe, almost, I-was-so-sure-we-would kiss?

I reread the note, grinning all the way through, then did
what any thorough woman would: typed David Remy into a
Google search. The Remys moved the summer before we
started eighth grade. That was right around the time I was
starting to wonder if I should try for that terrifying transition
out of the Friend Zone. But it also lined up with the bitter end
of my parents' marriage. David and I tried to keep in touch,
but the truth is he got lumped into a time that I was eager to
box up and put in the basement. I shifted at the counter, even
now eager to move on from those memories.

A social media account popped up on my screen first—like mine, David's was private—but below that were articles, speaker bios, and thumbnail images of a shockingly handsome man who appeared to be a very accomplished physical therapist. I squinted at the headshot, stomach fluttering. The David Remy I knew was a short kid with messy curls drowning in a usually stained polo shirt. This was a man: obviously tall with a tight haircut and arms that filled out every crisp button-down. *Wrong guy?* I wondered. Then I noticed a picture featuring those dimples, two half-crescent dips off the end of each side of his smile. My own mouth turned up instantly. *My David Remy.* According to the next link, he'd grown up to be tenured faculty at LSU, recently honored by the American Physical Therapy Association for work with a trauma-informed program developed for veterans. *It's too bad there's no such thing as a middle school reunion*, I thought, scrolling through the rest of his very long bio. Adult David Remy would have been the surprise star at ours.

I made a mental note to email him back something extremely clever after dinner at Charlotte's, then shut my laptop and bent over to slip it into my work bag. The whole room suddenly shifted with me. I squeezed my eyes shut against the bizarre dizzy feeling, then stepped a foot out to steady myself. With that, everything settled back to normal. *I pushed too hard during the run*, I thought as I brought my body level. *My blood sugar must just be low.* I reached for a banana from the bowl on my counter, a quick reset. Then I felt myself break into a ridiculous giggle at a ridiculous thought: *Or maybe David Remy can still make me weak in the knees.*

Chapter
Two

"LEAH, IS THAT you, finally?" Charlotte yelled from the kitchen.

"Oh, good. She'll know the answer," I heard Jeni add.

"If this is about intermittent fasting, I'm leaving!" I called out.

I had been serving as the walking WebMD to my cousin's friend group for years. Recent topics included *Is all Botox fine now?* And *How much bigger is it okay for your left boob to be?* But I was happy to oblige. This younger set had saved me from weekends of Turner Classic Movies and takeout these past few years while my high school friends were tied up with two-kids-and-a-Goldendoodle life. I entered the kitchen to find them huddled around one of Charlotte's color-coordinated charcuterie boards.

"It is about intermittent fasting. How did you know?" Jeni eyed me. She was still in running clothes from her own jog. I felt guilty that I never texted her to join mine.

"Educated guess," I said. "I see a dozen women a day, five days a week, one hundred percent of whom have the same social media."

"Right," said Anne, looking found-out. She spent a lot of time online promoting her own family business and even more popular home décor hacks. "So, what's the deal?"

"There's not enough peer-reviewed research for me to say it's good, which in my world means it's bad."

"Told you she'd say that." Charlotte gloated, popping a pepper from the red section of the board into her mouth.

"Well, I want to see whatever research there is," Rayna said as she threw her pile of curls into a clip. She was the contrarian of the group. "Kate Baylock lost fifteen pounds—"

"*Fifteen?*" Jeni interrupted.

"*Thank. You.* I thought the same thing when she told me," Anne added, eyes rolling.

The cool-clique lunch tables of my youth had become kitchen islands. I had stayed neutral then because I hated drama. The same rationale applied now, plus the fact that 75 percent of the women whom *these* women gossiped about were my patients. This meant I would not be sharing the surprise message from David Remy. Charlotte knew enough about him to make a mountain out of an email, and I suspected my status as single was a favorite topic when I wasn't at the island. Though, in fairness, the only three dates I'd been on in the past three years were to their credit as aspiring yentas.

I slid over to Charlotte's fridge to pour myself a glass of my favorite pinot grigio but stopped short at the sight of a man draping a black tablecloth over her dining room table. A man . . . wearing a *cape*?

"Did you hire a magician for the night?" I asked Charlotte, not at all kidding. Her signature head-tilt-nose-scrunch confirmed why. Charlotte had a bleeding heart that knew no bounds and a cherubic face to match. She'd recently been hostess to a town-council hopeful, a fledgling yoga teacher, and three foster dogs that were currently yapping in her yard. They were in addition to the two she and her saintly husband, Beau, had already adopted.

"Not *exactly*," she said, then she turned to the group. "Okay! Surprise activity for tonight! The other day the incredibly charming Nova came into the coffee shop. We got to talking, and turns out he's an experienced astrologer looking to expand his online business with IRL group events. He just needs to figure out the timing of things, so I offered us up as a trial! He's in the other room to give us all mini astrology readings right now!"

The room erupted in oohs and aahs. My reaction was internal and opposite: I would have almost preferred a magician.

"I know we're not all into the woo-woo," she said directly to me, "but this will be totally harmless and fun. Nova will teach us a little about astrology, then give us mini overviews of our charts." I nodded to keep the peace.

"I'm game!" said Jeni.

"I follow a few astrologers online already," said Anne.

"I'll try anything once," said Rayna. "But you know Stacey Jackson had her astrology chart read and in six months she was divorced."

Moments later we were sitting around Charlotte's dining room table, which was now covered with a sequined map of the solar system. At the head was Nova, a man wrapped in a black silk—yes—cape/blazer situation dotted with iridescent crystals. His peaches-and-cream skin popped against raven hair with silver streaks. And he may or may not have been somehow glowing. The whole scene reminded me of far too many cult documentaries. I considered a silent prayer for a patient to go into surprise labor after eating Kunya Siam.

"Well, hello, *hello* there, friends. Are we open to beginning with a few deep and beautiful breaths?" Nova asked, his voice sweet and Southern.

I agreed along with everyone else. Being resistant would only draw attention. But somehow Nova's eyes locked into mine anyway as we inhaled and exhaled in unison. They were two oval pools of a blue-green I'd never seen before, and I lived at the ocean. *Very cult leader*, I thought as I tried and failed to break focus.

"Gorgeous," Nova finally said, then he opened a bedazzled iPad cover. "*So!* How much do any of us know about the great force that is astrology, or maybe our own astrological charts?"

His question opened a floodgate in my mind. All the thoughts about why I was so allergic to astrology started to spill out before I could stop them: that my mom talked my dad into naming me after my sign, Leah for an August-born Leo baby; that she stuffed my room with plush lions and sun wall decals and called my golden hair a mane; that I co-opted the obsession for years like any agreeable only-daughter would, asking for little lion earrings when I finally got my ears pierced and perfecting "Here Comes the Sun" for my first piano re-cital. But then my fourth-grade teacher made us all do presen-tations on our signs. I was the only Leo—*fiery, dominant, attention-loving, regal, filled with big emotions*, my report went.

The class took that and ran. *That's why Queen Leah always wants to lead the group projects* (not wrong). *Now we know why she cries the second she gets upset* (also true). Mom called them jealous. Dad called the school to say the project was inappropriate. As usual by that point, he made my life easier, and she did the opposite. I'd hated astrology ever since. I straightened in my seat, then refocused on the room. *Enough.* This was harmless, and it would be over soon.

"Seems like we need a quickie overview," Nova said to our circle of unsure faces. "Okay, each birth chart, a.k.a. the map of all the stars and planets at the second you babies took your first sweet breath, features what we call *the big three*: your sun sign, your moon sign, and your rising sign. Sun is the thirty-or-so-day phase in which we're born and the one that has all the fame, but the moon and rising are the real bosses of your life. Moon is the zodiac sign Mr. Moon was in when you were born. And rising is the super-specific position of the sun. *Very* personal. Changes every hour or so. We follow? *Gorgeous.*" Everyone nodded robotically. "Moving on! Your sun is who you are, a.k.a. your identity. Your moon is *how* you are, lifestyle and personality. Your rising is *why* you are, your big purpose. Why does this matter? Because if you live as your moon says, you'll become what your sun dictates, to fulfill the destiny your rising sign has gifted you and this world. Boom!"

Every set of eyes widened, fascinated. Mine narrowed, and Nova noticed.

"We're confused or we're questioning?" he asked me.

"Sorry. We're just a doctor, so . . . you know," I answered.

He did not appear to know. "But, Doctor, astrology is one of the oldest-known sciences, dating back to the third millennium BC. The *brilliant* Misters Galileo Galilei and Johannes Kepler were both working astrologers. At one time the word 'astrologer' was *synonymous* with 'doctor'!" He waited for me to react; I did not. "And we're moving on. *Respect.* Okay, I'll need your birth date, year, time, and location. Who wants to go first?"

I sat patiently for the very long forty-five minutes that followed, somehow maintaining control over my desperate-to-roll eyes. Rayna was a Libra, so *naturally* she'd ended up a lawyer. Jeni had a Pisces moon, making her life running a day care *perfection*. And double-Scorpio Anne had enough intensity to turn her parents' old auto-body shop into a thriving business, which was—yes—*gorgeous*. Finally, only Charlotte and I remained unconfirmed by this—sorry, but—total weirdo with an iPad he kept entirely hidden from our view.

"Hostess first," I tried.

"No, no," Charlotte said. "I already had him do a little of mine when we met. You go."

Nova batted his aquamarine eyes at me, far too eager. That color had to be fake.

"August seventh, 1983, five fifteen a.m., Los Angeles, California," I said, relenting in the name of getting this over with.

"Los Angeles . . . ," he said, as surprised as every man I've ever dated. Apparently I have an East Coast personality?

"Yes. My parents lived there briefly." It was the reply I found led to the fewest follow-up questions.

"Ooh, Dr. Leah is a Leo! *Gorgeous.*" Then he laser-focused on his screen. "Okay . . . *Okay.* Sun *and* rising in Leo. Oh, but then we have a *Cancer* moon and . . . okay. Oh, wow. This is . . . Wow. Wow. Wow." It was as if he were looking at a unicorn and/or ghost. Everyone laughed at the reaction. Meanwhile, I felt teleported right back to that fourth-grade hell.

"So, is she a good witch or a bad witch?" Jeni asked.

"She is a *blessed* witch. This is a *powerful* chart. I mean yes, we have this moon in Cancer, which, don't you worry, we will get to, but your sun *and* your rising signs are both in Leo . . . Unobstructed! That's *gorgeous* double fire with a clear path to *burn baby burn*. She is here to *get it*. Boundary breaking. Deeply creative. Writing? Producing something? *Definitely* on a stage somewhere. And with a huge focus on her own identity and experience." Every brow at the table scrunched along with mine. "But it's not going to be easy . . . Oof. This moon in Cancer is about nurturing, mothering, home, but to access it there needs to be so much solitude, introspection, even secrecy. I mean, with a chart like this, I can see you being—"

"The head of a hundred-year-old OB-GYN practice?" I asked, cutting him off, hopefully for good.

Nova seemed to short out. "*Interesting*," he finally said, somehow turning the word into an antonym for "gorgeous." "But no. That does not make sense."

The room went painfully silent. I caught Jeni mouth, *Awkward . . .* , to Anne.

I raced to cut the tension. "Well, maybe my parents got my birth time wrong."

"Or maybe some of this is up to interpretation," Rayna offered in my defense.

"Yeah, Leah's nothing like what I see people say about Leos," Anne added.

"Agreed," Charlotte declared with an affirming look toward me. "If anything, this sounds more like your mother." It was an innocent comment, but it still sucked the air out of the room. And my chest, to my surprise. "Shit. I don't know why I said that. I'm so sorry."

I stole a quick breath. "Don't be. You're right. My mom has definitely proven she's all about herself."

Nova silently considered the group, then me. He looked curious, if not a little concerned. I hoped but doubted it was because he'd finally been called out on his bullshit.

"Interesting," he said again. "You don't relate to any of what I said?"

"I don't. Nor do I like it," I said, desperate to move on. "But it's fine. I truly do not believe in astrology."

Nova nodded, certain in a way that made my ears heat up. "Mmm, but astrology doesn't care what you believe. She's like genetics, booping along behind the scenes your whole life. You can get way out of alignment for a thousand reasons, but something will eventually pull you back. Good news/bad news, Doctor: you cannot escape your chart."

"*Interesting*," I said with more than a hint of mockery. "Because it would appear as though I have." Nova had struck the wrong nerve.

He cocked his head, considering his next move. The rest of the group seemed to hold their breath, wondering if this was about to become a fight. But I was saved by a very specific ringing coming from my tote bag in Charlotte's kitchen: the sound of the hospital calling my phone.

"Excuse me," I said, thrilled for the exit. I got to my phone just in time to pick up.

"Sorry to intrude on your night." It was Karen, my head labor and delivery nurse.

"Oh, it's truly not a problem," I replied.

"ER just called up to us. A woman walked in and told them she thinks she's in labor, then mentioned LWM. But I checked and she's not one of our patients."

"Name?"

"Monica Shepard." It didn't ring a bell, but I was curious why she'd called out our practice. "I can have the on-call doctors handle it," Karen said. "But just wanted to check with you first."

A burst of Nova's laughter seeped in from the other room. "I'm five minutes away," I said. "I'll be right over."

Chapter
Three

KAREN WAS WAITING for me at the nurses' station, pink-rimmed readers holding back her curly bob, like always. But the concern across her face was rare for a woman with twenty-five years of experience. Now I was worried.

"I need to speak with you before you go examine her," she said. I motioned for the break room. Nurse stations shared a lot in common with kitchen islands.

"First, she's completely alone and says no one's coming. But more concerning, she just confessed to me that she hasn't seen a doctor throughout the whole pregnancy." Karen smoothed down the edge of her perfectly ironed scrubs top.

"Did she say why?" I asked, running through the short list of potential reasons, none good. Most of my patients requested *extra* appointments.

"No. She's very tight-lipped. I'd say she's scared, but she honestly just seems stubborn." Karen called it like it was, which was usually helpful. Right now, I wasn't sure.

"She's probably both," I said with a firm tone. "Does anything concern you from the intake?" Karen shook her head. "Okay, good. Let's be careful to follow protocol for any signs of abuse, but make sure we show her as much if not more care than every other woman we treat."

"Of course," said Karen, a twinge offended.

Monica was zoned out on her phone when we walked into her room.

"Hi there," I said. "I'm Dr. Lockhart. I was honored to hear you mentioned our practice when you came in." I kept my voice professional, figuring that would break through more than anything overly friendly.

"Yeah. Well. I googled 'OB-GYN near me' and . . ." She trailed off with a shrug, then went straight back to her phone screen. Karen had gotten the stubborn energy right, but up close I could see she'd left out one very important detail: Monica was young. Maybe not even twenty.

"Is there anything you feel like you need to be more comfortable right now?" I asked.

"Drugs." She said the word flippantly, but I'd been in this exact room with too many strong women not to see the pain behind it.

"Of course," I said. "And, Monica, I'm your partner in this room. My job is to make sure you and your baby are healthy, but I also want you to feel as safe and relaxed as possible. You can say anything and ask anything. Do you have any questions for me before we get going?"

She finally dropped her phone and looked me in the eyes.

Her own were deep black saucers that seemed wise beyond their years, and they were sizing me up.

"You've got this," I said, meeting her gaze. "And I've got you."

That line seemed to do the trick. Monica's face softened, then she shifted her body closer to me. "How much did I mess up my baby by not going to the doctor?" The question was delivered in a heartbreaking whisper.

I'd passed the test, a deeply gratifying feeling, but now I had to answer a question I hadn't faced in my entire career. I leaned in close for as private a moment as possible, then let instinct guide my answer.

"The female body is one of the most powerful systems in the world. And the most resilient. And I have a feeling yours is more so than most. Everything before today is in the past."

She nodded, almost smiling, then her face quickly contorted into a familiar scrunch: a very strong contraction was coming on.

I knew the motions of what happened next so well that the nursing staff and I had a running competition of calling the TOFC: time of first cry.

"She's finally ten centimeters, but it's her first," Karen whispered as we ran through our final prep checklist thirty minutes later. "I'm going with a full hour of pushing. TOFC eleven fifteen." She was undefeated this month, but I had a sense about Monica's spirit.

"Ten fifty, latest," I said, finishing my prep, then I moved to Monica's side for a quick pep talk. Jamie, our former-linebacker nursing assistant, was now in position, holding a cold compress to her head. "It's time to push, Monica. Jamie here is made of literal steel, so you can grab onto him and squeeze as hard as you need when I start counting."

"She's right," Jamie said, holding up his catcher's-mitt hand. "Unbreakable."

"Thanks," said Monica, hiding her nerves.

"Okay, Team Monica: on my count," I said, getting into position with Karen at the foot of the bed. "One, two, three, four, five, six, seven, ei—"

"I can't go to ten!" Monica was gasping.

"That's okay. First push is always the hardest. Let's take a ten-second break, then we'll try again."

Karen leaned into my ear. "Shoulder," she whispered.

I'd trained my staff to say as little as possible in these rooms, my way of keeping things calm for parents-to-be. The fewer people explaining every step aloud, the better, especially if one of the steps is a potential problem. "Shoulder" meant the baby might need to be shifted out of a tricky position. I examined Monica's body more closely.

"Yes or no?" Karen asked.

"Yes," I said.

"Fix or call?" was her follow-up.

"Fix." I could see that it was possible to carefully reposition the baby without issue, but we needed to move very, very quickly. "Listen, Monica," I said. "The baby needs to be adjusted a little so we can safely deliver. You're both okay. This is not uncommon. We'll do steady, deep breathing for a few minutes while I rotate the baby, then we'll push again."

"Is this bad?" she asked. I now noticed her holding on to Jamie's hand.

"It's just an extra step we need to add in." I did not lie to my patients, and "no" would not have been true.

"Chair, please," I said to Karen, but she already had one positioned behind me. I sat down, then tipped my body left to prepare. The room suddenly shifted with me, rolling like the chair was now a boat in chop. I grabbed on to the railing in front of me.

"What was that?" Monica asked. She'd felt the bed shake with my grasp.

"Nothing," I said, focused on keeping her calm.

"Are you okay?" Karen whispered. Three words.

I shifted my body back straight, and the world evened out. But my pulse was racing. *I haven't been running and have had plenty to eat.* I stopped myself. *The only thing that matters right now is delivering this baby safely.*

"Fine," I said to Karen. "Here we go," I called out to Monica. "I want you to breathe in and out slowly but try hard not to move."

"Is this serious?" I heard her ask Jamie.

"Dr. Lockhart has it all under control," he replied.

I took a deep breath and then tipped my body over again. Everything after that happened in slow motion. All sense of up, down, left, and right was gone after my waist hinged, gravity erased. If the chair was a boat, then I was overboard now, spinning round and round inside the crest of a massive wave. I reached my hand out, trying to find anything to grab onto, but everything was a blur. Then, *crash!* I smacked into the ground and the world went black.

Chapter
Four

"HELLO? *HELLO?* DR. Lockhart, can you hear me? I need you to stay completely still or we'll have to start over. Again."

I hadn't heard the technician, and it wasn't because of the booming churn of the MRI tunnel. My brain was two floors up in Labor and Delivery, where I'd been wheeled out on a gurney as Monica was rushed into an OR for a C-section. My chances of staying still were zero.

"Let's do that," I said into the speaker inches from my face.

"What? Start over?" She sounded frazzled, or maybe just rightly intimidated by the head of the ER rushing a fellow doctor into her space and then telling her to call his cell phone with the results.

"Yes. Why don't you take the next patient and then come back to me. I need to get in touch with my team about my patient. Then I'll be ready to go again."

There was a beat before the speaker cracked back to life. "I don't think I can do that, Dr. Lockhart. Dr. Grant gave me strict instructions to—"

"I'll tell him it was my fault. Just please let me out." I'd never had a panic attack, but I'd coached enough patients through them to know I was teetering on the edge. Cold sweat poured from my neck and hands as the walls surrounding me closed in even further.

"Um . . . let me just call Dr. Grant and—"

"No! Please just let me out!" I kicked against the machine like a toddler. "Hello?! Please! Stop the scan!" My heart was pounding so hard I felt it in my ears. I knew what I was supposed to do: close my eyes, focus on a still image in my mind—a flower, a sand dune—then find my breath. Instead, I started trying to wriggle my body down and out of this cage.

The speaker clicked on again. "Doctor," a new voice said. *Dad.* My eyes closed.

"Monica and baby Skye are all good. She's a lucky seven pounds seven ounces. Karen told me to tell you TOFC was eleven oh seven p.m."

"Thank you, Doctor," I said from the other side of panic. "Can you please get a message to her saying how sorry I am about everything?"

"One step at a time," I heard. With that, my body finally relaxed.

I survived the next half hour of total stillness for the scan, then somehow the extra four hours I spent waiting in the ER. My presence was offering excellent gossip, like a teacher's pet in detention. *I heard you were in here, what happened? Dan said he saw you on a stretcher! Is everything okay? What, are you testing out the beds?* I was so mortified I pretended to be asleep.

Dad found me with an extra pair of yellow fall-risk socks draped over my eyes sometime around five a.m. "Napping or pretending?"

I removed the left foot. "I haven't taken a nap since I was three."

"Me either," he said, lowering onto the chair next to my bed. He did not reach a hand out for our shake. He was more worried than his voice let on. Now I was, too.

"Everything came back normal with your scans and blood work. Dr. Grant's willing to sign discharge papers unless you want any further testing."

"I don't. Do you?"

"No. I still think what I thought when they called me after your fall."

Neither of us had said the word yet, but the kind of dizziness I'd just experienced, plus the little moments of it prior, minus anything at all showing up on a brain scan, meant one thing. "Why in the world would I have vertigo?"

Dad shook his head, equally puzzled. "And also, which kind?"

"That's definitely not a med school flash card I still have memorized . . ."

My father stood, chest puffed. "Of course you still do." I couldn't help but smile as my dad moved to stand behind me. The man had a photographic memory of every medical school textbook still on his office shelf. "I'll make this as quick and painless as possible," he said. "It's a movement test called the

Dix-Hallpike, and I am sorry in advance because you'll probably throw up."

Unfortunately, that detail did ring a bell. Minutes later, I was hurling into a bedpan.

"BPPV," Dad said, confirming what he seemed to have suspected. "Benign paroxysmal positional vertigo."

"'Benign' is a good word," I said, still miserably nauseous.

"Correct. Even better, this isn't a hereditary thing, so we can avoid a call to your mother. It's the rest of the name we need to worry about," Dad went on. "The 'positional' means this type of vertigo comes on when you move your body, mostly in tilting and bending motions." That made sense given the hurricane my body had experienced when my dad tilted me over just now, and what had happened every time I'd been dizzy before. "In this case, treatments are provided by a PT, so we'll know more about the timeline on this after you get in to see someone."

My head jerked up. "A physical therapist?" Even my compromised mind made the connection: *David*.

"Yeah. I like Ari Nassir at Shore Physical but want to ask around so we get the best."

"This is crazy. Remember David Remy?"

"David-across-the-creek? Of course. Why?"

"He emailed me yesterday. He's now this really accomplished PT and working on some project up in North Jersey for the summer." It was just a coincidence, but I couldn't deny how big of one.

"Good for him, but you don't want to travel for treatment if you don't have to. I'm not so sure how safe it will be for you to drive. We'll have to see what positions prompt the dizzy spells."

"It's not safe for me to *drive*? Then how in the world can I work?"

My dad's head dipped the way it always did right before very bad news. "You can't," he said. This was a rare circumstance when I did not appreciate our family policy of using the rip–off–the–Band-Aid approach. "I'll come back to run the office until this is resolved."

"What? No. You're retired. You've got fishing trips lined up all summer."

Now his face went firmer. "This is much more important than fishing, Leah. Last night was too close of a call."

A different kind of nausea rolled through me. Monica and Skye were fine, but he was right. My fall had put both their lives in very serious danger. "What if I still see patients at the office and you handle the hospital?"

I got a quick head shake. "This is about reputation and safety. I cannot have people finding out that you passed out during a delivery and were permitted to return to work. It's not how I do business."

We, I thought. But that wasn't fair. I knew how close he still felt to the practice. And rightly so.

"Chin up. We'll get through this," he said, giving my shoulder a pat. "Think of this like that time you popped your elbow out of place during that one week your mother put you in gymnastics. You're just a little out of alignment."

A chill ran up my back. *Out of alignment.*

"Right, Doctor?" Dad said, his arm finally outstretched.

"Right, Doctor," I replied, meeting him for our shake. *It's just a common expression.* I shoved Nova's face from my mind.

"All right. Let me see about those discharge papers for you."

Dad opened the curtain of my makeshift room. We both startled at the sight of Jean Bohm standing behind it, the head of HR for the hospital. I would have thought she was stopping by to see how I was doing, but the look on her face suggested otherwise.

"Hi there," she said with a polite smile. "Can I interrupt? I need to ask Leah a few questions, if you're feeling okay enough to talk?"

"I am," I said, suddenly the most nauseous I'd been yet.

"I'll just be a moment, Dr. Lockhart," she said to my dad.

"I'd prefer he stay," I jumped in.

Jean nodded, not surprised. "Of course, but I'm sorry that it's not good news. Monica Shepard just filed a complaint about your episode during her delivery. You know that means we're legally required to open a case exploring whether there was malpractice."

It was like my senses short-circuited with that word. I knew my stomach had flipped, but I couldn't feel it. I noticed Jean saying something, but I couldn't hear her. The metal taste that had been in my mouth for hours was gone. But I turned to my dad and watched with painfully clear eyes as all the color drained from his face.

Chapter
Five

I HAD DECADES of experience understanding the inner workings of the human body, specifically a woman's. Right now, mine was an infuriating mystery. I'd developed a running list of all the bending motions my body could no longer handle without throwing me onto a tilt-a-whirl. It was *way* too long. I was exhausted but couldn't sleep. I needed to eat but had zero appetite. All I could manage was sitting straight upright on the couch with my laptop, manically researching BPPV triggers. The results were frustratingly few: Chronic migraines. Recent head trauma. Several inner-ear infections they'd ruled out at the hospital. That left me with the worst option of all: D. *None of the above.* It was news I'd had to share with patients over and over throughout the years. *I'm so sorry, but we don't know why this is happening to you.* I understood why most of them reacted with overwhelmed tears. If I were the crying type, this would have been the moment. But right now, all I wanted to do was run—as far and fast as possible.

My body tightened. *Could I even?* If I could get my shoes on, the rest was fully upright. It should be fine. *It had to be fine.*

It took me fifteen minutes to lace up without too risky of a body shift, but soon I was able to take a lap around the living room. That was such an overwhelming relief I grabbed my phone and keys off the counter and ran straight out the door and down my trail, but I stopped five minutes in. Today was Sunday. The beach would be swarming. The Highlands was a town of roughly four thousand people, 75 percent of whom were either family, friends, or people whose babies I'd delivered. Ten percent of that set worked at the hospital, where everyone knew about my fall. Small-town math said very public places were not safe from questions I did not want to answer and shouldn't, given the open investigation. All we knew so far was that some family member of Monica's had shown up, heard what happened, and demanded to speak to someone. I could not have contact with Karen, Jamie, or anyone else on the floor during the episode until HR had spoken to them first, but I knew they were talking to each other and probably many other people in their lives and mine.

Dr. Lockhart was irresponsible. She made the wrong call. She can't be trusted.

I quickened my pace, then turned toward Ocean Boulevard. But more risky routes started appearing before me like I was in some kind of video game. First Avenue, for one, would be teeming with friends running weekend errands. The track at the high school was probably a safe bet. I could make like I was very focused on training for something to avoid conversation. *And then what? Repeat that everywhere, every day, until someone else's gossip trumps yours?*

It had been decades since I'd been forced to do this kind of social math. I was thirteen when my parents finally divorced. It became the biggest headline since their first round as fodder when Peter Lockhart came home from his prestigious UCLA fellowship with a golden-haired California bride and six-month-old baby. To hear my family tell it, there was nothing but celebration for Celia Luna—the breath of fresh air who wooed the shore's most eligible bachelor, then moved across the country to make a life in his hometown. Supposedly. I had very few memories of the blissful part of their *Romeo and Juliet* story. My mom was like a parody of a Californian: free-spirited, feisty, and indulgent. But all her fun and creativity always turned into a mess. Dad was raised by a navy doctor and preschool teacher, ruled by tradition, routine, and the belief that less was best. He colored inside the lines, if at all. I'd thought I'd be the one cheering loudest once they finally decided to part ways, but that's because I'd never been at the center of a Highlands gossip frenzy—or High *lands*, as my third-generation family proudly called it, like all the old-timers. I remember my aunt Kath trying to manage PR with the reveal that Celia was not technically a Lockhart. She'd never legally changed her name. But the rumor mill took that and sprinted. *She never liked the family. She tricked Peter into marriage for the money. Did she trick him into a quick pregnancy, too?*

I was in the middle of eighth grade, so already struggling with a brain that was not playing by its old rules. It didn't help that my equally fast-changing body made me look more and more like my mom. I made baseball caps my uniform so not even I had to see our matching gold hair. I quit cross-country for the season and stopped volunteering with the beach cleanup crew to avoid conversation. I walked to the library for a new book every single week, but only during the last thirty minutes they were open, so it was more likely to be empty. And I lost weight. More than was healthy and enough to give the town yet another gossip topic.

The final plot point for the peanut gallery came when my mom left to "spend some time traveling" the next summer. She came back nine months later to move out of her apartment across town. Her final trip was one-way back to Los Angeles. But that's when things finally got better for me. Dad was the hero single father; I was the brave little woman of the house. Mom was wrong and wicked; we were right and valiant. Soon enough someone else's problems became the focus of everyone's attention, and I vowed it would never be my turn again.

I blinked my eyes against the blinding sun ahead. I'd made it all the way to the municipal harbor. All the boats were already out for the day, leaving the docks empty, peaceful. Across the water was the outline of New York City, but my eyes went straight to a more important landmark: the tip of Sandy Hook park with its stately white-brick lighthouse, the very place we took the Remy family for a picnic the week after they moved to town. We were all fast friends, but shy David stuck to me immediately. By Christmas, the kids in our class teased that I was the only person he'd spoken a full sentence to since arriving. But they didn't realize our trust was a two-way street. David was one of the only people who knew my parents were struggling. Charlotte was too young to understand then, and I was too nervous to tell my girlfriends. An image of his sweet and steady face flew to my mind, stopping my stride. I grabbed the phone from my zipper pocket and rushed toward a nearby bench, eager to get an email out before I had time to second-guess it.

> Hi David—It's great to hear from you. I actually need to see a PT immediately.

Too desperate.

> Hi David—Thanks so much for reaching out. I'd love to catch up, but could we do that at your office first? I need to see a PT. Also, could this happen ASAP?

Accurate but awkward.

> David, hi! So good to hear from you. As it turns out your timing is really helpful. I'm experiencing some issues and need to see a PT. I'd love to have you visit town, but could we start our catch-up at your office?

Clear. Simple. And to the point. It was also effective. I had a reply message by the time I got home from my run.

> Hey. Any chance you could make it to my office tomorrow? I can see you at 11. Address is below. So is my cell just in case.

I read the response three times, lungs filling with enough air for my first deep breath in days.

Chapter
Six

I WAS SERIOUSLY questioning my decision to leave the Highlands for treatment after the seventy-five-dollar Uber from my house up to see David. The regret doubled when I started to feel what seemed like first-date jitters while waiting in his office, sensations I did not experience on actual first dates. Then he walked into the room.

"Leah Lockhart," David said, voice shockingly deep.

"David Remy," I replied, but I was just matching the line. In my mind, that name did not belong to the man filling out the door frame. I could not stop my eyes from the instinctual check for a wedding band. *None . . . interesting.*

"I'm so glad this worked out today," he said.

"You have no idea," I replied, then I promptly dropped my tote, bent down to pick it up, and lost all control of gravity. It took a few seconds of spinning before I could even open my eyes. They found David on the floor next to me, hand propped under his head like we were side by side on a beach blanket.

"It's only awkward if you make it awkward," he joked.

I was too furious with my dumb slip to laugh. "So I have vertigo," I confessed, pushing myself up to sit.

David touched a warm hand to my arm, stopping me. "It helps to give yourself a few moments before you move again." I collapsed back down, relieved.

"My dad diagnosed it as BPPV after my first big fall," I said. "He did some kind of horrific testing—"

"That made you puke?" David interrupted. I nodded, mortified to have provided him with that mental picture of me. "Impressive work. I hope he's doing well."

I opened my mouth, then closed it and nodded, not wanting to get into the full state of things. "Your parents?"

"Yeah, good too. Both retired, but we see them a bunch." *We?* "And . . . your mom?" David asked tentatively.

"Fine, I'm sure. Still in California. We do the courtesy holiday check-ins, which is just enough for me. Anyway, I've developed a list of all the dizzy-spell triggers. All bending motions, which supports the diagnosis."

David let me get away with moving on. "Good work. But sorry about this, Leah. It's tough."

"How tough?" I asked. "Because I'd like to get back to work."

His brow raised in a way that I did not like, then he started shimmying over to his desk, still on the floor.

"I'm sure I can stand now," I offered. "Or you certainly can."

"This is good," David said. "Tests my gross motor strength." He reached up for a notebook-and-pen combo on his desk, tipping it so it fell straight into his hand. "And lets me show off my impeccable hand-eye coordination."

That finally made me smile. David scratched a few things down on the paper. "Right. So, have you been in the Highlands this whole time?"

"Oh. Yeah," I said, not expecting that question.

"And you ended up at the family practice?"

"Of course."

He kept writing. "Nice. What were you up to before that?"

"Medical school?"

"Oh, so you went straight to the practice."

I didn't love his tone. "What does that have to do with my vertigo?"

"Nothing. I was just curious about your life."

"My life is fine," I said. "Great family, great friends—you remember Charlotte—and I've been running LWM since my dad retired this winter." I stopped, aware of the defensiveness in my voice. *It's David*, I thought.

"I didn't mean to sound like I was interrogating," he said. *And he can still read my mind.* That made me want to cop to the whole truth.

"I *was* running LWM," I said, finally propping myself up so I was fully sitting. "I passed out during a delivery, so my dad came out of retirement until I can clear this up." I stopped short of including Monica's potential lawsuit. But David's eyes were still so sympathetic.

"*Ugh*, Leah. I'm so sorry. How are you holding up?"

"I'll be fine," I said. "I just need to focus on whatever it takes to make it go away. And according to the Internet, you're incredibly qualified to help."

"You googled me?" asked David. With that, his dimples finally popped, swoon-worthy as ever.

"For verification purposes only," I said, feeling my cheeks flush.

He scooched over so we were seated inches from each other. It did not help my face settle. "First we need to figure out why the vertigo came on."

"Yeah. Bad news on that front. It's idiopathic, as far as I can tell. I can forward you everything I had done at the hospital."

David laughed out loud. "Aw, you did your homework and mine, just like old times. Right. So, BPPV is trickier when it's idiopathic. I can get really nerdy about it, if you'd like?"

"Please," I said, overwhelmed by a memory of him adorably geeking out, explaining how to make a lightbulb out of a potato during seventh-grade science. My crush grew tenfold that day.

"So, inside your ear is an organ called the vestibular labyrinth," he started. "In that organ are tiny, water-filled canals with teeny tiny crystal sensors that track your movement relative to gravity. Sometimes the crystals get dislodged from their correct spots and are stuck, floating rogue in the tiny canals and making them extra sensitive to head position changes. Think of your head as one of those handheld maze toys with the silver balls. Yours are out of their holes, and we have no idea why."

"I hate those toys," I said, then the reality set in. "Wait, are you saying my body is that game?"

David nodded, tentative. "But I'm a very good player. Like as good if not better than I was at Daytona USA in the boardwalk arcade. Also, you'll do similar, at-home exercises to speed up the healing. And we know how much you like homework."

His jokes were no match for my overwhelm. I went to throw my head into my hands, then remembered I could no longer do that without potentially falling over. "This is a nightmare," I said. "Sorry. Not the *you* part. The you part is nice."

"Thank you," said David. "I would have rather seen you for peanut butter shakes at Nicholas Creamery, but happy to help." That eased my insides up just a little. "All right. I'd like to lift you to the exam table just to be safe, okay?" Before I'd finished nodding yes, David had locked his two forearms beneath mine, lifted me to stand, and shifted me back down to a seat on the table without tipping my body an inch. It was masterful, and it brought back every first-date jitter from the waiting room. "Let's see if we can get a few of the movements in today. Get a sense of where you're at."

"Sounds good," I said, then I jumped a mile high at the sudden touch of his hands on my neck.

"Sorry. I should have warned you."

"It's fine," I said. *Cut it out*, I thought to myself.

"Okay, deep breath, then I want you to lean your weight to the right, almost as if you're going to fall over, but I'm going to catch you."

I tipped slowly, anxious. The room started to wobble ever so slightly. I tensed up just before David's arms whisked under and through mine until he was cradling me in the basket of his chest. "Good, let's try again," he said. I got maybe an inch further on the second round before tensing up. The third round was the same. David moved to quietly make some notes at his desk. I had a strong sense I'd gotten an *F* on my first test.

"Do you meditate?" he asked, finally looking up.

"Do you remember me at all?" I replied.

David surprisingly did not laugh. "I'll send you a link to one that will be helpful."

"I jog," I said. "That's very meditative."

"Not according to your body. You're locked up, especially through your center. Imagine trying to get the tiny crystals back in their tiny holes like this." David stood, then started moving like an imaginary board with robotic forearms. "No dice. We want this." Then he broke into what I could only describe as an impression of a man-sized piece of spaghetti: wiggling, loose arms, bendy legs. He even rolled his torso around like a mime with a Hula-Hoop. It was so damn charming I forgot he'd just told me I was "locked up."

"Well, I'll try anything to end this, fast. Before I came here I moved all the items in my lower kitchen cabinet onto my counter so I could grab a fresh garbage bag without risking a concussion."

David's eyes closed as if he were feeling my pain. "We'll get you there, Leah. I'd say eight weeks with your teacher's-pet ways. Plus, crystals will reposition as we go, so some movements will stop making you dizzy. Keep tracking that."

All I heard was "eight weeks." Two months of my dad having to come out of his hard-earned retirement while I sat around angsting over a potential career-ending lawsuit. I wasn't going to survive it. "I need something to do . . . ," I said to myself, not able to hide the panic.

"I'd say rest and relax but I feel like you need some kind of—I don't know—nerdy research project," said David.

"Hey! The world has tense nerds to thank for lots of things!"

That earned me an even deeper dimple reveal. "You're

right," David said, coming toward me again. "Here's one idea to kill at least the next hour: coffee with me right now to catch up on the past twenty years?"

"Is this not the middle of your workday?" I blurted out.

"I left extra time open for your appointment," he said. Adult David Remy was much smoother than I'd expected.

My heart pulsed in my apparently tight center. I looked into David's waiting eyes, then immediately away. I hadn't slept more than four hours any night since my fall. I was in no shape to be an impressive coffee date right now, even if it wasn't a real date. "Maybe after the next appointment," I said. "I haven't been sleeping well, so I oddly think I'm going take a weekday nap for the first time in my adult life."

David took a step back. Maybe disappointed? I was too thrown myself to figure it out. "Oh right. I didn't think about you having to get here," he said. "Let's do this. Next appointment I'll come to you. If you're comfortable we can do a session at your place, then I can see the old neighborhood. How does that sound?"

Like I have a week to prepare myself and my house. "Good," I said. "Thank you." I stood to leave, very, *very* slowly reaching down for my bag on the floor. David beat me to it, putting the bag handles directly inside my hand.

"This is all going to be okay, Leah," he said, eyes fixed on mine. "I promise."

The look sent a warm wave of hope straight through me finally. *I was right to come here.*

Chapter
Seven

THERE WERE FOUR texts from Charlotte waiting on my phone when I checked from the car home.

> How are you??

> Omigod you're with David call the *second* you leave his office.

> Wait. No. Just come to the shop. I made you a bunch of food.

> No. You shouldn't be lugging around food. I had Beau drop it off at your house. Come to the shop anyway!

I pictured my Tupperware-stuffed fridge and freezer, let out a sigh of relief, then redirected my driver to Coast Roastery.

Charlotte's coffee shop was tucked into a quiet plaza on the north side of town, my uncle Ted's addition to the Lockhart family legacy. He'd expanded to owning all five spots over the years, one for every member of his family. Charlotte had coffee and pastries covered, her brothers ran the sit-down and grab-and-go versions of an incredibly successful Italian restaurant, Ted still managed the hardware store, and my aunt Kath kept very close tabs on the flower shop she'd just retired from and left in the hands of a cousin. There was no chance of making it out of there without seeing at least 50 percent of them, but family was probably the best way to baby-step into talking publicly about my situation. Luckily the only person on site when I arrived was Charlotte, outside her café with a new chalkboard sign. "There you are! Hi! I've been so worried about you!" She started to wrap me in a giant hug. "Wait, is hugging okay?"

"If we remain completely upright," I said.

"*Ugh.* I'm so sorry, Leah," she said, gently kissing me on the cheek.

"Thank you for what I can only imagine is a week's worth of food," I said.

"More like ten days, and you're so welcome. We're going to get you better in no time!" Her eyes flickered. "Or David Remy is . . . I looked online, and *wow*. He really is the one that got away."

At least I could still roll my eyes without getting dizzy. "It was a good appointment, nothing more. I need him to cure my vertigo, not fall in love with me."

"See, you think that because you refuse to watch *Grey's Anatomy*. It can very easily be both. Especially given your history."

"Charlotte, we don't have a history. We were twelve!"

"Mm, and you think *that* because you refuse to watch *The Notebook*."

"Well, now would probably be the time. David recommended I find something to take my mind off things. Can I please—I don't know—pack your fresh chocolate chip cookies in those perfect little bags you put them in or something?"

"Sorry. I have Beau's niece Emma doing that. Ooh, but you can help me with something quick right now." She turned to the chalkboard. "What's better? 'Join us for Monday astrology readings with Nova' or 'Book an astrology reading with Nova every Monday'?"

I shook my head, frustrated. "I think it should say today's featured drip is Sand Dune Dark Roast. Charlotte, you're not responsible for that guy's career, and you don't want to turn your beautiful space into some weird psychic's den."

Charlotte's head shook. "He's an astrologer, not a psychic. And I know yours was way off, but everyone else at dinner got a lot out of what he said, me especially."

I'd left before hearing whatever Nova had said about her, but I read my cousin's face like a book now. "What did he say to you?"

She leaned in a little. "I just brought up the question of when Beau and I should start trying, and he reviewed all my transits and said it wasn't time yet. My better window to get pregnant will be in a few years when Jupiter transits my moon."

My head went hot. But the dots had finally connected on why Charlotte was so compelled by astrology in the first place. I saw it all the time. Perfectly logical women like my cousin engaged in all sorts of magical thinking when it was time for motherhood. Their feelings were more than valid. Their approach, not always.

"Why haven't you said anything, Char? You know I can help you think through this."

She shrugged, feigning uncertainty, then glanced away. My face fell as it clicked. *Sweet Charlotte.* She was one of the only people in the world who knew how much I wanted a family of my own. When we were younger, she used to talk about us having kids the same age and houses on the same block. I was very far from keeping up my end of that bargain. I'd just bought a condo across town and hadn't even frozen my eggs yet, too stuck on the statistics of their value relative to actual embryos. But I could not bear the thought of her waiting for me.

"Nova advising on your family planning was absolutely out of line," I said. "And—look—I know getting pregnant is the biggest decision, but I promise that if you want to have multiple children, the best time to start planning for that is now." The heat had traveled down my neck, where sweat was starting to pool. It was hot out, but this felt bizarre.

"I knew you were going to say that, but—sorry, Leah—you're just not a spiritual person. Bringing children into this world is a deeply spiritual decision. Beau and I have always talked about having two, but I just haven't been feeling ready, and Nova helped explain why."

"It's not spiritual! It's medical! Time to pregnancy and pregnancy risk increase with age," I yelled, shocking us both. This was not how I talked to anyone, let alone my cousin. I was just exhausted. I needed to get home. "I'm sorry. I just don't think it's appropriate for Nova to give medical advice. And I don't want him doing that from inside your place of business."

Charlotte nodded. "Well, I appreciate that," she said, then she glanced through the front door. "I'll go set that rule with him right after I finish this sign."

I flipped toward the shop door. "Wait, he's here?"

"Yeah. He's just inside checking the energy of the space to see where he'll set up."

The heat ran down my chest, through my middle, and directly to my feet. *Let it go*, my brain tried, but I was somehow already inside, ignoring Charlotte shaking her head at me from outside. She knew there was no stopping me.

Nova looked up from the table he was touching as if it had a pulse. He recognized me immediately and smiled with maddening delight. "Dr. Leah the Leo! What a *gorgeous* coincidence. I've been thinking about you."

"I need to speak with you," I said, approaching. "Wait. Why have you been thinking about me?"

He sat down and motioned for me to do the same. I did not.

"I felt very struck by you the other night, so I went back for another look-see of your birth chart again this very morning. *Ooh*, was it even more fascinating at a second glance! Did you know that you entered one of the most powerful transits of your lifetime this past February? Your Neptune squared your Neptune, a.k.a. it is time to let go in a very big way, or else."

"Or else what?" I asked, anger rising.

He flipped both hands over in a dramatic shrug. "Hard to say. These transits push us and pull us. Mysterious, even dangerous, things happen, especially if spirit is trying to get your attention."

I sat, but only so I could achieve a very direct eye line. "*Stop*," I said, my voice icy. "Stop giving women advice on their reproductive timelines and stop telling strangers they're in danger because of some planetary bullshit. Because—and I know you'll love this—I am going through something mysterious now. I have vertigo—a real medical condition. And the last thing I or any other vulnerable person needs is some mythical rationale that's going to throw their life even more off course. You are not a doctor."

Nova touched a hand to his chest like some kind of precious Girl Scout. "I'm so very sorry for whatever you're going through," he said genuinely. "But it makes perfect sense that you're out of balance, astrologically speaking."

"Of course it does," I said, wanting to kick myself for walking directly into this trap.

"You're so disconnected that you can't listen to yourself. And so you don't know yourself. *Kick–ball change*: your real self is rebelling."

The shop door opened. Charlotte had finally come to save me, or potentially Nova. "I know myself," I said in the most assured tone possible.

Nova questioned that with a squint of his infinity-pool eyes. "What does it feel like in your body when your subconscious is trying to speak to you? Example: when I know my heart wants something, my belly makes these little pulses, like spirit is tapping me to pay attention."

I stood to head toward Charlotte and away from all this nonsense. "My subconscious speaks to me through my brain, and right now it's telling me to go grab a coffee from my cousin."

"Come on. You're a doctor. You know about the amygdala and the cognitive alarm system."

I did. I was very surprised that Nova did, too. But that was not the point. I motioned to Charlotte at the espresso machine, clearly eavesdropping. "You are generously being offered a space here. Please respect that and do not do to anyone else in my town what you're trying to do to me. My vertigo has nothing to do with astrology." With that, I finally started to walk away.

"Can you prove it?" I heard over my shoulder.

It stopped me. I locked eyes with Charlotte. Mine narrowed. Hers got very wide. I flipped back to Nova. "Prove my vertigo is not about my astrological chart?" It was too ridiculous not to repeat.

"Yes," he said, as serious as I'd seen him yet. "And while you're at it, also prove that my reading of your whole chart is as wrong as you think it is. You have a birthday in a few months. The timing is pitch-perfect."

I started to crack up, honestly grateful for a good laugh over a ridiculous challenge from—sorry, but—a ridiculous person.

"I'm deeply serious," Nova said. "And I think you— Doctor—are the perfect person to tackle this little research project."

The strangest thing happened next. Nova's words transported me straight to my seat in Dr. Ival Storm's Foundations of Medical Research class. I saw her standing at her lectern as if time had rewound.

"I'm about to change the way you practice medicine with one sentence, followed by sixteen weeks of practicing it," she'd said. "Here goes: it's easier to prove something false than true."

As promised, she spent the next four months molding the way we thought about diagnoses. The key: never waste your time chasing down a positive premise. It's safer and more time-efficient to rule out what a presentation of symptoms *isn't* than to take stabs at what it is. I loved that class. There is nothing more gratifying than arriving at an answer after building a series of tests to deliver an accurate result.

That memory and this moment started to gel in my mind. I stared at Nova, remembering the details of his astrology mini-lesson at Charlotte's. My brain raced toward a Dr. Storm–approved approach to prove his ridiculous premise false. He was obsessed with this "transit" I'd apparently entered, and that was connected to a firm date, so a control . . . The corner of my mouth lifted. It was the sharpest I'd felt in days.

"So, in theory, everyone with my same birth chart should be experiencing this same wild Neptune life crisis thing?" I asked.

Nova nodded, curious. "And all the other transits in your life. Of course, we all experience things a little differently, but—"

"Can you send me a list of the most powerful transits in my birth chart?" I didn't need to hear whatever backpedaling he was going to attempt.

"Sure, but the transits are not the point of astrology. They're what happens to you, not who you are."

"I'm not interested in the point," I said. "I'm interested in the proof."

"Fair enough," Nova said. "May I know why?"

"May I know, too?" Charlotte added over my shoulder. I'd completely missed the fact that she'd joined by the table.

"Because I think Nova is right," I said. I was met by two shocked looks. "I do love just this kind of project, and I am in need of something to focus on right now. So, challenge accepted."

I felt my mouth expand into a determined smile. What could be more perfect than defending my life as I waited to get it back?

Chapter
Eight

I WOKE UP shocked to find I'd finally slept through the night. That gave me energy for a nice, long run. Then I leaped into another favorite activity: checking off items on a to-do list. First, I created a system for storing clothes that didn't require bending down. Then, I moved through the PT exercises David had sent me after our appointment. After that, I scrubbed every eye-level surface of my kitchen and bathroom. Each task took double the time given all the potential vertigo triggers, but I was keeping busy. I was going to get through this. And I now had delightfully tedious research to fill my open afternoon.

After another Charlotte-prepped lunch (she'd somehow managed to expertly freeze a meatball sub), I sat down at my kitchen table to do the absolute last thing I ever expected: read all about astrology. I'd already developed the hypothesis for my experiment—astrology has no verifiable impact on a person's lived experience—and a method: check data from my birth chart matches to compare against the predicted life experiences called for in our key astrological transits. I'd also given in and requested help from Nova on the info to use for data collection. Now I needed to figure out who exactly qualified as a birth chart match. I found the perfect book by a credible source, Dr. Alexander Bolter's *Mathematics and the History of Astrology*. From there I learned that I'd find an almost identical chart in everyone born on my same birth date (August 7) in my same birth year (1983) within one hour before or after my birth time (five fifteen a.m.). Using census data, I calculated that there could be as many as forty thousand people around the world who qualified. Of course, I'd have to find them and convince them to take the survey, but the prospects already felt Dr. Storm–approved. David was right, I thought as my fingers ticked across the laptop keys: this project had tweaked my type A nature and lifted my spirits. I also had to give the ancients credit where it was due: Astrology had started as a fascinating observation of what was happening down on Earth against a map of the stars above. It seemed my Leo sun sign wasn't some random guess at the qualities of a person born between July 23 and August 22, but a reflection of the high growing season, when powerful changes were occurring, thanks to the strong light of the sun. Ergo: Leos are powerful, bright, etc. etc. But I was thrilled to discover that what was called fact in the West was just one system. Chinese, Jewish, and Tibetan astrology were all different, as if I needed one more reason to delight in my little project to disprove it all.

I had no idea how many hours I'd been zoned into my computer by the time the email from Nova finally arrived:

Hello again! I've been through the lifetime of your
birth chart backward and forward. Below are the
four transits that have had the most impact on
your life.

Should have had, I corrected as I scrolled down to read. But
the heading he'd included stopped me: Powerful Transits for all
the August 7th, 1983, 4:15–6:15 AM Star Twins.

I let a Cheshire cat smile creep across my face. Survey collection requires careful marketing, and "the Star Twin Survey"
would immediately grab attention. I read on, now even more
energized.

Transit One: Between 1989 and 1991—An event or
events that made power dynamics in your life
clear, focusing your understanding of self

Transit Two: November of 2011—A struggle that
forced you to acknowledge something not
working in your emotional life

Transit Three: February of 2022—The experience
of a crisis related to your destiny

Transit Four: March 2023—A decision that
propels you to take action on your true
calling in life

I pictured Nova winking an aqua eye at me through the
screen. My own rolled. He had to know that a future date

couldn't be used for my research. He'd included 2023 just to taunt me. But I let myself do the math on my history relative to the rest of the dates.

I was only six in 1989. Who knows anything about power dynamics by that point? Or themselves? I now knew my parents had been at odds from the time I was very young, but my memories of asking to be excused from the dinner table at the start of yet another argument started around fifth grade. I knew because on those nights, I'd beam a lantern light out my bedroom window to signal David to meet me down by the creek, my favorite antidote. So astrology was 0 for 3 so far, but those stats changed when I considered what happened in November of 2011. It was the exact month and year that Cole and I broke up. I remember because I had to answer ten thousand questions about it from Aunt Kath at Thanksgiving dinner. We'd been talking for over a year about him pursuing residency programs in New Jersey so we could stay together. He secretly applied to one long-shot option in San Diego, got an offer, accepted, and informed me—in that order. He swore up and down that he'd come back to the East Coast once it was over, but my trust was too broken. And my instincts were correct. According to social media, he was happily married with twins a very short three years later. But I was more angry than heartbroken after we ended things. I couldn't remember even crying, and I never once considered that I'd made the wrong decision. If Nova wanted to call that proof of something not working in my emotional life, so be it. I wasn't willing to call the timing anything more than a coincidence.

February of 2022—The experience of a crisis related to your destiny. This was the easiest answer. If it had said May 2022, I might have flinched, but in February I was blissfully vertigo-free and months into an "authentic purpose" that had been decided many, many years prior. Case closed. But not for Nova, apparently.

> I know you're only interested in the transits, but I—of course—cannot help myself from passing along some of the personality and lifestyle traits of your gorgeous Leo, Leo, Cancer chart. These are as much a part of your journey as the dates. Know them. Explore them. Love them! They are your path to the best version of your short time on this earth!

> Blessings, Nova

I scanned the list he'd included:

> *I am meant to pursue a life of leadership and creativity.*

> *I am a deeply sensitive and emotional person.*

> *I need more alone time than most to recharge and tap into my intuition.*

> *I am guided by the pursuit of self-improvement and self-discovery.*

> *I must learn to quiet the opinions of others.*

I need childlike play, indulgence, and joy.

*Travel is key to my self-exploration and
development.*

I will make bold decisions to define my own path.

It sounded like the manifesto of a spotlight-loving diva. I
was proud of my leadership in the practice and our town, but
that was about the only thing I related to from this list. I had
thicker skin than most and preferred the company of others
over more time alone. If anything, I valued the opinions of just
a few key people—my dad and Charlotte, primarily—and
made my own decisions otherwise. And what did "childlike
play" mean? I read the list over and over, more annoyed with
each pass. Not only was I not this personality type, I did not
want to be. I much preferred myself to my astrological profile,
and I was perfectly fine if that disappointed one overly opin-
ionated astrologer and absent mother.

I loaded the three transits into the same online survey
builder we'd used in med school. Each transit would be for-
matted as a yes-or-no question—did you have *x* life experience on *y* date? If the response was yes, I created a field for
anyone to include further information. I'd use anecdotal research to further qualify respondents. Now to find at least one
hundred 8/7/83 needles in a whole-world haystack. The pos-
sibilities were endless, and—finally—the days ahead felt less
daunting. I took the very first step by posting a message to my
admittedly dusty social media account asking my small net-
work for any Star Twin leads.

A knock on my front door pulled me out of what had ended up being a five-hour research trance. Mission accomplished. I knew it was Dad with my favorite margherita pizza–and–Caesar salad combo from Franny's. A strange thought landed with me as I went to greet him: *Maybe don't bring up this project.* I dismissed it immediately. He would relate to my need for some mental exercise right now and always support my sticking up for science. But I opened the door to find a stocky man whom I did not recognize.

"Dr. Leah Lockhart?" he said, his face blank.

I immediately regretted nodding. "Who are you?" I asked, keeping my hand firmly gripped on the doorknob. My stomach lurched as he shoved a large envelope into the space between us.

"You've been served," he said.

Chapter
Nine

I PRESSED A hand to my knee to try to stop it from twitching. It was well into hour one of my third lawyer meeting in five days. Jim Cooper was an old and trusted friend of my dad who'd taken my case immediately. So far we'd been through a minute-by-minute recounting of what happened, then a lengthy interview about my entire career. Now it was time to talk about a strategy for preventing Monica Shepard from ending it with the malpractice suit she'd filed against me.

"Mom and baby are both perfectly healthy, so we're dealing with opposing counsel seeking emotional damages only," Jim said.

Dad sat across from him, nodding at what was apparently good news. He'd rescheduled another afternoon of patients to be my second set of ears in this session. Guilt was making it so I could barely make eye contact with him across the table. "Tougher case for her," he said. "But that doesn't eliminate the possibility of the hospital taking their own action against us, correct?"

I wanted to correct his use of "we" and "us." I was the one on trial here, but my dad's wrinkled brow across the table reminded me that was not true. If I was guilty, we lost the practice. I lifted my hand from my leg. There was no point trying to stop my body from shaking.

"As we now know, both nurses have corroborated the girl's claim that she saw your first dizzy spell before the fall," Jim explained.

"Monica," I said on instinct.

He mimed a firm "no" with the sharp cross of a finger through the air. The move matched the man in his dark, heavy suit and slick, corporate hair. "Humanize her and you'll start to feel empathetic, and that's when defendants make mistakes."

"Don't worry," Dad jumped in. "Dr. Lockhart hasn't had any contact with the plaintiff or staff since that night." But his comment didn't put me at ease. I'd gone radio silent on my entire team after they leaped in to save a patient and me. It felt beyond wrong.

"Good. Very smart," Jim said.

"Is it, though?" I asked. "I had a really good rapport with her. Is there any benefit in reaching out to talk this through? Offering her something to ease her experience?"

"An offer is settling, which is an admission of guilt. But I agree that we need to try and make this go away before it starts."

"And how do you do that?"

"We build up your credibility and take hers down."

My eyes shut. I'd taken an oath to do no harm to every patient I encountered. It made me sick to think that I might end up harming both a young woman and her baby in what was already the most overwhelming moment of her life.

"We're here for anything and everything you need, Jim," I heard my dad say. "Right?" I could feel him looking at me, so I opened my eyes and nodded.

* * *

I felt my dad's hand on my shoulder as we walked away from the building.

"Let me drop you home before I head back to the office," he said. I turned to find a worried look in his eyes.

"Thanks, but I'm good. I'll walk. Clear my mind," I said with as much reassurance as I could muster. The truth was I had absolutely nothing to do for the rest of the day. Everything *to do* had been put on hold by either a new request from Jim's office or my complete inability to focus.

"Smart," Dad said, nodding to himself. "Keep moving. We've got a great guy on this, and you know I'll do everything in my power to make sure we come out of it intact." His certainty should have been a comfort, but I was too numb to feel it.

"Thank you so much," I said.

We shook hands like always, then headed in opposite directions. I made it about five minutes down the road before my phone started vibrating. David was calling. My stomach clenched. *Shit, shit, shit. I'm supposed to be meeting him at my house for our second session right now.*

"David, hi," I said into the phone, already starting to

sprint. "I'm . . . long story. But I'll be there in—um—twenty minutes."

"Are you running?" he asked.

"I am. I'm so sorry. I forgot about our appointment, but I'm under three miles away. I'll be quick."

"Nope," he said. "I'm either coming to where you are or we can meet somewhere closer."

I searched the map of the town in my mind, stopping short when I realized the obvious and comforting answer. "Let's meet at the creek in ten minutes. My dad still leaves the side gate open."

I found David wandering around the oak-tree-shaded backyard.

"Hey," I said, startling him.

"Hey." He turned to me and smiled sweetly. "I forgot how pretty this little town is."

"Maybe it's time to move back," I said faster than I could stop myself.

David nodded. There was a thought I couldn't place behind his eyes, then they landed on our custom-built bridge. "Oh god, please tell me that all got smaller," he said, hurrying down the sloped lawn. "I thought it was the Mississippi River when we were kids."

I trailed him. "Unfortunately, I think we got bigger. But does the Mississippi have a bridge built from old boardwalk scraps?"

David laughed as he pulled his phone out to snap a picture, I assumed for his parents. "Remember how soaking wet our dads got trying to build this thing?"

"Remember my mom insisted we do a ribbon-cutting ceremony when it was done?"

"And she sang at it, if I recall?"

"'Let the River Run,' of course." Even I had to laugh at that.

David slipped off his boat shoes, then wove his body under the railing. His legs dangled so low he could rest them on the rocks below. I followed, successfully lowering myself down and slipping off my sandals without bending my torso.

"Someone's been practicing," David said.

"Just trying to live up to that middle school 'Most Likely to Succeed' status," I joked, finally landing my own legs to hang right beside his. Our feet lined up under a spotlight of sun poking through the trees above. It felt like unlocking a time portal straight back to the nineties.

"Man, it's good to be here." David looked out over the trickling water. "I'm jealous you have this right in your dad's backyard still."

I followed his gaze through the hidden gully of overgrown dogwood trees and ferns so tall they'd created a fence tucking us away from all the surrounding houses. *The Secret Garden* had been one of my favorite books growing up, a rare thing my mom and I shared. This nook became David's and my version of that sacred place. On this bridge, we'd hashed out everything from social studies projects and birthday party plans, to our total obsession with the movie *Big* after we'd rented it from Blockbuster one weekend. We were desperate to get our parents to take us to the real Zoltar machine on Coney Island. But it was the much bigger stuff that bonded us. His confession that playing sports against the much taller boys at school made him so anxious he felt like throwing up. Mine that I was desperate for my parents to just split up already. We always left the creek feeling better. Safer. Like at least one person in the world understood. Now here was my person again.

"Would you believe I haven't been down here in years?" I confessed as David tried to pick up a pebble with his feet. I couldn't honestly place the last time. *Maybe I should have come right here the day I got diagnosed with vertigo*, I thought. My gaze drifted out, then back to David beside me. His eyes seemed equally lost in his version of that exact thought. He turned to me with an almost sad look.

"I would," he said.

Before I could inquire into that ominous line, he was propped up on his knees beside me. "Okay. Disclaimer: this will be my first time doing a BPPV treatment session on a bridge, but maybe we'll have creek magic on our side."

"I need it now more than ever," I said.

David shifted over until he was behind me. "Here we go," he said, gently placing a hand on each of my shoulders. I was prepared this time, but that did not change the way his touch shot through my body. He tipped me left, back, and up, right, back, and up, in the smoothest motion. "Manageable dizziness?"

"Yes . . . ," I said slowly.

"No lies with me, Leah. It won't help the treatment."

I sighed. "Fine. It's actually worse today."

"Okay. Let me narrow the pitch." He guided me through those same moves twice again. It took everything in me not to vomit both times. "Wow. That bad?"

"How can you tell?" I shook my arms, trying to relax.

"I can feel your body clamming up. Let's do this. Close

your eyes. Take a deep breath and try to just release the muscles in your shoulders a bit."

David hugged his hands to the base of my neck, then he took his own deep, audible breath. My lungs caught it like a yawn, expanding. Then my body started to warm. He took another inhale; I mirrored it again, deeper this time. On the third go—heat building from my chest up through my head—I breathed so deeply that I was sure my whole body would explode. Then it did. I was suddenly sobbing.

David did not move either hand from my body, and he did not stop breathing as my chest heaved and my eyes started to fill with water. I tried to compose myself, but it only made my heart race more. Soon tears were rolling down my cheeks. *Why is this happening? Why can't I stop it?* I thought. Then words started pouring out of me, too.

"I'm sorry. It's just—the woman I passed out on during delivery is suing, and the hospital is doing its own investigation," I heard myself confess. "I was with my lawyer before this. And—I could lose my medical license, which would mean losing the practice." My head started to fall with the weight of it all, but I righted it in time to avoid the world spinning any more out of control.

"I'm so sorry, Leah," David said. "That's—" I was comforted by the fact that he had no words, too.

"I feel like I'm stuck in a nightmare, and I can't wake myself up. Or like I body-switched into someone else's life. This is not me."

He nodded. "Is that why you're doing this astrology project thing?" he asked. I shot back confusion, then remembered my posts. "I got back on social media to reconnect with more people up here, and I found you and your post looking for—what did you call them?"

"Star Twins," I said, wiping the last of the tears from my cheeks, thank god. "That's a long story involving a pushy astrologer who thinks my vertigo is because I'm living out of alignment with my astrological chart. I set up a control survey based on matching birth chart data to prove him wrong." David shook his head, laughing. "Hey, you were the one who recommended that I engage in some nerdy research project!"

"I was picturing you cataloging shell shapes or something, not disproving ancient star data."

"Please. I cataloged all the shell shapes when I was five." David cracked up even more. "I'm serious!" I said.

"That's why I'm laughing!" he replied. "So what does it even mean to be out of alignment with your astrological chart?"

"It means nothing as far as I'm concerned. But the *stars* say I'm supposed to be this boundary-breaking travel-lover with a big, bold life who needs alone time and play and a whole lot of other stuff that is the opposite of who I am and honestly would ever want to be." David reacted with a sort of squint that I did not like. "What?"

"Nothing," he said, but his tone gave him away.

"No lies with me either, David."

"Fine. That doesn't sound like the opposite of you to me."

My back shot straight. "What do you mean?"

"You started a student government in our elementary school, Leah. You were constantly trying to push back against school rules and dreaming up big ideas. We read

books to dementia patients once a week in fourth grade because you set it up."

"Well, that I still do when I have time. It's just being a good
citizen."

David shook his head. "It was more than that. You told me
you were going to go to college somewhere in Europe and
write books about your travels someday. And I remember you
never held back on anything. The second you even thought
about ice cream, you were dragging me to the creamery."

"Every ten-year-old is obsessed with ice cream," I said, ignoring the rest. I had memories of what David was saying, but
like impulsive dessert runs, they were little-kid ideas.

"Yeah. I guess," David said. I liked this new look on his
face even less.

"David, do not tell me you believe in some star-charted
destiny."

"I don't know a thing about astrology," David said. "But I've
had one too many experiences with stress on the body in my
work to chalk every single symptom up to science. And . . . I
mean no offense by this, Leah, but you're . . . I don't know . . .
you're just more—I guess *content* than I imagined."

"*Content?*" I threw my hands up. "I am content! What's
wrong with that?"

"Nothing." David shook his head at himself. "I'm sorry. I'm
not trying to be a dick. If you say you're happy with your
life—which is a great life—then I believe you."

"Yes. It is a great life," I said, avoiding David's eyes as I
slowly started to stand up. I couldn't remember a time when
he'd made me feel like I did now. *Which is what, exactly?*

David's phone rang in his pocket, saving one of the two of us, I wasn't sure which.

"Sorry, it's my daughter," he said, phone in hand. "I should probably take this."

That took care of instantly turning the tables. Our eyes met, mine shocked, his guilty. Apparently his lack of a wedding band was more complicated . . .

"Right. So I have a daughter," David said, letting the call go to voicemail. "Stella. She's five and amazing. And I also have an ex-wife. Erin."

"Wow. Okay," I said, recalibrating.

"Sorry. I couldn't quite figure out how to transition from *you have vertigo* to *I have a kid and ex-wife*," David said. "It's been tough, which is part of the reason I'm up here. Some distance felt like a good idea, though I'm trying to get back every other weekend to keep things consistent for Stella."

"That's good," I said, impressed.

David was standing beside me now, bracing himself against the beam of the bridge railing. His fallen face made me realize we'd both needed this creek session more than we knew.

"This poor bridge was probably not ready for our very dramatic return," I said, brushing my hand against the sun-faded wood.

David nodded. "Seems like we both need a reverse Zoltar machine, huh?"

A smile broke through me. Of course he remembered our shared obsession. The phone started ringing again. "Sorry, but I really should call Stella back. She just got home from a week of science camp because she inherited one hundred percent of my cool."

"Of course," I said. "Thank you for today. Promise not to cry my eyes out at our next session."

"Thank you," said David. "And promise it's okay if you do."

I watched his tall frame walk up and out of the backyard, hoping I could squash my crush on this man whose life was too far away and too complicated to mesh with mine.

That night I finally folded the pile of laundry that had been sitting on my bedroom chair for days. Two pairs of jeans. Two pairs of running shorts. Six T-shirts: three white, three black. Comfortable, convenient clothes. My mind went to David's comment—no, insult. Did he think grown-up me would dress differently, too? I slipped the items into their new dresser system, still lingering in that uncomfortable feeling from our creek session. But it prompted a thought. I grabbed my laptop from the kitchen and logged on to the Star Twin Survey for the first time since I'd posted it. I was hoping for a few responses— two or three people with my same astrology and zero connection to the transits Nova outlined, confirmation that I was right about myself and David was wrong. Unfortunately, zero 8/7/83 babies had found their way to my teeny tiny corner of the Internet. But one very interesting message had.

> Hey Leah, I'm Mikey. My girlfriend is a client of
> Nova's, and he forwarded me your survey. I'm not
> technically your full Star Twin—I'm 8/7 but born in
> 1998—but I want to help you promote your
> project. I produce the Andi Hour podcast, and
> she wants to have you on as a guest.

Chapter
Ten

"I KNOW MY talking points. I have my joke lines. I can do this," I said, flipping through my note cards for the hundredth time. Charlotte turned the volume down on the *Andi Hour* episode she'd suggested we listen to as she drove me to the show's Manhattan recording studio. "Thank you. I've listened to enough to know that she's a fast-talking firecracker, and I'm a camera-shy person who—apparently—still uses the word 'firecracker.'"

"Yeah. Maybe don't use it with Andi . . . ," Charlotte said. "But yes. You can absolutely do this. And remember, it's going to be worth it on so many fronts."

"Right," I said, grateful for that reminder as I turned the stereo all the way off to refocus on my notes.

Mikey's invite had turned out to be even better than his message let on. Andi Gold was a New Jersey native who dedicated one show a month to highlighting the lives of fellow Garden State Girlies (her term). She wanted me to talk about my life as a doctor and the incredible heritage of Lockhart Women's Medical during the episode, which Jim Cooper had cleared as an excellent credibility boost for the case. Then I'd plug the Star Twin Survey, which I'd committed to refocusing on in the name of my sanity. According to Mikey, the whole thing would be over in forty-five minutes. What he did not explain is that they'd be recording audio and video.

"You look fine," he said, giving my black joggers and gray T-shirt an unconvincing once-over in the show's extremely posh greenroom. He wore a vintage Rolling Stones T-shirt over skinny jeans with black leather sneakers that looked shined on the regular.

Charlotte shoved a lavender blazer into my hands. "Here," she said, barely looking at me.

"Where did you get this?" I asked.

"I brought it for you," she confessed. "And sorry. I knew the show also did video, and I didn't tell you so you wouldn't be more nervous." She turned to Mikey. "Don't worry. She's incredibly well prepared."

I went to protest but stopped. She'd done the right thing. "Thank you," I said, throwing the jacket over my top.

"Hey, birthday twin. Don't sweat it," said Mikey. "You're a Leo. You were born for this."

It was the last thing I wanted to hear. Then Mikey's words transported me to an image of the last person I wanted to envision in this moment: my mother. I could practically see her delivering that same line as she applied a second coat of crimson lipstick at the bathroom vanity before my one and only role in a school play. Orphan Number Three in *Annie*. Even I knew I'd been assigned to the background because my singing was god-awful, but Mom insisted I'd find my footing because *I was a Leo. I was born for it* and anything else that required a boldness she was desperate for me to embrace. Dad told me the truth after the show that night. "Better to be known for your brain than your voice," he'd said. It was the focus I needed then and now.

"Ready?" Mikey asked, pulling me back.

"Yes," I said as I touched a hand to the note cards in my pocket.

★ ★ ★

"God, I wish you were my doctor. I feel like I could actually tell you what's going on in my *down there*," Andi said minutes into the interview. My extensive prep was aided by the fact that she was dressed in the same XL sweatsuit as most of the nervous teenagers I saw for their first gynecology appointment. I'd simply sat down at the mic and treated her just like I would any new patient.

"The technical term is 'hoo-ha,'" I joked. It was smooth sailing from that point. I covered every note card I'd prepped and ad-libbed my way into an even deeper conversation about the benefits of small, experienced medical practices. Then I transitioned seamlessly into my Star Twin Survey pitch, explaining the premise and process, then selling it with my slam-bang stats.

"Listeners: do you know that Americans are spending upwards of two point two billion dollars a year on 'mythical services' *and* that revenue for astrology apps alone landed around forty million dollars as of a few years ago?" I said.

"That's *insane!*" Andi yelled.

"It is," I agreed. "Especially when you consider that anyone on the Internet can wake up one day and call themselves an astrologer." *Mic drop*, as the kids say.

"Okay, my fellow Jersey girls and beyond. I need you to get to work. Help us find Leah Lockhart's Star Twins."

"Yes, please," I jumped in. "That's people born August seventh, 1983, between four fifteen and six fifteen a.m."

"So, any predictions? Like, how many countries do you think you'll visit to meet your twins?"

That prospect had not crossed my mind. "Oh, I've got my survey all set up online, so I won't need to do any traveling," I said.

"Oh, sad!" cried Andi. "You have to *do this* do this. I mean, at the very least go meet the people you feel some kind of magic connection with, right?"

Now did not feel like the time to tell her and her very large number of listeners that I could not tie my shoes with confidence, let alone fly around the world.

"We'll see," I said. "Though 'magic connections' are sort of the whole thing I'm fighting."

Andi laughed. "Valid! Okay, I think we need you to come back on to tell us how it all turns out. *Omigod!* We'll have you back right after your birthday! *Omigod*, I cannot wait!"

"Sure," I said, caught up in the moment. But a return visit would accomplish my goal of getting the right message out to the public. A perfect wrap-up.

"Done and done. Okay, now I'm doing a new thing with every interview: a fire round finisher. Four questions. Four seconds to answer each. Sound good?"

"Sounds great," I said, fully settled in.

"Okay, number one: what's your favorite thing to do for a *really* good time?"

"Jog," I answered without a second thought.

"Wow. You heard me say '*really* good time,' right?" Andi joked. "Okay, two: go-to thing you put on to feel *so* good about yourself. Like *fully* in your skin."

"Um, my white coat?"

"Oh. Okay. A literal interpretation. But I guess that makes sense for you." Those greenroom nerves suddenly came creeping back. *Why did it feel like I was doing this wrong?* "Three," Andi continued. "Fill in the blank for what you want people to say about you in your eulogy. Leah Lockhart was . . ."

"God . . . Seriously? Okay. I guess *she was kind.*"

Andi wrinkled her nose disapprovingly. *What's wrong with being kind?* "Final question: what's something upcoming in your life that you're incredibly excited about?"

I froze. "Um . . ." Only two things came to mind: getting back to work and having my vertigo cured. But I did not think they were what Andi wanted, and I did not want to leave listeners focused on the fact that my life was currently a mess. "I . . . um . . ."

"Two seconds!" Andi warned.

"Oh. I go to Cape May for my birthday every year, so, that."

"Cute," said Andi. It was not a ringing endorsement, but at least our forty-five minutes were finally up. Andi thanked me with four air kisses, Mikey said he'd reach out to book my return, and Charlotte treated me to sushi on our way home.

I found myself staring at the ceiling fan in my bedroom long past midnight, more uneasy about my answers to Andi's final four questions with every click of the dangling light-switch chain. Worse, my mind kept pulling me to an image of David listening to the end of the podcast with the same almost-disappointed look he'd had at the creek. *Did I sound too content?* Why did that word now feel like a synonym for "boring"? I reached over to my nightstand and popped a melatonin. That would finally close out this day. *My answers were perfectly fine and very much me*, I offered myself as a final thought. But another one pushed its way through: *Why do I keep defending myself to myself?*

Luckily the episode served its purpose. The morning after it aired, I woke up to find survey responses from my first five Star Twins.

Chapter
Eleven

ON MONDAY I Zoomed with Annie, a Star Twin from north-
ern New Jersey with five true-crime novels under her belt, two
bestsellers. She was a *no, yes, no* on the transit survey and
the only thing we shared was straw-blond hair. On Tuesday I
had a phone call with Gio, a New York native living in DC and
aspiring to someday run for office. Charlotte and I once
joked about being the first co-mayors of the Highlands, but
that was about as much of a connection as I could muster.
Also, he refused to take the survey, citing public image concerns. Wednesday was Mei, a biology professor whom I liked
immediately. We were both science-minded small-town dwell-
ers who stayed clear of drama, leaving me incredibly disappointed when I explained this whole project started because
of the insane suggestion that my astrological chart gave me
vertigo and she said, "That doesn't sound insane at all."

Less than ten responses weren't going to cut it, especially
if they were all astrology-inclined already. I was prepared to

call this whole thing off. Maybe I could find a 10K, or better yet marathon, to train for as an alternate distraction. But a quick check of the database before my Thursday-morning run changed everything. There were suddenly twenty-five new responses. *How?* A message from one of them provided a concerning clue: Three people sent me articles about this whole search. So cool! Thanks for connecting all us Star Twins!

My heart was suddenly racing. *What articles?* Seconds later my laptop screen featured one long list of links to the exact same story: DOCTOR SETS OUT TO DISPROVE ASTROLOGY.

I clicked through to one from Bustle.com, hands shaking as I waited for it to load. It was just a recap of my *Andi Hour* episode. They'd included quotes from the recording but hadn't done any other digging into my life, thank god. The three next links were the same. Still, I felt queasy. *This was not the plan.* I'd envisioned slowly finding matches through personal connections and traditional data collection—emailing organizations, digging through social media. I was not looking to be the face of some public anti-astrology campaign, especially right now. I shut my laptop and left for the run, nerves pushing me further and faster than I'd gone all week. Unfortunately, they did not talk me out of getting right back on my computer immediately post-shower. At least the silver lining of this unexpected exposure was tons more intel.

So far 30 percent of respondents confirmed they'd experienced all three transits. Not affirming, but not nothing. But the anecdotal answers changed my tune: *Every astrology reading I've ever had has called out this 2011 transit. Obviously that's when I divorced my first husband.* And: *I thought I was going through an early midlife crisis back in February, but then I had an astrology reading that told me about this Neptune transit.* The only *yes* responders were already all about astrology. I'd need to find a more diverse survey set.

I flipped to social media, curious if there was any helpful chatter. Several messages were waiting in my inbox. Hey twin! Taking the survey! And Fellow 8/7/83 baby here! And Cool project, I'll share. But the start of one caught my eye: Thanks from a Star Twin and struggling doctor. I clicked through.

> Hi Leah. Seems like we're twins in more ways than one. I think a close to perfect match, too. Longer story but I'm on leave from my practice at the moment. At this point I'm desperate for any answers, even from the stars. Let me know if you ever want to chat. —Heidi

I navigated over to the profile page of Dr. Heidi Rosemont. It was private, but one detail that I could see jumped out immediately: she was born in Los Angeles, California. She was possibly even more of a perfect match. Heidi and I could have been born just fifteen minutes apart, maybe even at the same hospital. Now we were two doctors experiencing something similar during the same time in our lives. *How eerie . . .* I stopped myself. The brain is designed to jump to this kind of bridge building. That was especially true when things felt otherwise out of control. Like my entire life right now. I messaged Heidi, thanking her for the note and saying I'd be happy to chat.

I planned to take a break, my eyes blurry and stomach grumbling, but one new message popped into my inbox just as I was about to close out. I read it once, then twice, then a third time just to be sure.

> Hey hey, Ms. Leah. I'm your Star Twin Imani, and
> I'm also about to be your travel fairy Godmomma.
> Come with me on a retreat I'm running. Venice,
> Italy. Two weeks from tomorrow. My early
> birthday treat;) Check your email.

It was Venice, Italy, that knocked my back against the kitchen chair. *Of all the places in the world . . .*

Mom claimed she just needed space to get back on her feet once she and Dad divorced. She moved to an apartment just a few towns inland from the Highlands, but it turned out that was not nearly far enough. I thought she'd head off on some road trip, maybe go on one of the yoga retreats she was always talking about. Turns out she desperately needed back-to-back-to-back European vacations. I got a postcard from every single stop, including the very last, Venice. That one featured a picture of the Peggy Guggenheim Collection. I remembered because I had no idea who Peggy Guggenheim was and had to look her up in a library book at school the next day. But I also remembered because of the words she'd written on the back. *I think I'm finally done traveling for a bit.* I thought that meant she'd finally be home, but instead she left for California. Venice was the last place I wanted to visit, even for free. Who was this crazy Star Twin who wanted to take me there?

I quickly navigated to the profile of the woman behind this mysterious invite: @ImaniMichelleCoaches. She was a Master Certified Worthiness Coach, a job title that sounded straight out of a pyramid scheme. Her profile image was eye-rollingly "Leo": Imani lounging naked on a hammock, long, pink-dyed braids carefully placed over her bits. Her bio read: *I help women find themselves and their joy.* The rest of the page was filled with videos featuring her ranting about how women are ignoring their cravings, missing out on their greatest pleasures, and diminishing their worth. And of course, she alone had the answer to this "epidemic of unmet ecstasy." I found links to pricey online courses titled *Take the Stick Out of Your Ass* and *When Was the Last Time You Laughed So Hard You Cried?* She had more than one hundred thousand followers. *Of course.* Imani's world was proof of those stats I'd found on mythical spending. It made me suspicious about whether she was even my real match. But I was too curious not to check my email.

> Star Twin! Imani Michelle here. I'm an August 7th, '83 baby too. Listen, stop wasting your time shitting all over astrology and come with me to Venice. I have a JOY-ney starting soon, and someone just dropped out. How's that for the universe putting you on blast?! You cover the airfare (seasonably low round trip from NJ airports. Yes, I checked). I'll cover the entire retreat cost. Consider it a very early birthday gift so you can celebrate our actual day as the woman you're supposed to be. More deets via the link below. Or we could just talk about it all in person . . . I happen to be speaking in Philly tomorrow;)

I did not want to go to Venice. I did not want to go any-where with this woman. And I could not possibly travel a) with vertigo, and b) while my saintly father was holding down our practice in the middle of a pending lawsuit.

Oddly none of those facts stopped me from being pulled down the online rabbit hole of the mysterious Imani Michelle. I felt possessed. First stop: Imani's YouTube page, which was filled with video lessons featuring her standing in front of a vintage chalkboard set in outfits each more outrageous than the last (a full-feathered minidress, a red latex catsuit, a suit jacket covered in tiny mirrors). In one clip, she introduced the concept that if something in your life is not a *hell yes*, then it's a *hell no*. Another was about the way awe affects the brain, which she described as an "orgasm inside your head." Then, perhaps proving my sex cult suspicions, she talked about the power of an actual orgasm. I was impressed to see the words "dopamine," "oxytocin," and "norepinephrine" on the chalk-board. At least the woman had done her research. But she was the exact Leo diva I did not want to be.

"You're going insane," I said to my reflection on the laptop screen. "You need to step away, now."

The rotating image on Imani's website flipped to a shot of her belly-laughing with a group of women, all equally hyster-ical. I felt a sudden tingle in my shoulders. I wiggled them, figuring it was a kind of itch. The sensation stayed. It was as if all the nerve endings at the very top of my arms had been turned on. I'd probably spent too much time hunched over staring at a screen, I thought. Only I didn't feel cramped. I ac-tually felt perked up, like I could spend hours longer on this website. *Like I want to. Why?*

I closed my computer without replying, then spent the rest of the afternoon doing PT exercises and catching up on old medical journals before a long evening run. But I was still thinking about Imani and her offer as I went to bed. When I woke up, I threw on clothes, got in the car I was not supposed to be driving, and drove directly to Philadelphia.

Chapter
Twelve

UNLIKE 99 PERCENT of all speaking engagements, Imani's event was not in some hotel ballroom. It was on the roof of a defunct textile factory in Philadelphia's arts district. I sat down in the absolute last row of seats, feeling like my invite had left off the dress code. Everyone buzzing around the space—three-hundred-plus women by my count—was in color. And not just your standard primaries. These women had pulled from the Crayola Ultimate box. My jeans and white T-shirt stuck out more than the gold jumpsuit sitting to my left.

"Hello, hello!" said the woman wearing it. "I'm Bea. I teach high school science in Boston. How long have you been in the Imani orbit?"

People are here from Boston? "I'm—uh—not exactly in the orbit," I said, careful not to offend. "I'm here doing some research."

Thankfully the music turned up to twelve before Bea could ask a follow-up. Imani sauntered onto the stage in a sequined dress straight out of a Broadway show. She stopped at its center, appearing to float atop the skyscrapers in the background. It was impressive and terrifying.

"Thank you, queens! And welcome!" she yelled out to the screaming crowd. "Now I'm going to kick us off with a little trip back to childhood: who here remembers the movie *Alice in Wonderland*?" Most hands shot up around me. "Well, I honestly didn't, and so the other day I'm watching it with my daughter, and it gets to that part where Alice meets the creepy British caterpillar guy that asks her the same question over and over again. We know it?" Everyone nodded, this time me included. "Right. *Whooo aarrreee yoouuu?*" She did an impressive English accent. "I about fell off my couch, friends! This is a children's movie, and he is asking one of the most profound questions we can ever ask ourselves. Who are you? I thought that was powerful enough, then sweet Alice goes and confesses that she doesn't know who she is. Anyone remember what she says?"

Now the whole group drew a blank.

"This little girl says, 'I'm afraid I can't explain myself because I'm not myself. I cannot put it any more clearly because it is not clear to me.' I damn near cried my eyes out. My daughter was all, *What is happening, Mom?* And I told her: this is what I encounter with women every single day in my work. You know that you're not yourself. You're afraid that you don't even know yourself anymore. And you cannot figure out why. Well, I'm here to tell you that this is *excellent* news. This horrific, terrifying, out-of-your-mind feeling is the beginning of you being pushed to find out who the hell you really are. Congratulations."

The room was frozen, everyone letting that statement land. I caught tears streaming down Bea's face, then noticed cheeks being dabbed all across the room, and I surprisingly understood the emotion, even if I didn't quite feel it. Finally, someone started what turned into thunderous applause.

"Thank you. Thank you all," Imani said, waving her hands to end the cheering. "But I'm not done. Because I know some of you are out there thinking I sound like some bullshit guru that speaks in memes." I swear she looked right at me when she said that line. "So, what does it mean to know who you are? I know it sounds vague and heady and like the last thing you have time to figure out, even if you could. But I promise, it's the opposite. Now I'm about to tell you exactly what I mean and exactly how you're going to do it."

Imani proceeded to make good on that promise. Knowing yourself—according to her—meant discovering the list of things you specifically love most, from hobbies to meals to outfits to music. It meant understanding who you like to spend time with, who you don't, and why. It meant figuring out what makes you feel angry, elated, sad, sexy, nourished, etc., etc., etc. On and on she went, slicing what it is to be a human being into the thinnest wedges before finishing with the only piece left to prove her grand point. "Obviously this is not an overnight project. So now your final question is probably, why do all this work to figure myself out? What's it worth? Sorry, friends, but for this final part I've got to say trust me: your life will be more complicated, painful, and confusing if you don't and more joyful, fulfilling, and satisfying if you do."

The crowd went wild yet again. This time Imani didn't stop

them. But I sat motionless, batting around my own final question: what if you are sure you know yourself but keep being told otherwise?

Women started rushing to line up beside the stage for a Q & A. I stayed seated, not about to ask my question out loud. Not even comfortable admitting it to myself. But I watched the large group form, struck by the fact that not one looked like the sad victim of a crazed self-help guru. They were steady, poised, professional women, and they proceeded to ask fascinating questions about communicating boundaries to partners, practicing intuition work toward a new career, finding love after losing a spouse, and a dozen more issues that essentially boiled down to *Something does not feel right in my life. How do I figure out why and then fix it?* Imani's answer was almost identical no matter the question, but at one point she put it into words that struck me more than anything she'd said yet.

"You start very small," she said. "Look at your life and find one place where you are doing something that you know in your heart you do not want to do. And then choose to do what your heart wants instead."

My mind flew to an image of Monica Shepard. It was like someone reached into my head and brought her face straight to the front. Or maybe more like my heart. I shot a look up at Imani, so thrown I was almost willing to blame witchcraft.

I decided to wait in a different line to say hello after the talk ended. I'd come all this way. I'd thank her in person for the Venice invite, then head out.

"You came," she said once it was finally my turn. Her tone did not suggest that she was surprised.

"Hi, yes, I'm Leah. But you know that I guess," I rambled.

"Um. It was a last-minute decision for this astrology project. And I really just wanted to say thank you for the invite to Venice, but—"

"Why?" Imani asked. There were at least thirty women in line behind me, but she leaned in as if she had all the time in the world.

"I'm sorry?" I replied, stalling.

"Why can't you come to Venice?"

"Um, it's a long story, but I'm dealing with some vertigo that's being treated. And my dad is running our medical practice while I'm on leave, so I can't just go gallivanting off to Italy for a week."

Imani did not skip half a beat. "One: my mother had vertigo, and it didn't cure 'til she went *gallivanting off* to an all-inclusive in the Caymans. Two: you said 'gallivanting' like it's a bad word. Who taught you that? And three: if this father of yours loves you and wants you to heal, then he shouldn't stop you." I stood there unable to muster a single comeback. Imani took that as a sign to keep going. "Just answer without thinking: can you currently afford a plane ticket to Venice?"

"Yes," I heard myself say definitively.

"Do you have the *literal time* to go to Venice?"

"Yes." That was technically the truth.

"Do you want to go on this trip to Venice?"

I paused.

"First thought," Imani said.

"Yes," I said again. It was an honest answer, but a shocking one. I'd had negative feelings about Venice for almost my entire life. *Why in the world would I want to go?*

"Okay," she said knowingly, readying herself to greet the

next attendee. "Now, if you still say no to the trip, I recommend you sit down for a *long* talk with yourself about why." She gave my shoulder a tender squeeze with her perfectly manicured hand. "I'm not trying to bully you, Leah."

"Yes, you are." I couldn't help that, but it earned me a big, boisterous laugh.

"You're right, I am. But it's because I like you. Makes sense, since we're—what's your term? Star Twins? I think it's pure magic for us to have connected at all. Why end it at that?"

I smiled by way of response.

"The question was not rhetorical," Imani continued with a confident head cock.

"Oh . . ."

"I look forward to hearing your answer, in Venice."

Chapter
Thirteen

MANY THINGS GNAWED at me as I very carefully drove home from Philadelphia, but none more than my feelings about Monica Shepard. I'd been able to stick with logic after the last meeting with my lawyer, but now the thought of treating her like a problem to be solved made my stomach churn. *I* was the problem. I kept going back to Imani's direction for how to correct something that felt wrong in our hearts. But my situation was not cut-and-dried. I was the head of a business now, not just a doctor. I had to consider the security of LWM, not just the feelings of one patient. But ridiculous as it felt, I could not stop wondering if Imani was right, if I was somehow throwing my whole life off further by denying what felt true to me. There had to be a way for me to communicate to Monica that I'd never meant to hurt her or the baby, without jeopardizing my whole future in the process.

As I passed Riverview Medical Center on the last leg of my trip, I thought about that night and an answer landed: the intake. Monica's forms would have had to include a phone number. *I could call her.* Almost immediately, a second thought landed with the same clarity I'd had when I left for Philadelphia that morning: *I have to call her.*

Twenty minutes later I was pacing my kitchen, phone to ear. Three rings. The next would go to voicemail, and I could not leave one. I'd have to try again some other time. *No. I'll have to give this up.*

"Hello," I suddenly heard. My stomach dropped. I did not have a single note card prepped for this moment.

"Hi, Monica?" I asked.

"Yeah. Who is this?"

"This is Leah. Sorry. This is Dr. Lockhart from—"

"I obviously know who you are," she said. "Why are you calling me?"

"Because it's the right thing to do," I heard myself say.

She let out a "pffffft" on the other end. She probably assumed this was an angle. "Yeah, well. I'm not supposed to talk to you."

"I know," I said. "Same here. But I need you to know that I did not know what was going on with my body when I fell that night. I still don't. And if I had, I never would have walked into your delivery room."

"You're just trying to get me to drop the suit," she said. A baby started crying in the background.

"I'm not," I said. "I promise." The cry got more intense. Monica had picked up Skye, who was now shrieking into the phone.

"I have a good case and—ugh. Sorry. *Shhh, Skye, baby. You're okay. I'm here.*"

"Everything okay?"

"Yeah. I just have these cheap bottles that let too much air in when she eats, and then she gets all gassy."

"Lay her on her back and move her legs up and down like she's pedaling a bicycle," I offered.

Monica went silent for a moment. Five seconds later the baby stopped crying. "Thanks," she said, her tone softened. "Look, I'm not trying to ruin your life. I just really need the money."

"I know you're not. I just wanted to call because it felt wrong to vanish after what happened," I said. "I'm sure it was very scary."

"It was," Monica said. "Really scary." Her voice caught in her throat. My own tightened hearing her pain. "And I don't want it to happen to anyone else," she continued, "so no matter what happens with this whole legal thing, I need you to promise me you're going to do whatever you need to do to make sure it doesn't. Ever again."

"I promise," I said, then finished with two words I'd been trained over countless hospital HR sessions never to say in this exact scenario. "I'm sorry."

I slid my phone onto the kitchen counter after we hung up, desperate to be able to bend over and press my forehead against its cold surface. Then my phone buzzed. *Is she calling back?* I thought, tensing up. But I fully froze when I saw the caller's name. Dad. I let it go to voicemail. But he called right back. *Is something wrong?*

"Hey there," I said. "Everything okay?"

"I was going to ask you that," he said. "Are you on your way over?"

My mind raced—*Where and why?*—then it hit. "Oh no, Dad! I'm sorry!" I was supposed to be helping him shuck two hundred clams right now for the Fourth of July Clambake. "I was just—" *I cannot tell him about that call.* "At a lecture. I can jog over to you in ten minutes." And I cannot drive there.

"Well, I'll get started then." He was annoyed.

I made it to the house in seven minutes. Dad was in the backyard, where he'd set up the plastic card tables like we always did for this smelly mess of a project. He'd already gotten through a bushel of at least fifty clams. An extra layer of guilt washed over me.

"Hi, hi," I said, panting. I rushed to him for our shake, but his hands were too dirty. We elbow-bumped instead. "I completely lost track of time, somehow. So sorry."

I quickly grabbed gloves and a shucking knife, then got to work setting up my station.

"We'll get it done," Dad said, wiping his brow with a forearm. "So, what's this lecture you were at?" His shucking pace had not been interrupted. I hadn't even started.

"Oh, remember I mentioned I'm doing that little astrology survey? Well, yesterday I got contacted by a Star Twin I was curious to know more about, so—" I stopped, struggling too much with my first clam to split focus.

But Dad's brow suddenly wrinkled like something concerning had just clicked. "What's going on with this project of yours? The girls in the office were saying something about you being all over the Internet."

I almost sliced my finger open. "Oh. No. Just a few websites picked up that podcast I did." The brow wrinkles doubled. "Anyway, this woman seemed interesting for the project, and she was giving a talk in Philadelphia, so I went down." My heartbeat quickened as if disagreeing with how casually I'd just dropped that information.

Now my dad's whole face scrunched. "To Philadelphia? What'd you, take the train from . . . Red Bank?"

Thank god he said it first. I could not have even begun to guess how to get there without the car I'd risked lives driving. "Mm—hmm." *What am I doing?*

"Must have been an important lecture." I noticed he'd finished another half bushel. I hadn't picked up another clam since my close call.

"Um, she does research into—um—self-help, broadly speaking."

My dad wrestled with a tricky shell, then gave up and tossed it in the duds bin.

"Careful with all that stuff," he said. "It certainly never worked for your mother."

Mom was into self-help? I thought but did not say. His opinion about it had landed loud and clear. I took my time with the next shell, considering how to respond. How many times had we stood here side by side, opening clams and discussing every topic from the latest fertility treatments to whether we dared change the color of our office building from Grandad's original Newburyport Blue? We were partners. This was no different, right? It's just that the topic was me, and I needed his help.

"I've got to be honest," I finally said. "I'm willing to throw everything I've got at this recovery. David said I need to find ways to release tension from my body, so—I don't know—"

My throat felt oddly tight. "I'm just trying to learn more about how. Dot every *i* and cross every *t*, right?"

My dad looked up from his pile. "David thinks he can cure your vertigo by you relaxing?"

This was not the response I was hoping for. "Not exclusively. We're doing all the proper PT. But he also wants me to rest and meditate to see if that has any impact on my condition."

"Wow. Maybe you should take yourself on a tropical vacation."

I knew it was a joke. The edge in his voice from earlier had dissipated. But something in me was still triggered. It was seconds before I realized that the way he'd just said "tropical vacation" was the same way I'd said "gallivanting."

"The woman I heard speak today actually invited me on a retreat. In Venice," I said, surprising myself.

"Venice, *Italy*?" A clam dropped from his grip. He put his knife down. I nodded, feeling uncertain. I hadn't felt this way since I'd told him well-known bad boy Eric Cheney had asked me to the junior prom. I wondered if he also remembered Mom's postcard. Or had I managed to throw that one away before he saw it?

My dad shifted so he could get a good look at me. "You don't seem like yourself right now. This astrology stuff. All the risky exposure online. What's going on?"

He wasn't wrong. I had felt less like myself in the past few weeks than perhaps ever before in my life. But for reasons I could not put my finger on, hearing it from my dad made me angry. "I'm not myself," I said. "I'm really struggling. Vertigo.

The lawsuit. I don't want you missing out on your retirement. I'm a mess."

Tears gathered in my eyes, slower than the faucet I'd experienced with David, but still surprising. Not as surprising—it seemed—as they were for my dad to witness. He looked back at me, befuddled. Then his face went firm as he cleared his throat.

"You're not a mess. You're in new territory with your health and you're frustrated. Think about all the first-time moms we see at their first checkup after the baby arrives. Their whole lives feel off because they've stepped into a place they've never been before. When we see them for the six-month, they're fine."

I nodded, but not because I agreed. The six-month mark was when many of those women confessed to me that they were struggling with postpartum depression. I guessed very few ever shared that with my dad. Right now, I knew why.

We finished with the clams in a rare silence. Then I went home and sat in an Epsom salt bath, trying to stop thinking about Imani, Venice, and the weight of her invitation. Of course, I could let this go and move on with my life, but I felt connected to her in a way I could not explain. She'd challenged me, and I did not want to turn my back on that test. *Especially right now*, something inside me said.

A buzz interrupted my thoughts: a new text from David.

Hello. This is your gentle reminder to meditate today, which I can only assume you've been doing every day since our last appointment ☺ Hope you're hanging in, Leah.

He'd included the link to his recommended meditation track in the text. Now felt like as good a time as any to attempt a break from my brain. I clicked through. First came the stereotypical sound of a pan flute, then a voice.

"Welcome to this simple guided meditation." I jumped, splashing water everywhere. The voice was David's. He'd failed to mention that this was *his* meditation. I tried to resettle as he continued, but a steamy bath was rare enough for me without the added heat of David's voice joining me inside it.

"The goal of this session is to focus on the space between your breaths, that momentary pause after an exhale and before your next inhale. All you have to do for the next three minutes—just three—is count those pauses. Once you arrive at ten, start counting from one again."

In person he was light, goofy even. But this recorded voice was commanding. I let myself sink further into the tub, then did not fight the image of David seated on the edge of it, speaking these words to me in person. It sent the right kind of shiver through me, which I also didn't resist.

"Thoughts will come and go as you do this, especially if you're new to meditation. Think of those thoughts as clouds you're watching. Let them float by. If they're that important, they'll be with you after the meditation ends."

Despite the pan flute's presence, I felt oddly compelled to take this seriously. I breathed in and out, then paused. I repeated the pattern again. Thought came but did not pass like clouds. Every single one was about Venice. I was into my third minute when a familiar sensation bolted across my shoulders and sat me upright. With it came the question of whether this opportunity had come into my life for a reason, an idea I despised but was struggling to dismiss. *But isn't the opportunity to be treated by David the same thing?* And I'd only benefited from walking through that mysteriously opened door.

I listened through the end of his recording, following David's voice more than its direction. Then I dried off and started pricing out flights to Italy.

Chapter
Fourteen

"DO WHAT YOU *need to do* means he doesn't think you should go," Charlotte said. "My dad would have said the same thing. You have to read between the lines with them."

We were thirty minutes into a conversation at her shop that had gone very differently in my head. First I'd had to manage Charlotte's panic after she discovered my newfound "fame" online and her upset that I hadn't told her myself. When I finally got to my Venice plan, she insisted on joining as my chaperone, given the vertigo. After I delicately explained that I had to do this alone, she shifted gears to how completely unfair this decision was for my father, a thought spiral I'd been up and down myself.

"I think he's worried about me," I tried. "And I think he could be just as curious as I am about whether this could actually help." These were the answers I'd landed on to ease the weight of the guilt.

"I'm worried about you, too," Charlotte said, finally lowering her cleaning rag. "I'm so worried, Leah. That's why I think you're better off laying low right now. Go on a retreat with this woman when you're cured, if you even still want to. I looked at her website, and it's a *lot*."

Now I wished *I* had something to furiously clean. I'd expected my cousin would be the cheerleader she'd always been in my life. The fact that she wasn't left me uncomfortable and unsure.

"I'll think about it," I offered, mostly as a way to end this conversation.

After a long run, I texted Charlotte with the words I'd finally found to explain things in a way I hoped she'd understand: I think I finally see what you mean about some things being spiritual. And I know this sounds crazy coming from me, but I think this trip might be that. And if not, it will be over in five days! She showed up at my house the next morning with a bag of Italy-approved clothes.

"I still don't get it," she said. "But you don't do things on a whim, so I'm going to trust you that it's important." It did not feel like a true blessing, and that killed me. But it didn't stop me from boarding my flight the next day. I was wearing the black cotton jumpsuit she'd given me for the plane ride as I touched down at Marco Polo Airport, wondering if all of this could be worth the pit in my stomach I felt for essentially running away from my life. Then I saw Venice.

Approaching the city aboard the Alilaguna ferry made me feel like I was in the scene from *Mary Poppins* where they jump inside the sidewalk chalk drawings to inhabit an animated world. The Grand Canal was filled with countless boats whooshing by as if on parade. There were ornate palazzi everywhere, with turquoise and pink and crimson stucco façades decorated with spires sculpted into diamond points that made each structure look like a dollhouse of spun sugar. And the light. I'd lived minutes from the ocean my entire life, but here every street was a body of water. The midday sun above bounced off the canals below, sending flecks across the buildings like it was one massive disco ball. I disembarked the ferry and then stopped to snap a picture of this living artwork. A gondolier passed through the tunnel below me and right into my shot. Magic. Now I just needed to find the address Imani had sent me.

Using a map that made the city look like a piece of wedding dress lace, I quickly realized that I couldn't find any street signs—or any signs at all. With my phone dipping in and out of reception, I was forced to start using visuals as markers instead: a large, winged lion on a candy-cane pole at the corner of an octagon-shaped bridge; two giant flags with that same winged lion flanking a flamingo-pink palazzo; an open square with a fountain at its center featuring—naturally—the same flying lion spouting water from its snout. And then, just two turns later—*hmm*—that same candy-cane pole I was sure I'd left behind. It was time to stop at the equivalent of a gas station and ask for directions.

"*Ciao, parli inglese?*" I asked the small, square man standing behind a kiosk filled with touristy souvenirs. I'd crammed Italian phrases on the plane ride over. Chief among them: *Do you speak English?*

"*Sì*, yes," said the man.

"Great. I'm a little lost." He nodded knowingly. "From here, where is the S. Tomà ferry stop?"

"The San Tomà vaporetto. *Sì*. You make a left. Then your very next left. Then you go straight, and do not stop until the water."

"*Grazie*." I turned to leave, then clocked the same lion as a pin on his lapel. "*Scusi*, um, what is the meaning of the lion with the wings everywhere?"

He touched the pin as if for good luck. "This is for San Marco. The patron saint of Venezia."

"And why a lion?" I asked, my mind admittedly on the symbol of my sun sign.

"Historians will tell you that each of the four evangelists is represented by a different winged creature, and Mark was assigned the lion. But any Venetian knows that it's because this is the city of the Leo."

I shook my head. "Unbelievable."

"You don't like the *astrologia*?" the man asked, catching my tone.

"I don't," I replied. "And yet I cannot seem to avoid it. I'm a Leo."

"Ah! Brava!" He clearly liked the astrology. "While you're here, you have to believe. That is the spirit of Venice. How else would we have an empire city built in a lagoon? Here." He started to take the pin off his shirt.

"No, no. I can't take that."

But the man would not take my *no grazie* for an answer. He leaned across the counter and pinned it straight onto the lapel of my denim jacket. It wasn't until I made that first left turn that I saw the same little lion pins in back-to-back souvenir shops, but the sweetness of the gesture was not lost.

Twenty minutes and countless lions later, I dragged my

suitcase up to a building so grand I considered freshening up my day-of-travel hair before stepping inside. The exterior was the color of the best terra-cotta-colored sections of a sunset, and the interior surpassed it. I entered to find forest-green and pale pink marble floors, walls covered with oversized black-and-white vintage photos of Venice in baroque frames, and opulent furnishings in what appeared to be three living rooms just off the entry hall. Above me were half a dozen glass chandeliers that looked like upside-down flower arrangements in full bloom.

"Is that my Star Twin?" Imani cried from a room much further away. "Come, come! We're about to feast in the banquet hall!"

I followed the sound of voices past at least five more rooms until I found six women inside the Italian version of a *Downton Abbey* dinner party—a Charlotte-required watch. A dozen windows, all facing the Grand Canal, made one whole side of the room feel like a mural come to life.

"Oh my god," I said. Everyone laughed out loud.

"Six for six on the 'omigod'!" said Imani as she brushed imaginary dust off her shoulders. "Friends, this is Ms. Leah Lockhart." She stood to come double kiss me, then looked down at my jacket and winked. "Nice pin."

There was no point explaining, especially to Imani. I smiled at the rest of the group. They were all women, but that seemed to be the only similarity. A range of ages, hair colors, and clothing choices smiled back at me. I found an open seat at the center of the table beside a petite woman with tanned skin in a SPIRITUAL GANGSTER T-shirt, which did not ease my concerns about the kind of women who go on retreats.

"I know someone with my same birthday, too," she said. "Such a deep, otherworldly bond, right?"

I offered a fake smile and nod. *What have I done?*

"We're going to begin with the simplest intros," Imani said, pulling all our focus. "Just name, where you're from, and give an example of how loud you can scream." She watched all our brows furrow. "*Relax.* I'm not that much of a lunatic. But I do encourage screaming on your own time. Very powerful."

We went around the table. I tried to associate names with features to remember people. There was Claire the Canadian with the long, red curls. Naya from Boston who looked businessy in her blazer. Beth the Spiritual Gangster, who was obviously from California. And Sandy, who gave off Southern-grandma vibes and was in fact from a small town near Charleston. Imani from Atlanta launched us all right into our first order of business.

"As my OG knows, I always start with a decadent meal." Sandy smiled and nodded, seemingly—and surprisingly—the repeat customer. "This trip is about a lot of things, which will reveal themselves along the way, but you know one root of it all is finding your j-o-y. And food is one pathway to that joy."

The textbook image of a hot Italian chef (slicked hair, olive skin, perfectly tight pants) entered from a swinging door at the far left of the room. All the women clapped. I shot a look at Imani, wondering how the hell she'd just pulled that off.

"Friends, meet Marco." Imani double kissed him, too.

"*Ciao, belle donne,*" Marco said. "For the next three hours, I will tickle your senses very deeply." Naya let out a little church giggle, counter to her corporate vibe. We all caught it like a yawn, but Marco did not flinch. "Here in Italy, we believe that life should be savored. We take our time every day to slowly eat delicious food because it makes us happy. And what is the point of this short life if not to indulge every second we can, *sì*?"

Sì! we all echoed enthusiastically, but I wasn't sure I agreed with that statement. "Everything in moderation" was more my speed. Turns out that might have been because I'd never been treated to an eight-course Italian dinner cooked by a chef who looked like Marco.

Oh wow, was my reaction to our *aperitivo* of *sarde in saor*, sardines in an onion sauce. *Sweet Jesus!* I said for the first time in my life after tasting the *linguine alle vongole*. By the fourth course—*fegato alla Veneziana*—I was laughing out loud, delirious. It was the only appropriate reaction for liver that tasted like savory chocolate mousse.

"I cannot believe I've lived my whole life without eating in Italy," I said to Sandy and Beth across the table.

"It's my first time in Italy, too. Don't tell France, but they've got nothing on this," Beth said.

"It's my first time outside of North America," I confessed.

"Same," Claire chimed in, confirming my sense that she and I were the most alike in the group.

Sandy's eyes widened. "Oh, that breaks my heart! Travel is a must. I take an international trip every single year."

I bristled a little. "Well, I'm a doctor, so it's hard to get the time." I felt a pang of guilt for the reasons I had time now.

"Oh, you are! I'm an oncology nurse! Sweetie, I get it. But I just mark my two weeks off at the beginning of the year, then set aside a hundred fifty dollars a week to make it happen."

I opened my mouth to start in on the fact that I co-ran a

very-small-town practice without a ton of extra staff but stopped myself, realizing how defensive that all would sound.

"That's nice," I said instead.

Imani clinked her knife against her crystal wine goblet. "All right, my queens. Before our final course, I'd like each one of you to answer a simple question: Why are you here? We'll go around the table. Leah, would you like to kick us off?"

"No," I blurted out, surprising myself. Everyone laughed, including Imani.

"Fair enough," she said. "Sandy?"

"I'm here because Venice has been on my list for a long time, and I wanted to experience it the Imani way," Sandy said. It struck me that this buttoned-up Southern grandma—literally in a floral button-down—had found an idol in her polar opposite.

To the right of Sandy was Beth. "I'm here because I need to recharge in some beauty after a really tough year at work. I'm a prosecutor with the attorney general's office, and we just went up against a huge corporation. We won, but it almost killed me." The group did a little cheer as I studied Beth, embarrassed to have misjudged her.

Claire was next and nervous, which I found relieving. "I came because my best friend made me. I'm sort of struggling in my marriage right now, and she thought this would help. Also, she let me use her points for my flight, so—I don't know. Sorry. That's not a great answer."

Imani touched an arm to her shoulder. "I'm sorry you're struggling. And God bless friends with airline miles." We all smiled. Mine was directed at Imani, the generous benefactor of my own trip.

Finally, Naya answered. Given the shoulder pads on her gold-button blazer, I expected some kind of strategic rationale. Or maybe I just needed one. "I don't have a deep reason. I'm just here because I saw this on Imani's feed and it looked like fun." These women were one enigma after another.

"This is not a competition," Imani said. "But so far Naya is the winner." Then she turned to me again. I was even less ready after hearing all those answers. Every eye was turned toward me.

"I . . . um—" My nerves gripped the back of my throat, a sensation so odd I coughed. "Sorry. I just . . . This was sort of a . . . I don't know why I'm here," I finally stammered. More words started to flow out of me, not that they provided any more clarity. "I think it's maybe like a little personal test. There's some stuff with my mom around Venice, but that's . . . I don't know. I have a lot going on that doesn't make much—"

"Let me stop you," Imani said. "And apologies because my question was incomplete. I should have asked you all to tell me why you're here *if you know*. And I should have said that not knowing might be the best answer of all." She turned to Naya. "Sorry. Leah's the new winner." Then she offered me a smile so warm and loving that I felt my heart squeeze in my chest. It was the exact look I'd been hoping for from Charlotte.

"Thank you," I whispered back, truly grateful.

The group and I somehow managed to roll ourselves down the hallways to our rooms following that feast. We had the rest of the night off to settle in and, as Imani recommended, enjoy the massive clawfoot bathtubs in each en suite bathroom. I found myself too exhausted to do anything but a round of PT exercises, determined not to get behind. My phone pinged with a text from David just as I was finishing up. The Venetians would have swooned at the serendipity.

> Hope you made it to Italy without any
> issues. And I'm expecting a power ranking
> of gelato flavors upon your return.

I curled into the room's massive wingback chair to reply.

> Thank you. Just one near disaster
> trying to get my luggage off the conveyor
> belt. And TBD on the gelato. Not sure
> what we'll have time for on the retreat
> schedule.

The three dots of David typing crept across my screen immediately. My stomach did a little flip at the thought of us together in this moment despite the ocean in between. Then his reply appeared.

> Make time. Gelato is perfection, and you
> deserve it.

My eyes stuck on the word "deserve." *I don't deserve it*, I thought. *I don't deserve this whole trip.* But it was hard to hold on to that feeling with an image of David's smiling face behind his text. I knew his words were genuine. And maybe even that I needed them. I replied with an ice cream cone emoji, then a heart.

Chapter
Fifteen

THE NEXT DAY began with a breakfast feast fit for Marie Antoinette, or rather her Italian counterpart—platters of meats, cheeses, breads, and pastries that were like the fun house versions of everything I knew back home. I'd eaten Parmesan cheese my whole life; here it melted in my mouth like unctuous salt crystals. I'd seen mortadella in the supermarket; here it was a deep rust-red color I'd never encountered. Every Sunday after church, my grandparents would take me to get fresh cookies from Cozy Corner Bakery, but not a single one packed the vanilla, orange, rum, and butter flavor punch of the *bussolai Buranei*. I usually ate a protein bar for breakfast, *maybe* a yogurt if I had time. Today I spent forty-five minutes devouring three plates of food while talking about nothing but how good it all tasted. Focused on nothing but what and who were inside that room. It struck me how different this felt from standing around Charlotte's kitchen island eating the Italian-American version of these same foods while everyone gossiped about the info collected from their social media feeds.

As our pace slowed, Imani—today clad in a leopard-print tank dress, the leopards embroidered in gold—stood up at the head of the table.

"Friends! Time for today's adventure! I know it's the stereotypical tourist move, but it must be done: we're going on a three-hour private gondola tour through the entire city."

There was celebration all around.

"I don't think three hours is the stereotype," Beth said. Today her T-shirt read HEAVILY MEDITATED. I'd stopped myself from rolling my eyes at it when she came down to breakfast. Meditation had technically landed me on this retreat.

"Good point," Imani said. "People probably also don't get taken hat shopping pre-gondola so they look fabulous and have full sun protection for the ride. But we're doing that, too." The group erupted into applause, but I could only offer a fake smile. I didn't love to shop, nor was I sure how I was going to manage a rocky boat ride without a vertigo attack. Everyone else's wide, excited eyes left me feeling like I was still sitting in the back row on that Philadelphia rooftop.

Imani led us so quickly through the weaving streets of Venice, sans map, of course. With a tour guide, I figured I could relax into the views, but my eyes did not know where to land between all the one-of-a-kind sights—a storefront filled with powdered paint pigments, a massive Gothic church, a group of men carting garbage cans over canal bridges with a genius rolling cart contraption. I kept bumping into Claire, who was walking right in front of me. Finally, we arrived at Giuliana Longo, Modisteria a Venezia, a space no bigger than the small guest bedroom in my condo from the outside. An English sign in the massive front window said HATS TO MAKE YOU HAPPY SINCE 1902.

"Let's go be happy," Imani said, leading the way. The store was like a magic trick, somehow three times as big inside as it appeared from outside. My mouth dropped open as I gazed around to find every inch of it covered in hats—pinned to the walls, hanging from the ceiling, stacked on the floor. There were fedoras in six shades of pink and countless versions of brown. Panama hats in every size, all the color of a white-sand beach. Pageboy caps made of rich plaid. And an entire wall of the gondolier style, with the famous ribbon down the back.

Claire sidled up next to me. "I'm guessing this will be the first non-baseball-cap of your life, too?"

"Do the three black beanies that I wear when I jog in the winter count?" I asked, but I knew the answer as my eyes continued darting around this wonderland. *Maybe I just never found the right place to shop.*

"Here is your budget." Imani handed us each a small envelope. Inside, I quickly counted one hundred and fifty euros.

"This is too much," I whispered to her, assuming none of my fellow retreatants knew my time here had been gifted. "You have to let me pay you back."

"Don't tell me how to spend my money," she said, playfully but at full volume.

We became kids in a costume shop, trying on hat after hat, clapping and squealing and snapping pictures of each other's perfect finds. Sandy went red felt with a giant brim and an even larger black silk flower on the side. Beth chose a floppy straw bucket hat that fit her vibe perfectly. Naya naturally kept it classy with a black woven that had white ribbon detailing. Claire shocked everyone by loving the gondolier look too much to resist going full-on souvenir. And I found myself drawn to a medium-brim straw design woven by women in Tuscany. Imani made a beeline for my lion pin, taking it off my lapel and sticking it on the side of my purchase the second we left the shop. She was now wearing a lace fascinator with a sun-yellow papier-mâché bird on the front.

We walked to our gondolier launch spot, a hat shop promo on parade. I felt ridiculous—like we were kids playing pretend—but every time someone passing looked in my direction, they smiled. At first, I thought they were looking at someone else, but when I turned to check, my eyes landed on the four beaming smiles of the rest of the women in my group and my mouth turned all the way up, too. By the time we hit the water, I was as giddy as the rest of the group. Then I saw our chariots. My hand flew to my chest in awe. The black lacquered boat was like a bowing dragon inviting our group to board for safe passage along the rippling water. Also rippling: the man at its helm. He had the uniform of a Venetian schoolboy—a classic navy-and-white-striped shirt, with black pants and that brimmed hat with the black ribbon—but his body was built to shuttle six women through one of the most complicated waterways in the world. I honestly did not care if this ride triggered my vertigo. It'd be worth it.

"*Ciao, belle!* I am your captain, Giovanni," he said.

"*Ciao*, Giovanni," we all replied, our voices united in lust-filled wonder.

But once we were on our way, the sight of Giovanni faded into the background, paling in comparison to the views of Venice on display. Walking the streets of this city was enchanting, but sailing on the canals was a dream. The light danced across the water, just inches from the gondola's low sides, casting everything under a sparkling veil and highlighting each detail we passed, from the little black minnows darting beside us to the massive windows of each palazzo.

Giovanni wielded one giant oar, expertly maneuvering us through the frenzy of gondolas, ferries, and taxis about to collide, around impossibly sharp corners, and through passages so narrow he needed to use both hands to push the boat between buildings. Those were the little waterways that charmed me most—this city's version of a secret creek. I wished David were beside me right now to see them.

Our captain also somehow managed to talk us through the entire history of Venice. I listened intently, learning so many things that I did not know: that Venice was built on ten million underwater logs petrified into the lagoon sand; that the city spent over one thousand years as an independent empire, conquering regions quadruple its size; and, most fascinating to me, that it developed one of the world's first systems of medical care. One could even tour the historic Scuola Grande di San Marco, featuring a small medical museum exhibiting examples of their earliest surgical equipment.

"They say Venezia has *l'audacia*, 'audacity' as you say in English. It is a city that would not exist without big, bold ideas that the rest of the world rejected and creative people with the courage to make them come true."

Imani smiled proudly. That was why she'd picked this

location for a retreat, I realized. But my mind went to the image of another woman. *Did my mom learn this when she came to Venice? Did it inspire the moves she made when she left?*

Somewhere around hour two, we began drifting through a series of canals so serene, I considered taking a nap. Then Imani cleared her throat.

"Now it's time for the real activity of the day," she said.

"Uh-oh," said Sandy. She was the veteran of the group, so we all took note.

"Now, friends, you didn't think I'd take you on a gondola tour with no strings attached, did you?" Imani asked. This question was rhetorical. "We're going to use the deep tranquility of this moment to try a little vision-based meditation," she said. "You're relaxed. You're inspired. Your hearts are in the perfect place to ask what more they crave."

I felt myself tense up. The last time I'd asked my heart what it wanted, I'd ended up here. After such a huge leap of faith, what more could it have to say?

"Now let's settle into our places and close our eyes." We all complied with varying degrees of trepidation on our faces, mine and Claire's especially. "We'll start with two deep, cleansing breaths. In through the nose, out through the mouth." I followed the directions, my chest expanding so much it was like someone had sent a gust of wind into my body. It was so intense I feared it was going to explode into another sobbing session.

"Good," Imani said. "Now I want you to try and picture yourself in a simple, comfortable room. You're on a small, very cozy bed covered in plush white linens. The room is light, but it's a morning light. You're waking up, stretching out. You can feel free to stretch right now as you envision this if it feels right."

When in Venice, I thought with a shrug. I raised my arms over my head and alternated stretching left, then right, before letting out a yawn.

"Now, there's one door in this lovely room," Imani continued. "A magical door. It opens to absolutely anywhere you'd like. Any place, at any time, with any*body*. Doing absolutely anything you want. You own this room. You can come here any day or every day; it's yours. So right now, you're just going to focus on this one magic-door moment, just one thing you'll get up and walk through to find. No wrong answers. No bad ideas. You can walk through to jump in a giant swimming pool at a luxurious resort. You can open it to find another empty room with a best friend to gab with. Maybe beyond the door are your kids waiting for their bedtime story. What do you crave? What feels like it would be most joyful to you *now*?"

My mind was blank from the moment she stopped talking. I refocused on the room: the white sheets, the morning light, the door. I tried to picture myself standing up from the bed but saw nothing. *This is ridiculous*, I thought, then I remembered I'd flown thousands of miles to give whatever was supposed to happen here my best shot. I refocused, trying to imagine walking across this room and turning the doorknob I'd find. *What do I want to see behind the door?* I tried to bring my favorite places to mind. The beach. *No.* The hospital nursery. *No.* My jogging path. *No.* I started to panic. *Why can't I do this?* Finally, something started to materialize in the dark behind my eyes. Not a place, but a person, I realized as the image sharpened. *Me?* A shiver hit my spine but didn't stop the details from forming. The room was dark, but not where I was standing. I looked from that spot and saw a sea of odd shapes. An audience? Yes. I was standing on a stage. *But why?* The shapes in the audience sharpened to the faces of women. They were smiling. And so was I. And as I spoke my shoulders expanded with what I knew was the same sensation I'd felt the night I booked my flight to be here. *But this makes no sense.*

"When you're ready, begin to open your eyes at your own pace," I heard Imani say. I blinked mine open and found the rest of the group doing the same. Then I clocked that Naya, Beth, and Sandy were crying. I stared past the gondola's bow, stunned silent. "I hope that felt so *fucking good*," Imani said. Everyone laughed but me. Of all the images I could have daydreamed—walking back into my office, vertigo-free; winning yet another clambake trophy standing beside Dad; enjoying a Sunday off with Charlotte at the beach—why me on a stage?

"No pressure at all, but would anyone like to share what they saw?" Imani asked.

Sandy spoke up immediately. "I saw my grandbabies," she said, choked up. "We were at the community pool, which is a real shit place, to be honest, but when I'm with my Lucy and James, it's never bad—it's the best. Lately, I've been thinking about retiring a year or two early to spend more time with them; maybe this was my sign."

Everyone nodded but me, again.

"My vision was about family, too," offered Beth. "But weirdly, more the idea of a family I don't have yet. I had this image of a cabin in Tahoe: a fireplace, a little kid reading beside me on the couch. Definitely not something I actively think about, which was weird, but it was clear in the moment."

"I hear that," said Naya.

"Same," I heard myself add. Every head turned in my direction.

"Did you see something similar?" Imani asked.

"No," I said, squirming slightly in my seat. "I think my mind sort of—I don't know—" I looked at Imani at the front of the boat, and it finally made sense. "I saw a woman speaking onstage, so I guess I was picking up your frequency instead of mine," I joked.

"You don't connect with that same desire?" Imani asked, not letting me off the hook.

"Omigod, no," I said. "Sorry, I just mean I'm not a center-of-attention kind of person."

"Because you think that's bad?" Imani was genuinely curious, not upset. The answer inside me was yes. It had been yes since fourth grade.

"It's just not for me," I said.

"And yet of all the wrong frequencies you could have picked up on, in that moment, your mind was tuned in *there*," said Beth.

Claire jumped in on my behalf. "*Okay*. I saw a field of golden retriever puppies. It was lovely but I'm not about to adopt ten dogs."

"Maybe you're supposed to give it all up and become a vet," I said, joking.

"Maybe she is," Sandy fired back. "All things should be on the table for all of us."

"Of course," I said, trying to right things. "I'm just saying, you saw a vision of your grandchildren. I think we can all agree that's a much more worthy reason to run through an imaginary door."

"Does that make all my speaking work unworthy?" Imani asked.

Shit. I'd dug myself in even deeper. "No. I'm sorry. It's just not the life for *me*. And it doesn't make sense anyway. I already have a career."

"And you love that career?" Imani asked.

"Yes, of course," I said. Now I was pissed. "Look, I'm not interested in having my vision picked apart while we float through one of the most beautiful places I've ever seen with my eyes open. We had five minutes to think, and it was only the second time I'd even meditated in my whole life. I'm sure I did it wrong."

I hoped that would close the conversation out. But Imani was not done. "I've had visions after a five-minute meditation that saved my life."

"Ooh, can you please say one?" Naya asked.

"Okay, I once saw myself alone in an apartment reading a book in a giant, cozy chair. A month later I started spending weekends at a place all my own to recharge from hectic life with my kids. I believe I saw that image quickly because it was urgent for me."

"You spend weekends away from your kids?" I blurted out.

"When I need," Imani replied, matter-of-fact.

Sounds like meditation makes you selfish, I thought. Then, immediately: *I'm here because of it.*

Beth finally broke the awkward silence on the boat. "I do

get how difficult it can be to feel out of control of your thoughts, Leah. It's like you want one thing but your brain keeps insisting on another. I've struggled with that for years in therapy. It's a big project. Maybe this is just the start of it for you."

Claire almost jumped out of her seat, sending the boat and all of us in it rocking.

"*Gentile, per favore!*" our captain cried out, rushing to steady things with a swoop of the oar.

"Sorry," said Claire. Then she eyed me, more lit up than I'd seen her yet. "Beth said 'project' and I finally figured it out: you're *doctor sets out to disprove astrology!*" My stomach dropped. "I knew the whole Star Twin thing sounded familiar when Imani introduced you, but I couldn't remember why." Everyone but Imani exchanged confused glances. "Leah's doing this big research project to prove astrology wrong, and I came across an article about the whole thing. So cool."

Naya did not seem to agree. "Disproving *all* of astrology? How?"

"I'm more interested in *why*," Beth added, clearly Team Naya on the topic.

I suddenly felt like I *was* on a stage, and I did not like it. "Um, I developed a survey. But it's really only focused on my astrological chart. This is just a personal project." That was the opposite of what I'd claimed on *The Andi Hour* and was publicly on the hook to revisit on her show the week of my birthday.

Sandy's eyes went skeptical. "Oh, so that's really why you're here with Imani?"

Is that the dock I finally see? "No. We just met through that," I tried. Now not even Imani looked convinced.

"Well, I think it's amazing," said Claire. "Why shouldn't all the woo-woo shit we're sold be put to the test?"

That point finally seemed to appease the group. *Thank you*, I mouthed to Claire, but Imani was not done.

"So then—I'm curious. What does our astrological chart say about being onstage?" she asked.

"Oh. I don't know." A memory flashed through me as I said those words. With it came a shiver. *Nova told me I should be doing something onstage during his very first rant.* "I'll have to check," I told Imani. But I feared she could see straight through me.

"*Allora*, okay, *ragazze*," Giovanni said, giving the gondola one final shove. "Our journey is *finito*." Music to my ears.

Chapter
Sixteen

"TODAY I'M ANNOUNCING the plot twist of this trip," Imani said once we'd finished our breakfast banquet feast the next morning. "And you're not going to like it." Everyone but Sandy looked nervous. "Drumroll, puh-*lease*: there are no plans for the rest of this trip." Now everyone appeared very confused. "This is not a drill. You each have three more days in Venice. We'll meet here for breakfast every morning. We'll meet back here at seven for dinner, which I've already got covered. The rest of the time here is yours to fill as you see joyfully. You'll each receive an envelope of per diem money, which is what I would have spent on planning additional activities like museum visits, walking tours, and most definitely more gondola rides. But I didn't! I truly want you to do whatever you wish. Take a three-day nap and blow it all on a Gucci scarf if that's what your heart desires. My only rule is that you cannot take this money home."

I felt a prickle of annoyance. I'd officially flown thousands of miles, upsetting the people who mattered to me most, for a vacation I could have taken myself, at any time. My sentiments were shared by Claire, according to her scowl.

"I was ready for those looks," Imani said in our direction, confidence unshaken. "But I promise you will get more out of this experience than you know. The discomfort of having to fill your own time, in your way, with absolutely no one to answer to but yourself, will serve a much greater purpose than being shuttled around to some Venetian glass-blowing demonstration." She slowly sipped her cappuccino to make it clear that was the end of that.

"Glass blowing sounds fun . . . ," Beth said, visibly anxious.

"For real, or because it's the one suggestion I offered?" Imani asked. Beth's nervous eyes grew wider.

Sandy stood, chest puffed. "I freaked out my first time, too. I recommend a walk to think it over. Then your best bet is the rule of first-thought-best-thought!" And off she went. Naya was frantically on her phone now, likely searching for Venetian glass blowing. Beth whispered to her, "Do you think we're allowed to do things together?"

"Ask her . . . ," Naya said.

Imani had already heard the question. She lifted her hands, palms facing out, and leaned back slightly in a gesture that said, "I'm out, this is your call." Beth and Naya huddled.

Claire stood, surprising me. "I can't leave without seeing the biggie sights in St. Mark's. Anyone want to join?"

The practical answer was yes, but I found myself oddly unmoved by the idea of snaking through a long line of tourists on a very sticky day. "I'm going to think about it," I said. "I'll text you if I change my mind."

I poured another cup of coffee from the sterling silver urn, then went to look out from the wall of windows. Below, the Grand Canal was alive with the morning rush of boats carrying everything from market veggies to schoolchildren. Maybe it was the energy of that view, or the strength of Italian caffeine, but I decided the very first thing I'd do with my days of nothing was test my premise that jogging brought me joy.

My typical route was a wide-open path with beach on my right and dunes on my left. Running in Venice was like being inside a video game. Corners were tight and often came up by surprise. Every few yards was another bridge. And it was impossible to keep up any consistent pace because I kept wanting to stop and look at something. It took me over forty minutes to go what could only have been half a mile until a tiny alley opened up to giant St. Mark's Square. We'd passed around this area on prior walks, but this time I'd entered from a different vantage point. Directly in front of me was a sight that made me stop so short the man behind me almost slammed into my back.

"*Scusi*," I said, then I stepped to the side and looked up, squinting until the full building came into view. It was a massive gold clock on an equally large tower, but rather than numbers, it appeared to have images or symbols on the face. I stepped closer, then stopped short again. They were all the signs of the zodiac. The clock tower in the center of the most important square in Venice was dedicated to astrology. *Unbelievable.* I grabbed my phone and searched *clock tower, Venice, Italy*. Results popped up immediately for the Torre dell'Orologio.

"The clock tower is one of the most famous architectural landmarks in Venice because of its large, one-of-a-kind astronomical clock, a masterpiece of technology and engineering that tracks the flow of the city against the map of the stars above it."

It was a stunning structure, but given the connection, I felt almost cosmically obligated to take a tour. I was starting to wonder why the expression wasn't *when in Venice*.

Minutes later a very over-it Italian tower attendant informed me that the clock tower experience booked up several months in advance.

"We have one time that is first to come, first to be served at twenty hours if you'd like." He did not wait for me to do the conversion from military time. "Eight *di sera*."

It was currently eleven thirty in the morning for Americans *and* Italians, meaning I had more than eight hours to fill before doing the one Venice-based activity I had come up with for the day. With nothing else immediately jumping to mind, I started off jogging again, this time moving away from the Grand Canal.

I dipped inside the wedding lace of the city now, happily wandering at a crawl along streets as narrow as my arm span. I spent at least an hour looking for just the right souvenirs for my family in the Venetian equivalent of a Jersey Shore shell shop: every item was in the shape of a gondola, from candlestick bases and can openers to pencils, pens, and of course, thousands of souvenir magnets. When nothing felt quite right, I continued, directionless, though I realized I couldn't technically get lost because I didn't have anywhere to be. That fact should have been comforting, but I felt twitchy with anxiety. This day needed to be worth more than an aimless, hours-long run. Eventually, I came to a dead end, where I was shocked to see a group of people had gathered. For a moment, I thought maybe they'd all gotten lost, too, but the sign on the side of the building enlightened me: PEGGY GUGGENHEIM COLLECTION. I winced. I'd accidentally found my way to the exact location from my mom's postcard. But the view wasn't right. What I saw was a courtyard with brick walls and an enclosed garden flanked by citrus-colored buildings. The image I remembered—a stone building with a classical façade that opened onto a wide canal—was nowhere in sight.

Curiosity pulled me straight into the ticket office, then through the courtyard, past ivy-covered walls and massive, modern sculptures. I followed the flow of visitors through the doors and into the main galleries. That's when I learned that the museum's entrance was actually at the *back* of the building. The true front of the palazzo sat directly on the canal, accessible through double doors leading out onto the expansive terrace. The sun shone through their stunning wrought iron pattern, making shadows on the walls that looked like a flock of birds in flight. Stone steps led straight down to the rippling canal waters below, where the traffic was much more serene. Every vessel here seemed to be one of those ritzy private water taxis, captained by tanned men chauffeuring tourists in large sunglasses and silk scarves. The postcard picture was from their view, looking at the museum from the water. It was all so stunning that I couldn't resist taking a rare selfie.

"I can take that for you," a silk-scarved women offered.

"Oh . . . okay. Thank you," I said, handing her my phone.

I leaned against the thick stone of the front steps and smiled.

"*Buongiorno!* Do I have the twelve thirty group?" a young American woman called out. She was standing at those distinct door gates. I'd expected an older Italian tour guide who looked like an American librarian. This girl looked plucked straight out of whatever the coolest part of Brooklyn was these days.

"Hello, everyone. I'm Margot, one of the Guggenheim fellows. We're a group of international interns who live here in Venice and work at the museum. An incredibly lucky group."

There were murmurs of agreement from everyone, me included, to my surprise. This city was overwhelming, but it had captivated me so far.

Margot launched into her well-rehearsed presentation. She explained that Peggy Guggenheim made an offer for this palazzo the day she saw it, immediately turning the backyard into a garden, exhibiting modern sculpture by artist friends. An avid collector, she soon began opening her home to the public as an art museum, free of charge, *while she was living in it.*

"Peggy offered viewings of the collection three afternoons a week from Easter to November until she died in 1979," Margot explained. "She was a pioneer in that way and a true champion of modern art. She was also a rebel. Peggy was always working to demonstrate independence from her powerful family, from how she spent her money to how she wore her hair, so it's no surprise that she chose to support lesser-known, boundary-breaking artists from the beginning. She defied the male-driven art establishment and didn't care that her tastes were often touted as ludicrous. Eventually, the haters caught up."

Maybe that's why my mom chose to send a postcard from this museum, and not your typical Grand Canal or St. Mark's scene, I thought. I couldn't deny that like Peggy, she was an original. She'd once painted our front door Tiffany blue just because she wanted to feel extra fancy. She wore different lipstick colors on her top and bottom lips. She threw dinner parties for her own made-up holidays: First Flower Blooms Day and Leah Got Straight A's Eve.

"Any questions before we move inside?" Margot asked.

"Did Peggy Guggenheim have any children?" my photographer in the scarf asked.

"She did," said Margot. "A son, Sindbad, and a daughter, Pegeen."

"Did they also work in the art world?" the woman followed up.

"Sindbad lived a more traditional life: he was married, had a family, and worked in publishing and also insurance. Pegeen seemed to live a more complicated life," said Margot. "And had a very complicated relationship with her mother. By most, if not all, accounts, Peggy Guggenheim's priority was her commitment to art and not her role as a mother."

My neck was suddenly hot. That was the connection to this place that mattered much, much more. Peggy Guggenheim probably felt like a living defense of all my own mother's selfish life choices. She came here and decided beauty and art were important enough to outweigh love and connection. That's exactly what she chose, a life teaching yoga to strangers in sunny California instead of one with her daughter.

I heard the muffled sound of a new question from the group. I tried to refocus on those words and ignore the rage building inside me.

"I was wondering," a bespectacled man said. "Do you know the meaning behind the palazzo's name?" He pointed to a gold plaque on the wall. I craned my neck to read the embossed words—PALAZZO VENIER DEI LEONI. *Leoni?* As in lion?

"Yes, great question," I heard Margot say. "Peggy bought the building from the Venier family. They were a force in Venice for generations, so it's assumed the *dei leoni*—loosely, 'of lions' in Italian—was to reinforce that status and connect them to the great, symbolic animal of the city."

"Enough!" I said to myself, unfortunately at a volume others could hear.

"I'm sorry?" Margot asked, trying to make eye contact.

"No, no, *I'm* sorry." I could not tell this group of strangers that I—a doctor—was now certain the universe was taunting me with yet another Leo connection. Or maybe it was the ghost of my very alive mother—can a living person actively haunt a location they once visited in the past? Instead, I just turned and ran left when Margot directed everyone to the right.

In the courtyard, I found an open bench and sat down, throwing my head into my hands, overwhelmed. Suddenly the ground shifted toward me; I'd completely forgotten one of my biggest vertigo triggers. I could feel my body moving forward in slow motion as I tried to reach for stability, but my head was spinning way too much. My only option was to curl myself into a tiny ball and hope to god it would quickly pass.

"Hey, Star Twin. You okay?"

I recognized the voice was Imani's, but I did not see her—or anything at all—before toppling completely and landing smack onto the inlaid floor.

Chapter
Seventeen

"DO YOU THINK they'll let me do my own stitches?" I asked Imani, trying to lighten the mood.

"Why bother? Italian tailoring's the finest in the world," she said.

I cracked as much of a smile as the giant gash on my forehead permitted. "Thank you so much for coming here with me," I sighed. "Here" was an Italian urgent care clinic that Imani had shuttled me to in one of those very fancy water taxis, which the museum staff insisted on calling. She even tried to lend me her rainbow-striped silk scarf when I mentioned seeing them on other riders. I refused because it completed her own outfit too perfectly to remove.

"Thank goddess I strolled myself over to the PGC when I did. That's probably just some Star Twin magic in the works," she said, winking in jest. I'd gotten the sense over the past two days that Imani was more about personal than spiritual power.

That, plus her overwhelming generosity, had endeared her to me.

Moments later I was called in for six impressively tight stitches. It helped that Italian doctors were as swoon-worthy as Italian chefs and Italian gondoliers and that mine let Imani stay to serve as my translator, even if she only communicated via Google Translate. *How strong is this hospital-grade Tylenol? What exactly can she do to prevent a scar? Do you have a favorite spot for live music in the Dorsoduro neighborhood?*

After I was discharged, Imani looped her arm through mine and walked me at an absolute snail's pace back to our retreat's palazzo, by my request. I needed the air, and the chance to shake off whatever had led to my future souvenir scar.

"It's not my policy to pry, but if it's helpful, we can talk about anything you might need to get off your chest," Imani said knowingly as we made our way through a cobblestoned *campo* that a group of boys was using as a soccer stadium. *Vai, vai, vai!* they screamed at each other.

"Oh, are you perhaps referring to why I was curled into a possum pose when you found me on the ground?"

"Not gonna lie—I just thought you were wasted."

A laugh popped out of me. "You know, you're not entirely wrong—I'm sort of permanently drunk right now." With that I finally explained the details of my vertigo and even how mysteriously it had come on. Imani didn't press for much info, listening to what I was willing to divulge, then saying, "Thank you for sharing that with me," when I went quiet. Her total lack of judgment was so welcome, I suggested we sit down for an afternoon espresso, where I told her much, much more.

The only thing I held back was the details of my lawsuit, too ashamed to add that into the mix. When I finished, Imani sat back in her iron bistro chair, looked me dead in the eyes, and said one very shocking thing.

"Why aren't you crying?"

"What do you mean? Like, right now?"

"Yes, right now. Forget crying. You don't even look that upset. You just told me a painful, confusing, overwhelming story about your own life—happening *right now*—and you recounted it like it was a day at the beach."

When she put it that way, it did feel a bit strange. "This is just how I've always been," I said. "And then I'm sure I locked it in even more as a doctor. It's my job to be the calmest person in the room."

Imani shook her head as she sipped her espresso. "You're not calm. You're numb."

"*Excuse* me?" So much for being nonjudgmental.

"You know, I wasn't sure about us being Star Twins before, but now I see it. We both found a way to override ourselves. I have my own version of your story. I wrote myself a gorgeous life when I got out of college: married a great man, had two beautiful children, and used my English degree to make a difference at a wonderful school. I had a teacher like that growing up, and I wanted to be just like her, which was also the opposite of my parents. Longer story. By thirty, I'd checked off every dream on my list, and I numbed out of it by drinking a bottle of wine every night. Minimum. It got so bad I came very close to losing my kids."

"I'm really sorry to hear that," I said. Tears were forming in her eyes at the memory. "Is that when you got the weekend apartment?" I asked, regretting how I'd reacted to hearing about that yesterday.

"No. That came after a lot of healing, thanks to a lot of help."

"Oh no," I said, my least favorite dots connecting. "Please do not tell me that you went to an astrologer."

Imani rolled her eyes. "I went to a rehab! Way more expensive, but worth every penny. That's where I learned that you can't outsmart your emotions. I'd been living with unprocessed shit from my childhood that I continually denied. I had different dreams for my future that I ignored. I really struggled as a mother and pretended I was fine. It catches up with you." Her eyes suggested she meant that "you" for me.

"You think my vertigo is your drinking?" I asked. If so, Imani was making the same argument as Nova, just from a different angle. I didn't know whether to be struck or put off by that fact.

"All I'm saying is I know your type. I *am* it. Your heart is as strong as your brain, so they're bound to battle. I'm honestly surprised this is the first mysterious ailment you've experienced."

She delivered that last comment almost offhandedly, but my mind went immediately into detective mode. *Is it the first?* I raced back through time: a few small running injuries; a rough flu during college; some pretty run-of-the-mill IBS. Even more puzzled, I crossed my arms to reach a tiny itch on my shoulder, and there it was. Chills ran through me as if confirming: For four long months in my third year of med school, my arms and legs were covered with a sudden, inexplicable rash. I got tested for every allergy, fungus, and bacterial infection. I removed every single fragranced product from my life, changed laundry detergents, and even tried using natural deodorant. Then one day the rash was gone just as quickly and bizarrely as it came on.

"Something did happen. Right after Cole left for California," I said under my breath.

Imani perked up. "Family member?"

"No. Boyfriend," I said, confused.

"Oh. I just figured since your Star Twin Survey said you were from California."

"I am, yeah. And my mom moved back there when I was in high school. But that's a much longer story."

Imani cocked her head. "Sounds short to me. What I'm hearing is that your body had a powerful reaction to your boyfriend leaving you, headed for the same place you'd already been left once for by your mother?"

I froze. The connection had never, ever occurred to me. "He went to a different city," I began. "And she'd been there for a long time. And—"

Imani was nodding. "And you decided it wasn't a thing." Something suddenly occurred to her. "Didn't you say something about your mom when I asked everyone why they came on this trip?"

I nodded, stunned. Then I felt my throat start to tighten. Imani gently placed her hand on top of mine as if she somehow felt it, too.

"You need to give something inside you more credit, Leah. It knows a lot more about what it wants and why than your mind has caught up to yet."

She gave my hand the sweetest pat, then stood up to find

our server. One more piece of this fuzzy puzzle settled into place as I watched Imani walk away. Cole left and that bizarre skin issue emerged in November 2011, the second major transit Nova had included. What was the description? Something about emotions? I grabbed my phone and pulled up his email.

> A life struggle that forced you to acknowledge
> something not working in your emotional life

Maybe what wasn't working in my emotional life was the failure to acknowledge any emotions at all.

I was quiet as we walked on, crossing the wooden Ponte dell'Accademia, connecting the more bustling San Marco *sestieri* to our quieter neighborhood to the south. Imani stopped us at the top of the bridge, leaning her arms over to rest and take in the view: two gondolas floating in sync against the postcard-perfect Venice landscape. This was the shot I would have purchased if I found it at a gift shop. I followed Imani's lead, much more willingly than I had on day one.

"Makes you understand why people say travel is the only thing you buy that makes you richer, right?"

I nodded, but I'd never heard that expression. Right now it rang true.

"I have a confession to make," I said. "And I feel awful about it after everything you've done for me: I never even read your response to my Star Twin Survey. I was—shall we say— *thrown* when I found you online and never went back to check it."

"I have a confession, too," Imani said with a coy smile. "I didn't take your survey."

I flipped to face her. "You didn't?"

"No, ma'am. I don't do astrology. Nothing against it, it's just not for me. I go to church. I have my apartment. I confide in my husband and my best friends. I've got my ways of knowing who I am, and when I might be losing her."

I stared back at her, struck. Imani didn't know anything about our sign, and yet she'd somehow found a way to embody exactly the traits predicted.

"All right. We need a photo with this view of heaven-on-earth," Imani said. "Grab your camera."

I started to set us up for a selfie, the moon positioned directly between us. But Imani took over, her long arm making her a much better photographer. She snapped a dozen shots, then kept the phone to review them.

"We're gorgeous," she said, then I watched as she accidentally went one too far and discovered the picture I'd taken earlier on Peggy's terrace. Imani looked at it, smiled, then held my phone up so I could see.

"There," she said. "This is the *you* that you should be chasing."

A woman beamed back at me from the screen. Her smile was so wide that her eyes narrowed with delight. She looked filled with total joy. I barely recognized her.

Chapter
Eighteen

IT DIDN'T DAWN on me until I woke up the next morning that I'd missed my window to try to tour the clock tower the night before. I went downstairs to find I'd also missed the window on today's breakfast. Imani had left me a note in the middle of the empty banquet table: *Leftovers for you in the kitchen. Be gentle with yourself today, but no less indulgent.*

I made myself a plate of cured meats, aged cheese, and this magic sugared donut with surprise Nutella in the center. Then I sat and ate it very, very slowly, imagining Chef Marco smiling proudly at me. I added gondolier Giovanni and urgent care doctor Maurizio to my audience, because why not. Somehow a full hour passed in which all I'd done was take tiny bites of mostly bread while sighing with delight. As I tucked a strand of hair back, I brushed the large bandage on my forehead and remembered the giant gash on my face, one that was not going to be healed by the time I returned to New Jersey. Grabbing my phone to check in with Dad, I weighed how to explain that he had—of course—been right about the risks of traveling with vertigo.

"Hello there, Doctor," he said, tone even.

"*Ciao*, Doctor," I said. "Just calling to see how you're doing there."

"Eh, I'm okay," Dad said. "Caught some kind of bug from one of the kids at Junie's christening this past weekend, so I'm home."

"Oh no. Sorry to hear that." It was Friday. If my dad was home, then the office had to close for the day. In other words, he was really sick. "Want me to text Charlotte to do a soup run for you?"

"It's okay. We rescheduled patients for the weekend, and Edie offered to work it with me," Dad said. A wave of guilt washed over me. "You learning a lot over there?"

The feeling doubled. "I am," I said, hoping he didn't follow up for any specifics.

"And all's okay with the vertigo?"

"Yes," I lied, again.

"All right, then, good. You take care of yourself, and I'll see you soon. Remember we've got a meeting with Jim the day after you're back," said Dad.

I hung up feeling like shit.

It would be ten hours before there was another open time slot to see the Torre dell'Orologio. I strolled St. Mark's Square again to start to kill time. There were plenty of other landmarks to keep me occupied, from the Doge's Palace to St. Mark's Cathedral. I couldn't bring myself to get in line for either. Instead, I kept walking, trying to figure out how I was supposed to know what I wanted to do. Shop? *No.* Take some kind of class? *Meh*. Go back for a full day in bed? *Oddly appealing but such a waste*. I remembered Giovanni mentioning the medical museum, but not even that compelled me. Eventually, I came to the water at a vaporetto stop called San Zaccaria, where a large sign said VAPORETTO TO MURANO/BURANO. Murano I knew from the famous glass of the same name, on full display in the bouquet chandeliers covering the ceilings of our palazzo. Burano was currently an unknown.

A small line of tourists stood waiting for the next boat. I approached a couple in matching University of Minnesota T-shirts.

"Excuse me, hi, I'm just wondering—have you been to Burano? Is it just another island in the lagoon to walk around?"

"No, no, dear," the woman answered. "It's this incredible—" The husband touched her arm, and she stopped short.

"Let her be surprised, hon," he said. She agreed with a smile and mimed zipping her lips.

On that cue, the boat arrived. *When in Venice*. I boarded for what turned out to be a lovely forty-five-minute ride through the open waters of the Venetian Lagoon. Eventually, we approached a small island. The docking area reminded me more of the ferry stop back home than of any of the grandeur of mainland Venice.

"Go immediately to the right, dear," the woman whispered just before stepping off. "Best view for your first visit."

I did as she directed, taking a small, graveled path that hugged the shoreline. There was a tree-lined park at my left where two older ladies chatted on a bench. I saw a mother walking with little kids in the distance, then a man holding a fishing pole and bucket walking toward me. They were small-shore-town sights I knew well. The difference was every single person was in oddly bright clothing. The ladies wore matching tomato-red housedresses. The mother was in Barbie-pink pants, her white shirt covered in a pastel pink cotton candy scarf. Each kid was in a school uniform of deep navy pants and a sky-blue top. The man's bucket was highlighter yellow. *Is there some kind of dress code here?* I wondered as I rounded the bend. *Maybe there's a summer festival going on?*

I turned the corner, stopped so short I almost fell over, then double-blinked. In the distance were row after row of very old, impossibly quaint two-story town houses in a rainbow of colors so vibrant they looked like they'd been colored in with markers by a kindergarten class. An electric yellow that felt straight off a nineties tracksuit. The red from a clown nose somehow lit up from the inside. Bubblegum pink, and clementine orange, and a turquoise that reminded me instantly of Nova's eyes.

"What is this place?" I asked aloud to no one. I spent the next hour answering the question for myself, moving in slow motion around every inch of this tiny town-sized island. The rainbow row houses were not limited to the first street. Those colors were everywhere. Every house. Everything. To make matters more magical, Burano was a city built like Venice, with dozens of canals connecting patches of land. I'd thought the light dancing off the water in the Venetian canals could not be surpassed, but it was nothing compared to this shower of rich color: the sun poured across the island and ignited every façade, making each of the buildings explode. I spent five full minutes moving back and forth between the shadow and sunlight views of an orange house; I couldn't get over how the color changed so dramatically within a two-inch shift, left and right. A country-club chic woman passed by with her seemingly disinterested daughter, who surprised all three of us by copying my move and smiling for what looked like the first time in a long while.

"Incredible," she said to me. "I think if I lived here, I wouldn't need Zoloft."

We laughed, but I got it. A silly, almost childlike energy imbued Burano. It made me want to skip. Or eat a giant ice cream cone. Or, I thought—irony not lost—sing "Here Comes the Sun" at the top of my lungs. Why not do all those things? What was stopping me? I was completely alone, and nobody here knew me.

I found a place to skip, and *good grief* was it fun, trotting up and down the street and into the air. My hair bounced. My arms flung. I felt so alive. Now for some gelato. My only obstacle was wanting more flavors than could fit into a single cone. And so—I ordered *three* cones! *David would be so proud*, I thought as I savored each and every one.

Feeling full to the point of a mission-critical lie-down (*very* carefully this time), I found a bench in the shade of a tall canal bridge. And then, without too much thought, I hummed that very old favorite song of mine until I drifted into a nap. I woke to the sound of someone else's tune: the same fisherman I'd passed earlier was whistling as he cleaned shrimp on the ground beside me.

"Oh, sorry," I said, immediately trying to move. "Am I sleeping on your—" I stopped myself from continuing in English. "*Scusi.*"

"It's perfectly fine. We share everything here," said the man. His accent was not even Italian. Australian maybe?

I sat up slowly, stretching my arms overhead like the day was starting all over. "Do you live here?" I asked.

"Since the eighties," he said. "Met an Italian girl on my gap year and . . ." He opened both arms as if to say, "You see the rest."

"I'm not familiar with this island," I said. "What's the history?"

"Ah, welcome, then. It's simple really. The homes of Burano were painted this brightly by the wives of fishermen many, many years ago. It sometimes gets so foggy here that the men couldn't find their way home. The colors were meant to be their map. But they made everyone so happy that it changed the whole spirit of the island." That tracked; it had changed my whole spirit in the last few hours.

"Back home, people usually book a spa day when they want to recharge," I told him. "Maybe they should just come here instead."

The man nodded, barely looking up from his giant yellow barrel of peony-pink shrimp. "If I've learned one thing in my years traveling—and especially living here—it's that there's nothing more contagious than culture."

My doctor brain loved that metaphor. So many things really could be considered "viral." But his words struck me deeper given all the things swirling around my own life, if not my own body. I sat back on the bench, turning them over in my mind, oddly wishing Imani were there, imagining what she'd ask me to push all my thoughts forward. *What culture have you caught that isn't truly you? What culture do you want to pass on?*

✦ ∙ ✦ ∙ ✦

I stayed on the island for as long as I could without missing my chance to see the Torre dell'Orologio again. Now I understood what the woman I'd met on my way over meant when she said it would be my *first visit*; I would be back.

After a mad dash to St. Mark's, I lucked into the very last slot on the eight p.m. tour. A bookish guide directed our group of six tourists up the narrow wooden stairs and into the first room, which had once housed the family that cared for the clock's intricate mechanics. Standing with the massive levers and gears of the clock face, I felt shrunk down, humbled. The entire system had been designed to track not only the minutes and seconds of our twenty-four-hour clock but also the position of each constellation in the sky during the given season of that year. Our guide explained that they'd been included because of just how closely Venetians tracked the stars. Yes, this was a port city that relied heavily on the night sky for maritime navigation, but it was also a community closely tied to the fortunes of those stars.

We finished on the top balcony of the tower, above the gold clock face. From my position, it was hard to see every constellation symbol on the façade, but the lion for Leo was in my direct eyeline. It was late July, almost Leo season. My season. I glanced up at the inky sky, realizing I had no idea what the real constellation of Leo's stars even looked like. Beside me was a woman in a silk sari, Burano-bright purple. She was holding her phone up to the sky. On its screen, I saw star shapes that moved as she shifted where the camera was pointing.

"Excuse me, is that showing you where the real constellations are?" I asked.

"Oh, yes," she said. "It is an app, so incredible. Come see, you can have a look with me."

I moved closer just as several dots connected, and the image of the crab appeared.

"That's Cancer," she said.

"My moon is in Cancer," I replied on instinct. I had become a person who easily said *My moon is in Cancer* to complete strangers. But this one lit up at my comment.

"Like my son! Very powerful moon placement." She continued to move the phone around, searching the sky.

"Do you know where Leo is?" I asked.

She repositioned without a beat. I saw a group of dots come together, then form into the shape of a lion right before my eyes.

"Do you have Leo in your chart, too?" the woman asked, clearly not a novice.

I nodded. "It's my sun and rising signs."

She almost dropped the phone. "You are Leo, Leo, Cancer?" Her eyes scanned my face. "What is your birth year?"

"Nineteen eighty-three," I said. "Why?"

"And time?"

"Five fifteen in the morning. Are you an astrologer?" I braced myself for another Nova-like reaction to my chart, but the woman was just staring at me, seemingly in disbelief. When she finally spoke, it was to exhale a phrase that I can only assume was the Hindi expression for *Holy shit*, before dropping her phone and saying, "You are the Star Twin to my son."

"Holy shit," was my reply.

Chapter
Nineteen

THE MOTHER OF my Star Twin was squeezing my hand so tightly it started to sweat.

"*Abir!*" she screamed to the other side of the tower. "Get over here now! I cannot believe this!" Then she turned to me and oddly *raised* her volume. "We were just with him in Istanbul to celebrate his birthday early—*your* birthdays!—and now here we are with you! It is fate!"

Abir—her husband?—finally appeared. She grabbed his arm with her spare hand. "*Montu,* this girl is the birth chart match to our Sai!"

He lit up. "Really? The same year?"

"Five fifteen a.m., too," I added. Honestly, their excitement was contagious.

"She must meet him!" Sai's mom said.

"She must!" Sai's dad replied. He grabbed his phone, I assumed to call Sai right then and there. She brought hers to my face, navigating to show me photos.

"Here he is! He is very handsome. And very successful. He is a pop star musician! And he has just moved to Istanbul because he was compelled to go there because—*oh, you know!* It is your Neptune transit!"

I did know. And Sai was, in fairness, handsome. The rest of the details sounded very proud-mother lens.

"It's gone to voicemail," Abir said, visibly disappointed. "But please give me your phone, and I will write him a text from you. Then you can coordinate when you will go see him."

I did not have the heart to ruin this moment by explaining there was no way I was going to fly to Istanbul and meet their probably-not-a-pop-star son. But there was also no way I was willing to rain on their parade by refusing to hand over my phone.

"Who do I say is texting?" Abir asked.

"I'm Leah," I said.

"Leah the Leo!" the mom screamed, of course.

Abir read aloud as he typed. "'Hello, Sai. I am Leah, your Star Twin. I am here with your parents in Venice. We met by fate. Now I must meet you. I can come—'" He turned to me. "When can you go?"

"Um, soon . . . ?" I offered, again just trying to be kind. He nodded, pleased, then pressed SEND on the most madcap outgoing text of my life.

*　*　*

Back at the palazzo, I found a few of the women, Imani included, up enjoying after-dinner drinks in one of the living rooms.

"There she is. How was today?" she asked.

"Oh, you know, the usual Venice stuff," I said. "Had my mind blown on Burano, saw the most breathtaking clock in the world, and then ran into the parents of another Star Twin who insisted I go meet their son in Istanbul."

All eyes went wide.

"When?" Beth asked. She'd traded her woo-woo-themed T-shirts for a full-length red silk dress. Everyone was being transformed by this city.

"Like fifteen minutes ago," I said. "On the roof of the Torre dell'Orologio."

"No. When are you going to Istanbul?" she asked.

"Now! It's a hop and a skip!" Sandy jumped in. "Ooh, *honey*, your first time in Italy is about to become your first time in Turkey!"

I carefully collapsed on a chaise. "I'm not going to Istanbul! It was a stretch for me to come to Venice." Today had finally been the right kind of dizzying. Imani placed a glass of sweet-smelling liquor in front of me, curiously quiet.

"Wise. These people are total strangers," said Claire.

"Right," I said, but her logic struck me differently than it had earlier. I sipped my drink. The rich liquid traveled through my body, unwinding me. "Though, they seemed like very sweet people."

"It begins," said Imani with a knowing smile. That struck me differently, too.

Ever-efficient Naya was already on her phone. "Wow, it's less than two hours to fly there. That's like—what?—New Jersey to Florida."

"And a hell of a lot cheaper than flying from New Jersey to Istanbul." Sandy's position was clear.

"No. This is crazy. I'm in the middle of this retreat," I argued.

"Where you've been directed to do whatever you want," Beth reminded me.

"Fair point . . . ," I said, then my brain jumped to some quick math. "I could miss one day of Venice and add one day of Istanbul and only be away for an extra twenty-four hours."

"Wait. You're not really considering this, are you?" Claire asked, judgment clear. Now I knew why I was suddenly bumping against her: she was reminding me of Charlotte.

"Maybe I am," I said.

Now Imani smiled wide. I put my drink down on the black marble coffee table. "Okay. Come on, sensei. What's the lesson here? I want to go, so I just go? It feels joyful, so I just do it?" I sat back in my chair and sighed. "Like, must be nice to be able to pop over to Istanbul, right?"

She did not get the chance to respond because Sandy smacked her glass down on the table, turning every head. "'Must be nice' is my trigger phrase," she said, nostrils flaring. "If I had a dime for every time someone used that line on me about one of my 'whims,' I wouldn't have to save my hard-earned money for these trips that expand my life every single time. 'Must be nice' is code for 'Don't be who you are, be like me so I feel okay about myself.' When people *must be nice* me now, I say, *It is. That's why I do it.*" She downed the rest of her drink. We broke into applause.

"Looks like I should have put Sandy on your case from go," said Imani.

"There is a book deal in your future," Naya chimed in.

"Oh, I'm already writing it," Sandy said. "It's called *Must Be Nice, My Ass*."

That sent us into a total fit. Even Claire. It was only after I stopped laughing that I finally let my mind land on my body, specifically my shoulders. They were tingling, the same feeling that had led me to both Philadelphia and then Venice. Then I heard an actual buzz coming from my bag. I grabbed it to find a new text on the screen.

> Hey Leah and hey maan aur pitaajee! This
> is wild! I'm free as a bird all this week.
> Come party in Istanbul, Star Twin!

"Okay," I said to the group, "who wants to help me search for flights?"

*   *   *

At nine the next morning, I was en route to the airport for my flight into Sabiha Gökçen International Airport, which technically sat on the Asian side of Turkey's capital city. I'd be crossing a second continent and city off my international travel list. As for my family, I'd decided the best plan was to get safely to Turkey, then rip off the news Band-Aid over a phone call.

I distracted myself over the flight by checking in on the Star Twin Survey. The last time I'd logged on, not one of the three transits had more than a 35 percent yes response. But now all three hovered near 50 percent, from a total of sixty-five responses. Any sample size under one hundred wouldn't provide accurate results, but the trend was still shocking. And in a way, I was a part of the trend, having connected my mystery rashes with my ex.

More Star Twins were finding each other in the comments of my original promos. A few were negative (*So over all this astrology hype* and *Leave it to a Leo to study Leos . . .*), but most were from people genuinely thrilled to be connected, who shared way more details with each other than my survey had addressed. A mini poll from an @BrieWhitehall caught my eye: Heyo Star Twins! Let's all answer these life stats to see how we line up. She'd listed: "Town," "Work," "Hobbies/Passions," and "Relationship Status." My mind went straight to the gondola meditation. I wondered how many of this set had an aspect of performance in their lives. Brie had given me a ten-twin head start with the responses to her post. By the time the beverage cart had come and gone, I'd come up with a list of thirty-two twins whose careers I could cross-reference. An absolutely shocking nineteen of that set did something involving a stage, from a literal opera singer and motivational speaker to several actors, three litigators, and a person who wrote that their greatest passion in life was the church choir. That was well over 50 percent. I was surprised to see a name on the list that I recognized—Heidi Rosemont, the doctor who'd messaged me about taking leave from work. I couldn't decide whether or not to count her, given the fact that she was a physician, but the only six photos on her profile all showed her playing the piano and singing. To me, that signified a level of importance high enough to count for my purposes.

I went back to our message exchange, wondering if Heidi'd written back, thinking I could really use a Star Twin perspective more in line with my own. Or so I thought.

> Hey Leah. Let's have that chat. Honestly, you
> opened a whole can of worms for me with this
> whole astrology thing, and I'm thrown. Let me
> know when you have time. Thanks —Heidi

Same, was my reaction. I didn't feel in any position to provide counsel given my loose grasp on everything going on in my own life. And Heidi's suggestion that I was to blame for her own confusion left me uncomfortable. Best to keep a kind boundary.

> Hi Heidi, I'm so sorry for the radio silence. I'm also
> sorry to say that I doubt I can offer much clarity
> on the astrology front, though I definitely relate to
> that floundering feeling. Would be happy to
> commiserate—in the meantime, hang in there!
> —Leah

As soon as we landed in Turkey, I flipped out of airplane mode to finally call my dad, but it went straight to voicemail. The same happened when I tried him from the customs line thirty minutes later. I made a mental note to try again from the cab into the city center, but my first views of Istanbul were too consuming to do anything but stare out the cab window. The city was as jaw-dropping as Venice but with whites and blues versus pinks and greens, towering buildings in place of rows of palazzi. Its skyline was dotted with ancient spires and imposing domes crowded alongside stacked-stone structures with roofs in terra-cotta tile or what looked like pure gold. I rolled down the window once we approached what had to be the center given the dozens of street carts selling everything from flower crowns to fresh figs. Gone was the mix of sharp salt and earthy olive oil. Here, it smelled like a shaker filled with cinnamon, nutmeg, and pepper had been dusted over the air.

I dropped my bags at my hotel and then headed to the meeting point Sai had texted—the world-famous Spice Bazaar. It was teeming with people, but I quickly noticed a tall, handsome man. A flutter hit me in the gut. Sai was in black skinny jeans over boots, with a tight vintage Prince T-shirt, and his mom's phone photos had not done justice to his chiseled face. It was not hard to imagine throngs of female fans screaming at this man.

"Yo, Star Twin!" he said, walking toward me. I feared my rumpled travel hair gave me away. "Welcome to my adopted city!"

"Thank you so much for having me," I said. "You are officially the witness to and reason for the most insane thing I've ever done in my whole life."

"Ever?" He shook his head. "That explains a lot. Come. We'll eat and talk and see sights and talk and eat more and maybe dance at a boat club during sunset on the Bosporus."

Sai grabbed my hand as tightly as his mother had, pulling me into the buzzing crowd. The buzz inside me told me that coming to Istanbul had been the right decision.

Chapter
Twenty

SAI TALKED AS fast as he walked, which was only slightly slower than he ate. We *Very Hungry Caterpillar*–ed our way through the stalls of the market as I collected data on his life, which was easy because he was a captivating storyteller. And—fine—because he was very nice to look at while he did it. The mouthwatering food didn't hurt either. Over a soft Turkish mozzarella-style cheese stuffed with roasted pistachios, Sai explained that he'd arrived in Istanbul three months ago. He knew zero people in the city and canceled a show in London to make the move, but "it had to be done." While taste-testing six different types of Turkish delight, Sai ran me through his upbringing in tiny Hampi, India, where he'd dreamed of being a musician from age five, taught himself guitar at seven, and left for Mumbai to try using Bollywood as a way in by sixteen. I learned about his extensive list of self-care rituals over melt-in-your-mouth grape leaves (including his motto: *Always indulge in food*) and his commitment to creating music while I drooled over the buttery, crisp layers of my very first baklava. Had four days of international eating turned me into a foodie?

By the time we finally sat down for late afternoon Turkish coffees, it was very clear that one thing connected every single decision of Sai's life: his astrological chart. He had been raised in a culture that not only believed our destinies were determined by the position of the stars the moment we were born but lived in deference to that idea.

"So you're not even willing to consider the possibility that astrology is bogus?" I asked, sipping coffee so strong it made the hairs on my arms stand up.

"Three of my six uncles are astrologers," was Sai's answer.

"Well then, help me understand it all better. In your family, is an astrologer essentially a therapist?"

"I don't think so," Sai said. "A therapist just asks questions and gives suggestions, right? With astrologers, you get answers and direction."

"And you're saying these answers always work out?"

"What do you mean, 'work out'?"

"I mean no astrologer could ever be wrong?"

Sai downed the rest of his coffee in one gulp. "How could they be wrong? They're reading what's already in the stars."

I sat up straighter in my café chair, caffeine fueled and surprisingly ready to dig in even more. I got the sense Sai was the right kind of rival, quick on his feet and not easy to offend.

"Let me try again. Are you telling me you went from zero to successful musician with total ease because you follow our astrological chart so precisely? That you're happy every day because you live in line with our Cancer moon or whatever?"

Sai considered my question—perhaps for the first time—then motioned to the waiter for our check. "I'm happy knowing I'm doing what I was put on this earth to do, even if it's difficult. I'm happier when I do what our moon dictates, especially during all the alone time and travel. But what even is success? I make music. I support myself. That's my calling, and I'm aligned with it, so I'm a success, no?"

"I mean, sure, but I think we can agree that there's a difference between doing what you love and really succeeding at what you love. And if astrology is real, then you should be really succeeding, right?" I wondered if Sai realized this was my way of asking whether he was the world-famous pop star his mom had suggested.

"No," said Sai. "I don't have a record deal. I don't even have a next show lined up. Does that make astrology fake to you?"

"Maybe . . . ," I said, trying not to offend.

Sai shook his head. "See, I knew that's where this was going. You Americans are as judgmental and status-obsessed as they say."

"Hey!" I said. "That's not fair. I'm just saying that if being in alignment with your astrological chart is supposed to mean life opens all the doors, then I'd assume—"

"That I'd be more successful by the global standard for our Instagram-obsessed generation—rise to the top of my career, marry the perfect woman, buy a house and fill it with kids. I get it. And I agree. It's not fair."

That shut me up. I'd been proudly focused on checking off boxes and was stressed about the ones I hadn't. I'd never considered the question of who wrote the list or what it would be like not to have a list at all.

"Ha! I made you think!" Sai said with a cocky smile. He was up on his feet before I could agree. "Okay! We finish with *dondurma*!"

Before I could protest on behalf of my stomach, he'd grabbed my hand and led me back out into the warm open air. We wove through a maze of curved cobblestone streets until we arrived at what looked like a boardwalk ice cream cart. Behind it was a portly man with a curled-up mustache, a cherry-red fez, and a matching red vest. In his hand was a massive silver sword.

"Ready to be ten years old again?" asked Sai.

Before I could answer, the cart's owner dipped his sword into one of the stainless-steel buckets and returned it with a glob of ice cream on the point.

"Vanilla is good for you?" he asked.

"Sure," I said, not knowing what to expect.

He touched the scoop to a massive stack of ice cream cones at his right, then lifted the sword. Everything was stuck together—the cone to the scoop to the sword.

"Is this taffy or ice cream?" I asked Sai.

"Both. But neither," he said, shrugging.

"Ready?" the man asked. I would have said "For what," but before I knew it, the cone/scoop/sword trio had been lowered down in front of me. "*Üç, iki, bir!*" The man started spinning the sword like it was a fire stick. "Catch!" he cried, smiling so wide his mustache whiskers almost poked him in the eyes.

I reached a hand out for the cone. He swooped the sword left. I tried again. He swooped right. I prepped both hands to grab. He somehow got the sword over my head, then through the loop of my arm. It was like a bizarro version of the boardwalk arcade claw game, and it made me laugh like a giddy little kid.

"I'm too full to even eat whatever this insane ice cream is," I said to Sai, reaching and failing three more times. "But I have to win!"

By this point, the man had managed to touch the still-solid ice cream to both my cheeks. Sai swiped his thumb against my skin, taking it off in one swift movement.

"Young lovers," the man crooned.

"And we're twins," Sai added, looking for a reaction.

The man raised an eyebrow and stopped moving just long enough for me to finally grab my cone.

"Ha!" I said, then I closed my lips around what could only be described as marshmallow-taffy-cloud heaven.

"Nice diversion tactic," I said to Sai, handing him the cone for a bite.

He replied with a flirty shrug. "Leos are best matched with other Leos."

"I'm sure," I said with my own coy smile back.

We strolled back toward the center of the city, then found a bench with a perfect view of the imposing Hagia Sophia.

"I'm in Turkey," I said after yet another bite of pillowy perfection.

"And I'm starting to understand how big a deal that is," said Sai. He'd finally turned the conversational tables on our walk, asking me questions about my work and life. I'd kept to the basics, not eager for his take on my vertigo and all the trouble it had prompted.

"You know it's true that we don't have an easy astrological chart," said Sai. "The double Leo demands we do and be so much. And the Cancer moon can be isolating. Confusing even. But my parents always told me it was selfish to reject what the stars decided."

I appreciated the first part of what he said. The second made my forehead wrinkle. "*Selfish?* How?"

"You've been given this life for a reason, put on this earth to do something specific. Trying to override that is just playing like you're a god. Choosing yourself and your wishes over your destiny. Selfish."

Despite my years dutifully sitting in a church pew, I'd never fully bought into the idea of a great power pulling all the strings from above. I favored free will and the people behind peer-reviewed research. But something in me wanted to keep debating this latest point. Being with Sai filled me with a different kind of charge than I felt sparring with David, I realized as I watched his long legs stretch straight out from the bench. With David I wanted to impress. With Sai I wanted to win.

"Okay. I'll play ball," I said. "Let's say I have some magical, amazing destiny waiting for me to accept it. What if I just *choose* to honor my family by running the practice my father and grandfather built?"

"So then they're God?" he asked. *Point: Sai.* And one I was eager to move on from.

"But what happens when your astrological path—"

"*Our* astrological path—"

"When it impacts other people? Like your lovely parents. How do they feel about you living around the world from them because the planets just happened to be powerful right now?"

"They miss me, of course. I miss them, too. But they know

I'm not meant to be with them like my sister is. Her astrological path is connected to home, laying down roots, serving family, so it makes sense."

My arms flew up. "How convenient! The son of the family gets an astrological destiny that lets him travel the world, and the daughter gets to be home cohosting every holiday?"

Sai shot me his most confused look yet. "But Nitara loves to cohost the holidays—" We finished the sentence in unison but with very opposite tones: "—because of her astrological chart."

Turns out the best way to win an argument is to start from the premise that you're never wrong.

Sai and I broke from the daylong debate to stroll the plaza connecting the sixteen-hundred-year-old Hagia Sophia to its twelve-hundred-years-younger counterpart, the Blue Mosque. The area was serene despite being packed with tourists, everyone showing deference to the holiness of the space. It helped that the sun was starting to set, bathing everything in a dimmed glow. Sai helped me turn a scarf into a proper head covering, then we got in a line to enter the Hagia Sophia. I took in the chatter of fellow visitors from all corners of the globe as I looked up at the massive structure before us, humbled by its magnitude. Just then a crackling sound pierced the still air.

"Early evening call to prayer," Sai whispered.

The sheer volume of the voice calling out over the entire city gave me full-body goose bumps. I wished I could understand the words of the haunting melody, but it didn't diminish their impact. My head dropped and my eyes closed on instinct. Without sight, I felt even more connected to everyone around me, so many bodies vibrating at the same frequency.

I peeked while the prayer continued, curious to see how this city looked at a complete standstill. Almost instantly, my eyes landed on a large sign mounted to the side of a curve-topped building just beyond the mosque. It was a poster featuring three men wearing long white dresses and extra-tall cylindrical hats. They appeared to be dancing. But it was the words above them that drew me in: COME SEE THE WORLD-FAMOUS WHIRLING DERVISHES.

From some deep recess of my mind, I remembered: *My mother used to call me a whirling dervish.* I couldn't place when and had no idea why, but I could hear her singsong voice clear as day now. "Come here, my little whirling dervish." She said it all the time.

I was squinting to read the poster when the prayer ended.

"Beautiful, right?" Sai asked.

"What do you know about the whirling dervishes?"

He followed my eyes. "Oh yes. They're incredible. And—" He checked his watch. "We could go see them for the six p.m. show if you'd like. The mosque will be here tomorrow."

"But I won't be. I have to leave for the airport after breakfast."

Sai shook his head. "Twenty-four hours in Istanbul is not enough."

"This was a bonus stop," I reminded him.

"Then I guess you have a choice to make: the dervishes or the temple."

I looked up at the stunning building. "I can't come to Istanbul and not see the mosques."

Sai considered me. "Who writes all these rules you love so much?"

It was as if he'd somehow become possessed by Imani, and it had the same impact. "I think I need to see the whirling dervishes," I said.

"You think?" Sai asked.

"I know."

Chapter
Twenty-One

WE ENTERED WHAT looked and echoed like a cavern. Rows of simple wooden benches were arranged in a hexagon around a large open floor. The rest of the space was made of stone, making the room cooler than the sticky summer air outside, and slightly eerier.

"This was one of the first things I did when I came to town," Sai whispered to me as we filed into the seats. A mix of tourists and locals were doing the same. "Makes sense that you wanted to come, too."

"Why this?" I asked. *Did your mom also call you a whirling dervish?*

"The music. I heard it coming out of this building on one of my strolls through town and had to hear it live. I didn't know anything about the history then, but it's such a fascinating story."

"Can you give me the overview? I have no idea. I just saw

the sign and remembered my mom calling me a whirling dervish when I was little."

"Interesting . . . ," said Sai. "So in the ninth century, I
think, Sufism was developed in this part of the world."

"Oh sure," I said, high school history flooding back.

"So at some point along the way, a group of really spiritual
guys inside the religion—most famously the poet/philosopher
Rumi—landed on this way of expressing their connection to
God through dance, specifically this turning, spinning motion repeated for long periods. It's essentially their form of
prayer in motion, like a moving meditation."

David would be fascinated by this, I thought. I grabbed my
phone to snap a quick photo so I could describe it to him later.
Just then the lights in the room dimmed. Two teenage boys
wearing long tunics started lighting the votives in ornate glass
sconces hanging along the walls throughout the room. They
glowed amber now, and the air suddenly filled with the
peppery-sweet scent of incense. Next three men with
instruments—a flute, a guitar, and a small drum—entered
from a long hallway, taking their places on chairs set up at the
edge of the dance floor. They bowed to the audience, then
launched into an enchanting melody—long, airy notes from
the flute combined with jazzy guitar riffs that sounded almost
improvised, all held together with the beat of a slow, steady
drum. I understood why Sai had followed this sound.

The low, pulsing tune was so captivating that I almost
missed the three dervishes entering. Their slippers glided
across the floor under those long tunics, making them appear
as though they were floating into position at the circle's center.
Sai sat up straighter on his bench, ready for the show. He

couldn't help tapping a hand on his knee in sync with the drum, then he took my hand and made it do the same. I settled into the warmth of his grip, finding myself breathing to match his pace.

A single dervish, the oldest of the group, moved forward into the center of the stage. First, he slowly stretched his arms up and out into the shape of a wide V. Then he stepped to the side with his right foot, gently pushing off the ground in a heel-toe motion. His left foot met the right, then tucked behind it, turning his body in a smooth circle. It was as if the spin came from the ground up. After that first turn, the rest of the group followed. Their movements were all slow at first, in line with the rhythm of the trio accompanying them. But soon the speed increased. My eyes darted, and I felt like I was watching the rippling ocean waves at home as the men ebbed and flowed. It was mesmerizing. The dancers seemed so deeply focused and yet totally lost in their trance; all three sets of eyes were somehow closed despite how quickly they were now turning. I did not understand how they could continue at this pace without toppling over, especially given my still-delicate relationship with balance. It was as if they were both here and not, moving their bodies and yet outside of them.

Time became elusive. At one point, my eyes relaxed their focus, morphing the men into blurry white shapes. Entranced, one thought swirled around and around in my mind: *What did my mom see in me that made her think of this?*

Soon the music started to slow. Eventually the youngest dervish decreased his speed to match, finally coming to a stop. The second followed. As the eldest completed his final turn, I scanned their faces, wondering if they could be three generations in one family. Then the group bowed gracefully. Every single body in the audience dipped in reply, even mine. I came up from the bend with only the slightest bit of a wobble. My skin pricked with chills. Had the whirling dervishes cured me? I bent again to check. The room shifted like usual this time, but with only a small wave, not a massive crest. Relief flowed through my limbs. Was I on the way to recovery? Was this trip the reason? I shook my head. Was I losing it?

"What did you think?" Sai asked as we exited onto the darkened streets. It felt fitting that night had arrived while we were inside.

"It was one of the most incredible things I've ever seen," I said. But I held back the thought behind that: *I should call my mother.* It had been years since I'd felt anything close to that desire.

I wrestled with that idea through our decadent dinner of mezes and kebabs, and even more so once I was finally alone in my hotel. I couldn't stop myself from staring at my reflection in the bathroom mirror as I washed up. *Who or what did my mother see in me when I was a child?* I had to know.

I reached for my phone, typed in Mom. The last texts we'd exchanged appeared on-screen.

Happy birthday sweetheart.
Thanks.

Above that was almost an identical back-and-forth at Christmas. I slammed the phone down on the vanity, furious with myself. I'd sworn off letting my mother upset me years ago, specifically after the hell she put me through at med school graduation, insisting on a seat away from my dad and grandparents, photos nowhere near them, her own dinner with me to celebrate. It filled every moment of what should have been a joyous occasion with tension. I looked back up at my myself, taking a breath to calm down. What did it matter what a woman who barely knew me had called me thirty years ago?

Chapter
Twenty-Two

THE NEXT MORNING I shot awake in a panic. *I never tried my dad again.* I raced to grab my phone off the nightstand. One new voicemail was waiting.

Hey there, Doctor. All's good over here. Dragging a little but headed into the office. You land late tonight, so how's pizza tomorrow night to catch up?

I did the quick time-zone math in my head, leg twitching under the covers as I considered having to finally explain that I was in Turkey. I tapped his name at the top of my contacts, then my finger flew to the END CALL button. I was leaving Istanbul in a matter of hours. I could get away with never telling my dad I was here. My stomach churned at the thought of lying, but I was able to quiet it with another thought: *It's easier for us both if I just leave this little detour out.* The same philosophy he'd taught me for handling irrelevant medical details our patients were better off not knowing.

Sai and I planned to meet for breakfast near my hotel be-

fore I headed to the airport. But I still had an extra hour to see
more of the city. This was where being a runner came in very
handy. Ten minutes later, I was pushing up Edirnekapı Hill.
The running map online had promised a full view of Istanbul,
and it delivered. I was finally able to see the quieter, residen-
tial neighborhoods beyond the tourist center. There were low
stucco buildings, many with laundry drying out the window;
small courtyards with tiny versions of the grand Spice Bazaar;
and dozens of cats lounging in every open patch of sun. Finally, I came to a low, industrial-looking building amid the
ancient stone structures. Outside was a line of people sitting
on produce cartons, most of their heads hung in what looked
like exhaustion. It snaked around the building, with no end
in sight. A sign on the door put all the pieces together: INTER-
NATIONAL MIGRANT HEALTH CENTER. The door of the building
opened. A petite Asian woman stepped out wearing classic
blue scrubs under an equally familiar T-shirt.

"Hey, go Scarlet Knights!" I called out on instinct, pointing
to my own Rutgers tee.

She clocked me, then my top. "Hi. Wow. Small world!"

"Even smaller. I'm a doctor, too," I said.

She nodded, then looked down the very long line. "Any
chance you're free today?"

I shook my head, but she didn't see, too wrapped up in her
work. I watched her take in a quick breath, fix her topknot in
two swift moves, then call out to the group in what sounded
like fluent Arabic. A smile grew across my face. Seeing her
commanding the moment—and with her own smile—filled
me with so much pride that I lingered for several more minutes before finally jogging away.

★ ·★·
·★·

"Sorry I'm late," I said to Sai, who was waiting for me outside the café. "You could have sat."

"I'm outside because I don't want to go in. I want you to move your flight back so we can go on a spectacular river cruise down the Bosporus this afternoon. Killer views. Delicious lunch. And a dance party on the top deck. We must."

"Lovely as that sounds, *I* must fly home."

"You're already here. What's six more hours?"

"Potentially hundreds of dollars."

"Worth it," Sai said.

I was prepared to hold my ground, but those words stopped me. What—quantifiably—would it be worth? I was supposed to land back home tonight. If I moved my flight, I'd land tomorrow morning instead. Half a day's difference. I wasn't working. I wasn't partnered. I could manage the costs. So then going home was about what? Making sure I didn't have too good a time? I was going home out of guilt. I wanted to stay. I could feel that desire in my shoulders.

"Okay," I said. "Let's look into timing options."

"We Leos are very convincing," said Sai, pleased with himself.

By this point, I was accustomed to his unbreakable confidence and found myself surprisingly charmed. It felt worth it just to spend more time as the beneficiary of his affirming worldview and undivided attention. And smile.

Fifteen minutes later, I had a new flight home. Thanks to the time difference, I could leave Istanbul at ten and land in

Newark at two a.m. And it could all be explained away with a flight delay. A harmless lie.

"First, more good news: it's a gorgeous day for a sail," Sai said, leading us toward the river. "The bad news: you can't wear that American tourist costume."

My eyes rolled. "Worse news: you cannot tell a woman what to wear."

"I respect that. But can you take her to a gorgeous dress shop on the way to the water and see if she changes her mind?"

"You can try."

I had not anticipated the wonder that was Gürbüz Vintage. The kaftan was a foreign concept to me before I walked into the shop. After a few minutes inside, I was holding a massive stack of them to try on. I found myself positively giddy as I spun around the mini stage in front of the three-panel mirror wearing a canary-yellow silk kaftan covered in gold embroidered flowers. They were Ottoman tulips, a talisman against harm, according to the salesperson. I liked the dress before the good-luck connection. I liked it even more when Sai looked at me in it and said, "Wow." If only Andi Gold had been there with those lightning-round interview questions. *I feel most badass in an outrageous silk kaftan that I'm about to wear on a party boat sailing between two continents.*

We weaved through the swarming streets, the fabric of my dress flowing like a queen's train, until we arrived at the water's edge. I saw what I now knew locals called the First Bridge, connecting the two halves of this city across the Bosporus strait. Its hundreds of thin suspension cables were covered in small lights that made the structure look projected onto the water below. A constellation.

"I'll now confess I've been wanting to do this since I got to town but haven't had anyone to join me," Sai said as we boarded what was certainly more yacht than boat.

"Anyone, or anyone good enough?" I asked with a brow lift. I'd never flirted that confidently in my life, but the words had fallen out of my mouth with ease. And they worked. Sai was rendered speechless for the first time since we'd met.

We headed immediately for the sleek bar at the boat's stern to order drinks—a traditional Turkish liquor that smelled like lighter fluid to Sai and a sensible white wine to me. I didn't want to push things too far, especially since Sai was still unaware of my vertigo.

"So, we haven't talked about how the whole astrology project you mentioned in your text is going," Sai said, draping himself against the boat railing. "Have you found a lot of us Star Twins?"

"Yes," I said. "Not enough to prove or disprove anything yet, but we're getting there. You'll have to take my survey. It's about our key life transits."

"Ah, like the Neptune square from earlier this year?"

"Exactly," I said.

Sai nodded casually. "That's when I broke off my engagement."

My wineglass almost went overboard. "Wow. Okay. Sort of a big reveal," I said. "I mean, I'm sorry to hear that." I held back from what I wanted to say: *If astrology is so foolproof, how did you end up with the wrong fiancée?*

"We were together for five years. I really thought she was the one for so many reasons—we had the same ideas for the future, our personalities were compatible, and yes, our astrological charts were, too, since I know you'll ask." I shrugged, guilty. "But something in me said no. So, here I am."

"And you broke up in February of this year?"

"No," Sai said, "I went to look at rings for her in February and couldn't find a single one I liked. Once I had my monthly chart reading, I realized what was going on with the transits. That shopping trouble was the very start of my subconscious giving me a nudge."

This was probably the moment in our heart-to-heart where I should have shared my own life shake-up, even if the vertigo hadn't come on in February. But as I looked into Sai's warm brown eyes, then past them to the movie scene behind us, I realized that I wanted to stay in this moment. We were aboard a luxurious boat, sailing against the skyline of an ancient city five thousand miles from real life. Reality was much more interesting than astrology; my dress and his eyes didn't hurt either.

"Now you're telling me astrology likes to play hard to get?" I joked to keep the mood light. We crested a wave just as I did, tipping me off balance. Sai caught my waist with his hand. Then he left it there.

"No," he said. "It just only makes real moves when the time is right."

My pulse quickened—I was sure he was going to pull me toward him—then the boat's speakers crackled on.

"Yo yo, everyone! Time to get this party started!" the DJ called out.

A spark ran through Sai's eyes. "Let's go make this party our own," he said, keeping his arm right where it was as he guided me toward the stairs and up to the main deck.

I thought he was being metaphoric, but as we reached the

dance floor, Sai walked straight up to the DJ, showed him something on his phone, then came back with a very proud smile. "I just booked myself an early release party."

I started to ask what he meant but stopped when the DJ abruptly cut the music.

"Ladies and gentlemen, you're not gonna believe this—we have a *very* special surprise for you aboard today. The whole scene's buzzing about this dude and this new track about to drop—even Harry Styles is a fan. This man is a true original and he's here with us right now—so please, make some noise for Mr. Sai Bakshi!"

He pointed toward Sai, prompting every head on the boat to turn in our direction. Once they spotted him, it was all over: the deck exploded into applause.

"You didn't tell me about Harry Styles!" I said.

"Well," he said, shrugging, "it's nothing serious yet. I just submitted an EP to his label, that's all . . ." He shook his head, smiling, seeming almost bashful.

"Not that commercial success matters," I teased as he pulled me onto the dance floor.

What followed was two hours of a type of carefree, dance-like-no-one-is-watching joy that I don't even recall experiencing at my high school prom. Sai's music was killer, dancey and catchy with tons of the nineties synth sound I'd loved growing up. Planted in the center of the dance floor, I taught the Running Man, the Roger Rabbit, and the Cabbage Patch to everyone on board. Eventually someone else took over, leading us all in a Turkish belly-dancing lesson. I caught Sai looking over from across the deck, his head tilted, those warm eyes fixed firmly on me. I flashed an inviting smile and turned my shoulders slightly but didn't take my eyes off him while he navigated through the crowd.

"How is this not all the success we need in life?" Sai yelled as the DJ masterfully mixed one of his songs with "Like a Prayer." I answered by pulling him close to me, channeling an inner Madonna I never knew I had.

"I'm so glad you convinced me to stay," I whispered in Sai's ear.

"Not as glad as I am," he replied, wrapping me in even tighter.

Minutes later, we were pressed up against each other in a hidden corner of the boat, hands grasping and lips racing like teenagers. *Maybe this will cure me?* I thought as Sai ran his mouth up and down my neck. My body did feel like it was finally releasing after a very long, very tight grip. So much so that I was sure the buzzing against me was coming from inside it. A tingle of elation I could not control.

"Is that your phone?" Sai whispered into my ear.

"Oh," I said. "Maybe. But it's fine."

On the third round of ringing, I snapped to. *Someone is trying to reach me.*

I grabbed the phone from my kaftan pocket, then my stomach dropped: *David?* I stepped back from Sai as if he could somehow see us, as he started calling for the fourth time. Something had to be wrong.

"David, hi. What is it?" I whispered into the phone.

"Hey, Leah." His tone was measured, but I could hear the alarm in his voice. "I'm so sorry to call you like this. I popped in on your dad on my way to the Sandy Hook Lighthouse, and he started having severe chest pain. We've got an ambulance on the way, but I thought I should call you."

I stumbled back further. "He wanted an ambulance?"

"What's going on?" Sai asked, but I pushed him away, running to a quieter corner of the boat. "What are his vitals? He had you take them, right? There's a whole doctor's office worth of equipment in his living room closet."

"BP's only one forty over eighty but all the other symptoms are there. We didn't want to risk me driving him and then—"

Ice ran through me. I couldn't let him finish. "Absolutely, that's the right thing to do. Can I talk to him?" I was pacing now, caught between the calm of what my doctor brain knew—*BP is stable, medics can and will handle this*—and my daughter-self feared: *My father is having a heart attack, and I'm half a world away.*

"I . . . I don't know, Leah. He's pretty—" David tried.

"David, I need you to put me on speaker so he can hear my voice," I said, trying not to scream.

"He's here, Leah," David said.

My heart raced up to my throat, but I quickly shoved it down. "Hey there, Doctor. You're going to be okay. Just deep breaths and hang on until the paramedics get there. You know it'll probably be Dan Palumbo and Mark Banya, and they'll take really good care of you even if you have to hear Dan's bad jokes, right?" I had fifteen years of experience talking to panicked patients and no fucking clue what else to say at this moment.

"We should go, Leah," David said. "I'll keep you posted."

"No. No, please keep me on the phone. I want to listen when the paramedics assess him." I heard sirens in the distance. Help was close. "Dad? Can you hear me?"

"He's nodding," David said.

"Okay. Thank you so much, David. I'm going to get on the first flight I can. Istanbul's a major airport, so I should be able to get out immediately. I'll be home as soon as humanly possible."

There was a pause on the other end of the line. "Istanbul?" I heard just as the paramedics knocked on the front door. It was the only word out of my dad's mouth before the phone disconnected.

Chapter
Twenty-Three

AS HARD AS we tried, the staff of our cruise would not agree to end it an hour and a half early. I sat on the bottom deck for all ninety excruciating minutes until we were back at the dock. Two and a half hours later, I was finally at the airport with all of my luggage and another changed ticket, racing through the terminal at breakneck speed to make it to the gate. I'd tried calling David, then Charlotte, then the entire ER team at Riverview before we took off; no one responded. Faced with the reality of an eleven-hour flight, without the hope of an update or any distraction, I did the only thing I knew would temper the spirals of guilt and fear until we landed in the States: guzzled mini bottles of alcohol until I fell asleep.

Thirteen and a half hours later, my cab pulled up to River-view. I hadn't gotten more than a text from David saying He's stable and another from Charlotte saying Where in the world are you?? since I took off. I had to assume she now knew where I'd been. I stepped out of the car, shaking from anxiety and a very bad hangover. The first person I saw as I ran toward the ER was Jack Wayland, the hospitalist.

"Leah, hi," he said, giving me a confused once-over.

"Tell me," I said. He motioned for us to step aside. I went numb.

"Pulmonary embolism. He'll be fine. Just needs blood thinners and two weeks of vacation. Why didn't you take him wherever you got that fancy thing?" He gestured at my body.

I whiplashed from relieved to mortified. I was still wearing the bright yellow kaftan. But there was no time to explain that as Charlotte walked up.

"Hi. You're here," I said, running to her. "Why weren't any of you picking up your phones?"

Her face was stone as she noticed my outfit. "Because we were here. With *your dad*. Why were you in Turkey? What happened to Italy? And why is there a giant Band-Aid on your head?" I'd never heard my cousin use that tone of voice, and I'd known her since the day she was born.

"Oh god, Charlotte. I'm sorry. It's a long story and—"

"Yeah, well, I think you should go tell it to your dad. He was up all night worried about you, which is the last thing he needs right now." I was talking to a stranger. All I could do was nod back. "Room one eighty-four. My parents are up there keeping him company."

"Thanks," I said.

"Call me later," Charlotte replied. It was clear she had much more to say.

I saw my uncle Ted and aunt Kath walk out of Dad's room

as I made my way down the hall. I slipped into a doorway and waited until they were gone. Then, chest clamped, I finally opened the door to Dad.

"Doctor," I said. He was sitting up in bed, cheeks pink and eyes wide. My eyes welled with tears.

"Hey, hey. No need for that. I'm fine," Dad said.

"I know. I'm sorry." I grabbed a tissue off the tray table, shoving it over my face. "I just . . . I didn't know, and I couldn't get a hold of anyone and—" I stopped, realizing how ridiculous it was to be defending myself right now. Instead, I just added a second tissue to my eyes and blew my nose so my dad didn't see me crying.

"They only kept me overnight because they think they've got to give me the Cadillac treatment. I already signed discharge papers, so they should be up in a minute to finalize everything. What happened to you?" He motioned to my forehead.

"Oh, nothing. Just nicked my head on a cabinet at the hotel." *Another lie.* Meanwhile, the one I'd *not* gotten away with hung over me like a dark haze. I sat down on the vinyl chair beside my dad's bed. "I'm sorry I wasn't here," I said. "And that we didn't connect about my extra stop in Turkey."

Dad shook his head. "And that you were planning to completely blow off the meeting we had scheduled with Jim today?" My head fell. In my excitement over Istanbul, I'd forgotten what should have been—what *was*—the most important thing going on in my life. *Who am I?* "What could have been so important that you ran off on a second trip, solo, without any time to let anyone know?"

It was not a rhetorical question. I wished I could come up

with a reason that would meet his approval. There was none. "An opportunity came up last-minute to meet a Star Twin, and I felt compelled to go. I wanted to explain it all to you on the phone, but we kept missing each other."

His eyes narrowed as if he was examining me more closely. "Compelled to go meet a new Star Twin? I feel like I'm talking to a stranger."

The edge of disdain in his voice was so sharp that I had to look down at the floor. "You're not," I said, but even I feared that was not convincing. And maybe not even true.

"Good, because we've got some things to figure out now," Dad said. "I'm supposed to be home for two weeks of recovery, but I think I'll be fine in one. That still means we've got to shut down with a full schedule at the office and two deliveries this coming week." My heart sank. "I assume you didn't make much progress on your recovery while you were traveling," Dad said.

His tone made me bristle. "I actually did make some improvements—"

"Improvements aren't enough. We're already walking on thin ice and can't afford even one misstep. We need you back, but only if you're one hundred percent."

"Let's really think this through," I said. "We're both in need of real recovery now. I think our patients will understand if we need to bring in help until we're well."

"I don't know," my dad sighed, exasperation in his voice. "There's plenty of competition for care these days. We don't have the luxury of finding out how many issues our patients are willing to excuse."

I knew he was right. And worse, that every single issue was because of me.

"I'm sorry. I never should have gone on this trip. I'll talk to David and map out what we can do to ramp up my PT and get me back to the office as soon as possible."

That finally softened my dad. "Good. And chin up," he said. "We'll get through this as a team, like we always have."

Those words did not soothe me as they usually did. How had I lied so easily to this man who gave me everything? Learned to braid my hair? Cut the crust off every sandwich? Laced up my running shoes in his secret way so they'd be extra tight for race day? I didn't give a shit about Imani's or Sai's opinions about the best way to live my life. I'd acted selfishly, and I'd let us all down. I'd forgotten our name.

"We'll have to think of something nice to give David," Dad said, pulling me back to the room. "He rode in the ambulance with me and waited 'til Ted and Kath got here last night."

"Of course. I should call him now, actually," I said. "You okay here for a minute?"

Dad nodded, much lighter now. I wished I felt the same.

David answered my call immediately. "Hey. You're back? How is your dad?"

"He's doing fine. It was an embolism, not a heart attack, but you probably already know that. Thank you so, so much for being there."

"I'm just glad I popped by to say hi to him last night. Where are you now?"

"At the hospital, why?"

"I'm still in town. Stayed with the Millers last night."

"Oh wow. I didn't realize your family stayed close to them."

He hesitated slightly. "We didn't, really . . . but I got in touch with them yesterday so I could stay to see you as soon as you got back."

My eyes welled up. I was exhausted, overwhelmed, and still a mess from that miserable trip home, but I desperately wanted to see David. "We should be getting discharged soon—I'll get my dad home and then text you once he's settled in. Meet at the creek?" I asked.

"Peanut butter shakes are on me," was David's reply.

Chapter
Twenty-Four

IT WAS NINE p.m. by the time my dad allowed me to help—very minimally—with getting him to bed. I considered texting David to reschedule for the morning, then remembered we had a well-honed strategy for meeting at our spot after dark. I slipped downstairs, hoping my dad's night-fishing lanterns were still in the basement. Luckily my type A father had them in a box labeled LIGHTING—fully charged. I turned to head back upstairs, but the box just to the left caught my eye: LEAH MIDDLE SCHOOL. I froze. *If I saved them, they're in there.*

At some point, I'd bundled all of David's pen pal letters together in a bright blue hair tie. I found them cinched up, just as I'd left them, in chronological order. That meant that the last one he'd sent would be right at the top. I started to unfurl the first envelope and hesitated. *You're about to see David anyway, this can wait.* But I'd been around the world and taken some serious detours within the past five days; what harm could a little trip down memory lane do to me now?

David's scratchy handwriting stood out against the worn paper. *Hey Pen Pal* was scrawled across the top like always. Below followed a paragraph about his new turtle, his new soccer coach, and how it was "so steaming hot" in New Orleans that he and his mom fried an actual egg on their sidewalk. He was "beating the heat" by watching *Big* in their den—with a fan in front of his face. And then—to close—I saw three short sentences and realized what I'd dreaded this whole time: *I really miss you, Leah. If my parents agree, can I come back up to visit you this summer? Maybe we could go hang out somewhere?*

That was the question I'd left hanging for two decades, and even worse, I'd somehow managed to erase the memory that it even existed. David had asked to visit and take me on what would have been our first real date. I'd known that's what he meant by *go hang out somewhere* when I first read it. I'd never replied.

I found David in the backyard, cell phone flashlight in one hand and tray with two giant milkshakes in the other. He smiled at the sight of our lanterns floating toward him, or maybe it was just at me.

"How are you?" he asked.

"Not great," I sighed, too tired to be anything but honest.

David replied by handing me one of the milkshakes, then looped his arm through mine.

"They don't make them like this down south," he said, taking a sip.

"You mean your poor child is growing up without this bliss?" I asked after gulping down my own.

"Sadly. Though she might be up to visit last-minute this weekend."

"Fun." I somehow fought the urge to say that I'd love to meet her.

"I just need to figure it out with a talk I'm giving at Columbia."

"Fancy. What's the talk about?"

"Long story, but I'm basically explaining the work I've done focusing on preventative PT with the military to a group of business school students studying medical venture capitalism."

"Those words do not sound like they should go together."

"I didn't think so either, then I started getting huge grants from insurance companies because my work actually saves them money in the long run. There's a lot of interesting stuff like that going on between money and medical people."

"I would not know the first thing," I said. "We're still making the switch from paper to online patient records."

"You're welcome to come to the talk, though I know it's your birthday weekend. Big plans?"

My face fell. "Yes. Cape May with Charlotte, who's furious with me right now." I shook my head. "I never should have gone on the trip."

David shook his head, too, sorry to hear that, it seemed. "I get it," he said. "I was saying the same thing a week into my work up here."

"What changed?"

He looked down the backyard toward our creek. "I remembered what made me come in the first place," he said.

My skin pricked with curiosity—*what exactly did he mean?*

We'd made it down to the water. David hopped onto the bridge, hooking his lantern to one of the posts, then leaned against the railing. I followed to stand beside him.

"Do you want to talk about your dad?" he asked, as if reading my mind.

"Not really," I said, then I dipped my head in disgust. "Ugh, how bad is that?"

David considered me a little too closely for my liking. "What happened to him is not your fault, Leah," he said.

I looked away, my chest suddenly tight. "I don't know. He's under way more stress than he has been in years, and that is definitely because of me." It pained me to think that the last time was probably when my mom left.

"But it's still not your fault," David said, then his face shifted. "Sorry. I did some counseling when things were at their worst with Erin. There was all this stuff about what we do to people intentionally versus what happens to people because of things we can't control. I wish I could remember it all better, but the therapist had this very intense way of staring at me when she was trying to focus that I found wildly distracting."

"Impression, please." I was desperate for a mood shift. David's deep brown eyes locked into mine, then they expanded—and kept going—until he looked like a crazed killer. "Oh god, stop, that's so creepy!" I cried.

"Yeah, now imagine it with blood-red lipstick!"

That made me laugh. "Well, sounds like she still taught you something valuable. And I appreciate it," I said. Then the comfort of the creek made me go further. "You know, you were right about something else, too. I'm starting to realize that I did change a lot from who you knew when we were growing up. I'm just trying to figure out how and why."

David's brow raised. "Interesting. Have you considered engaging in a broad-sweeping personal astrology experiment as an option?"

"Ha! I wish I'd considered it more carefully. I feel like I opened Pandora's box. And now it's sort of spilled out onto my entire life, if that makes any sense."

"Too much," David said, nodding. He looked down to the water below. "I've been dealing with my own version of it, in a way."

"Oh?" I asked, flipping around so that my back was leaned up against the railing.

David considered for a second. "I've been trying to figure out how I married the wrong person."

"Oh wow, we're going there," I blurted out.

I got a laugh, thank god. "Creek cone of silence?" he asked.

"Always."

He flipped his body so we were face-to-face. "Erin's really attached to status. Her family's big into politics down in New Orleans, so that makes sense. That's never been me, but when she showed an interest in me . . . I don't know." He scratched a fingernail into the wood, thinking. Or maybe stalling. "It was hard after I left here. I was an outsider down south, and the shortest, skinniest kid for a long time. I didn't get a ton of attention from girls. So when she picked me, I just . . . I figured she knew something I didn't. I jumped and didn't look back."

It was hard to think of him as anything but the sweet, goofy kid I'd adored, and the incredibly attractive man next to me now. "Are you saying you didn't really pick her? Or wouldn't have if she didn't make the first move?"

David turned away, thinking again. After a moment he seemed to come to a conclusion, then he lifted his eyes to mine. "All I know is the boy I was on this creek bridge never would have ended up with that girl."

A silent exchange passed between us. My breath quickened. I was sure I felt David start to lean ever so slightly into me. There was that slow, magnetic pull between us—a kiss in the millisecond before two lips touched. My heart started beating through my hands. I knew I wouldn't stop it. Then something else did.

"Hello? Who's there?!"

We both jumped at the yell coming from his old backyard, then the flashlight beam that followed. My eyes quickly spotted our current across-the-creek neighbor, a gossip queen of the Highlands, which was saying a lot.

"Duck!" I whispered, dipping below the railing.

"Why? We're grown adults and this is your family property," David said, still standing.

"It doesn't matter." I pulled him down to my level. The thought of even five minutes with Sherry Heinz was too unbearable.

"Hello?! Come out, or I'm calling the police!"

David's eyes turned ten years old. "Then we have to make a run for it." He whisked me up in one silent swoop. We raced over the bridge, up the hill, through the thicket of ferns, and out the driveway gate, flying like kids evading the cops on Mischief Night. Both of us were gasping for air by the time we made it to David's car across the street, laughing so hard it was a miracle Sherry hadn't tracked us.

"*No!*" David cried, looking back to the house. "We left our shakes down at the creek."

"Just means you have to come back for more," I said, still panting.

"Please," said David.

We were under just enough of the light from the old street lantern above for me to see David's dimples as he smiled at me. *How did I ever think I could stop myself from falling for him again?* He leaned in. I closed my eyes on instinct. But instead of his lips on mine, I felt his arms around me. Our bodies came together like two magnets finally close enough to fuse. It was a hold, not a hug, and it was exactly what I needed.

"Thank you," I said once we finally parted.

"It's going to be okay, Leah," David said. "I should get back home, but I'll text you to find time for another PT session. Let's at least try to finally clear this vertigo."

He gave my shoulder a squeeze and then turned to open the car door. I reached out and spun him back around.

"I'm sorry I never replied to your last pen pal letter," I blurted out. "I think I couldn't have you come up here and then leave again. I couldn't have anyone else leave again."

David nodded, as if maybe he'd known that all along. "This might sound crazy to you," he said, "but I think I ended up getting back here at just the right time."

I answered with a smile. It didn't sound crazy at all.

Chapter
Twenty-Five

JET LAG WOKE me at six. I laced up and started to run my usual Hudson Trail loop but was dragging, spoiled by the brand-new views from my last two jogs. A few paces from the top of the beach, a thought struck me. I raced back, got in my car, and took the bridge over to Sandy Hook state park. I hadn't made the short drive for a run, picnic, or even stroll in longer than I could remember. What followed were the slowest three miles I'd run in years, taking in the bay and city skyline from a completely different angle. I loved it so much that I ran two more, then faster than I had in months. I'd always thought of myself as someone who craved consistency as a runner, but exploring here felt like it had in Venice and Istanbul—like with eyes open wider I could suddenly move with more propulsion. After I finished, I popped into town to grab a bag of bagels for my dad. I did not know how to put my life back together, but I knew part of the way back was making amends with the most important people in it.

He was finishing up a phone call in his study when I walked in. The tight line of his mouth made me fear it was with his cardiologist.

"Hey, Doctor," he said, finally entering the kitchen. I'd set up a full bagel bar and had coffee brewing. "Thanks for all this." He came toward me with an outstretched hand for our shake. At least that was back to normal.

"Everything okay?" I asked.

"It will be," he said, grabbing a plate. "I was just on with our lawyer." *My lawyer*, I thought, my brain jumping to correct him. "I wanted to run some questions by him now that I'm going to be out for the week. Every move we make is critical with this case."

"I feel like I should have been on that call," I said.

"I've known Jim a long time," was Dad's answer. "We think the best course of action, given everything, is to get you back to work."

"When?" I asked.

"As soon as possible. I'm still going to have the team at Shore OB-GYN cover deliveries while I'm out this coming week, but if the vertigo has calmed down enough, I'd like you back in the office for regular appointments. Consistent care from the Lockhart team. That's who we are. That's what we do. That's the message we want to send our patients and certainly that girl's lawyers."

"Monica," I heard myself say.

"How does that sound?" he asked, ignoring my comment.

"I have to check all my vertigo triggers again," I said.

"Good. Do that and let me know. Today's Tuesday." He lit up, realizing something. "And your birthday's Saturday. Perfect gift to have you back in action that Monday morning, right?"

Say yes, my brain commanded, but I couldn't even get my head to nod.

Dad took a bite of bagel, satisfied. I turned to make myself a cup of coffee, hiding.

"I'll take a cup, please," he said. I poured another, then brought it over to join him at the table.

"I wanted to say one more thing." Dad took a sip. I tensed. "I didn't mean to be so short with you at the hospital. I should have never compared you to your mother. I've just seen some changes in you lately that made me nervous."

"What kind of changes?" I asked, regretting it immediately. I was surprised to find I'd almost expected his statement, but I had not been prepared to feel a wave of defensiveness.

"Frankly, you putting yourself before almost anything else. I hope it's just a phase. And, look, I understand it to a degree— you've been thrown for a loop, you're desperate to get better— but after what I just went through, it's clearer than ever to me what really matters in life. Like I told you on my last day back in February, running a practice that honors the work we do requires putting that work first. I hope all this doesn't mean you're not up for that job."

A chill ran through me. "January," I heard myself say.

"What?"

"Your last day was in January."

Dad looked back at me, confused. "No. It was after Uncle Ted's birthday party. February second. But that's not the point."

"Right," I said, calendar boxes racing through my mind.

We had the retirement party on January 26. *But then he stayed on for an extra week to see Jenny Bayless through her delivery.*

"You understand what I'm saying," I heard my dad continue. "Promise me this is all just a phase you're going through."

According to my astrological chart, February versus January was the real point. If there was any truth at all to what Nova had claimed about this year's transit, then my dad leaving the practice might have been my version of Sai's failed engagement ring purchase, the first domino to fall.

"Leah?"

Dad's eyes bore into me. One part of my brain was screaming at me to just answer yes and move on. Tell him what he wanted to hear. This was just a phase. But I could not look this man in the eyes and lie again.

"I don't know if it's a phase," I said. The truth, finally.

It was not the reply he was expecting. It seemed to shake him for a moment, then he reset with a nod. "You're off to Cape May with Charlotte this weekend. Maybe take a boat ride off the point while you're there. My treat. Some time on the water'll do you good. Set you back on track." That was that, as far as he was concerned. But my insides did not agree. There was a fist in my chest now, but I didn't know if it was anger or sadness.

As we ate our breakfast sandwiches, Dad asked me about the food in Italy, but nothing else about the trip and certainly not the Turkey portion. I didn't offer. On the surface, everything between us was back to normal, but I felt as far from him across the dinner table as I had close to David on the

creek bridge last night. The pit in my stomach at that difference stayed with me until I was back at my condo.

I went immediately to check the Star Twins Survey. There
were seventy-five responses now, but I surprisingly didn't
care about looking through the transit stats or anecdotes people had included. I wanted their names. The only people in the
world who might understand all the madness I was feeling
were right here in this location I'd created, ironically, to deny
any connection between us. Were they going through *just a
phase*? Was any one of them on the other side? I had an email
address for every single person who had submitted, but what
was I going to do? Send them a message asking if they also felt
insane? Pop them a note to see if they too got the sense they
were finding themselves and losing themselves at the same
time? My mind went to Heidi Rosemont. I knew from her last
message that she was struggling. I found our exchange and
sent along a new message.

> Hi again, Heidi. Sorry I was short in my last reply.
> This astrology project has really thrown me, too.
> If you're still interested, I'd love to finally have
> that chat. Happy almost birthday to us.

I sat, blankly staring at my sent message, still desperate for
help. Moments later, I reached for my phone and texted the
absolute last person I'd ever thought I'd be asking for advice.

Chapter
Twenty-Six

NOVA WAS WAITING for me down by the marina, clad in a red linen romper and holding a giant fan hand-painted with bright orange flowers. "There she is. I'd say I thought you'd never call, but that would be a lie." He winked, of course. It reminded me that we had one piece of unfinished business.

"I need to know something before we talk," I said. Nova replied with a "Go ahead" bow. "Are your eyes real or colored contact lenses?"

He batted his lashes. "One hundred percent real. I consider them an extra nod from the great creator that I'm *one of a kind*."

I do not know why, but that reply endeared Nova to me for the very first time. We made our way down to the rows of docks. "So, how are we?" he asked.

"We don't know . . . ," I said, sighing.

It was only then that I realized I'd essentially booked a session with Nova so he could give me advice on what the hell I was supposed to do with all the confusing thoughts clouding my mind. *Who am I, really? How am I supposed to know for sure? And what if I don't like her?* I shook my head as the irony of this moment landed, but that's just how desperate I'd become for answers.

"That's a good sign," he said. "Don't overthink the answer. Just give me the word-vomit version."

My first thought came in the form of a desperate question: *Where does this end? I need to know if the universe is going to take my medical license away and destroy all my relationships to teach me some grand lesson, because if so, I'm not going to survive.* But I said something else.

"This whole project really fucked me up."

"YES! There she *is*!" His fan flew up with a flourish. "Sorry. Proceed."

I let my frustration keep leading. "I've had weird shit happen, weird memories come up. I've made insane decisions and told a lot of lies to people I love. I'm having instincts and desires about things that feel good but do not fit my life. I'm suddenly resisting the idea of going back to work. Oh, and I've felt more emotional in the past months than I have in years."

Nova took that all in with a more serious face than usual. "You feel like you knew yourself and now you don't, even though this new you is eerily familiar."

"Yes." He'd picked up on the same feeling I'd confessed to David.

"You feel like your life was simple and clear and now it's not."

"Extremely."

"You feel like you made everyone in your world happy before and now you're not so sure."

I nodded, surprised by how completely true that felt.

Nova sat down on one of the benches that lined the walkways of the marina; many of them were engraved with dedications to family. Somewhere just a few docks over was the one we'd purchased for my grandparents. FOR GERALD AND RUTH LOCKHART, WHO GAVE ALL OF THEMSELVES TO THIS BEAUTIFUL PLACE. My dad's bench could read the same someday. Would mine?

"You may be shocked to know that I've been through what you're going through," Nova offered. I couldn't stop myself from shooting a look at his neon-pink toenails in bedazzled white rubber Birkenstocks. I *would* have been shocked. "Seven-year-old Neville did not prance around his tiny Southern town dressed like this."

"*Neville?!*"

"The *third*, honey. So you can imagine how well it went over when I changed it to Nova. You may also be shocked to know that I knew nothing of astrology when all that happened. I was just a little boy who liked glitter, capes, and other little boys. And I thought, *Surely this is wrong. I am wrong. I am having bizarre thoughts—bad and inconvenient ones that go against everything I've been taught to believe. How could they possibly be right?* Obviously I wasn't getting a well-rounded education on puberty in the South circa 1999, so I figured it was when your brain goes haywire for a few years before you grow up and become a real man like all the other Nevilles. Those Nevilles own a chain of Chevy dealerships, to give you a mental picture."

"I'm guessing you were never Employee of the Month?"

"I was never an employee at all. Try as I might, I could not seem to get rid of myself. He was just screaming at me too loud to ignore. It is deeply uncomfortable to feel conflicted about yourself. It's worse to decide you hate the version that feels most correct."

That part wasn't so hard for me to imagine right now. "So what did you do?" I asked.

"I surrendered at sixteen, got kicked out of my house, and haven't spoken to a single Neville since."

My hand flew to my chest. "That is not what I was expecting."

"Thank you. I am a natural storyteller. It's an Aries thing. Anyway, that's why I'm so sympathetic to your situation."

This reveal was somehow more surprising. "Wait, *you're* sorry for *me*?"

"I have twenty years of experience learning how to accept myself. My insides live on the outside. I couldn't hide. You got sidetracked thanks to what I'm guessing is a little bit of nature and a big bit of nurture and have been lost somewhere inside yourself for decades. Sorry, love, but the longer you wait to know her, the harder she is to know. You're—what, two months into this whole experiment?"

Had it really only been eight weeks? Nova's first challenge to me was *prove that your astrological chart has nothing to do with your vertigo*, but his second was what I thought I'd built the whole Star Twin Survey around: *prove that your astrological chart isn't you*. From the very beginning, he'd tried to explain that this was all about me—only about me—but instead I'd set out to prove that it was about everyone else, from my Star Twins to my family.

My head jolted up. A very big lightbulb had just finally gone off.

"I reversed the experiment," I said as the details flew together in my mind. "The right methodology is single-subject, not group against control."

Nova looked pleased but in a smug way. "Bravo, Leo," he said.

"You knew that all along?"

His fan fluttered proudly. "Think of your Star Twins as identical twins who were raised in totally different houses, with totally different parents. Meeting them will bring you a sense of connection, but it's not the right path to knowing yourself."

"Wrong subject. Wrong control," I whispered.

"Exactly. In the more revealing study, the old Leah is the control, and new Leah is the subject."

My ears perked up. "That's some more very scientific language," I said, remembering it was not the first time I'd heard it from Nova. "Now are you going to reveal that you've already conducted this exact type of experiment? Perhaps on yourself?"

"No," Nova said, whipping the fan closed. "I'm now going to reveal that I went to med school and was a practicing psychiatrist for six years."

I grabbed the fan straight out of his hand. "What?! Then gave it all up to be an *astrologer*?!"

"First, watch the tone. I've heard enough of that in my time."

I nodded, silent.

"Second, I have some . . . let's just say 'boundary issues' as a personality. Neutrality is not in my chart. But the truth is I fell in love with astrology, followed that passion, and feel I actually have a greater impact on people through this work versus the other."

That idea was still landing with me when a confession slipped out of my mouth. "My shoulders tingle."

"Oh," Nova said, looking down at them. "Should we get out of the sun?"

"No. That's what I think happens when my spirit—or however you described it—is trying to talk to me. My shoulders get all tingly, like they're filling up with energy."

Nova's eyes glistened, or maybe even teared up. "*Gorgeous.* Like the stars themselves twinkling through you . . ."

I stood up. "Nope! Too far!" But I was already laughing. Nova rose to join me, then insisted we walk along the rest of the docks so he could spend time manifesting the boat of his dreams.

"The SS *Neville*," he announced, adding a powerful explanation in response to my look. "He's how I got to me."

Leaving the marina, I had the beginnings of a plan for how to both crawl out from all this astrology haze and finally clear the air with Charlotte. I'd use my birthday weekend away with her to talk it through and figure myself out, maybe even using the prompts from Nova's original email as a guide. Who better to help me untangle it all than the person who knew me best?

As I approached Coast Roastery, my phone buzzed. It was a reply from Heidi.

> Hi Leah—Good to hear from you, and good
> timing. I'm actually on your coast right
> now. I've never been to New York City and
> decided to make a special trip for our

birthday. Not sure how close you are, but
if you're up for meeting let me know.
Maybe even Saturday for our birthday??

I dropped the hand holding my phone, stopping short in the middle of the sidewalk. I couldn't be in Manhattan with Heidi if I wanted to mend things with Charlotte in Cape May. *And shouldn't that be my number one priority right now?*

Chapter
Twenty-Seven

"I WAS TOO harsh at the hospital," Charlotte said, hugging me tightly the second I arrived. "You've never been through this kind of medical scare, and it made you question everything." Then she rushed to serve me a piece of my all-time favorite lemon tart with a shortbread crust.

"And so you start digging into astrology and—power of suggestion—you think that's the answer to recovery. I get it. I bought into it, too," she continued, showing me to a table in the back to sit.

"And then you go on a big trip for the first time, *alone*, get total vacation brain and start making crazy decisions that you would never make under normal circumstances," she concluded, popping up to make me a decaf latte. She thought caffeine would be unwise.

"I'm not sure they were *crazy*," I tried once Charlotte returned with the beverage I did not really want, but she put a hand up to stop me. She was not done.

"Everyone needs to go a little haywire every now and then. Remember when I dyed my hair red in college? I couldn't figure out my major, and I was losing my mind, and I had a mini snap. This is just your version of that—on a way bigger scale—but I'm here for you. We're going to have a totally rejuvenating trip down to Cape May. Your dad already sent me money to take you on a boat ride. I booked us fancy massages. We'll get you back to being our Leah for your birthday. It's actually perfect." She did a little *clap clap* of her hands. *Done*.

Up until this moment, I had not considered what the opposite of my shoulder tingle felt like. But my stomach had gotten tighter and tighter as Charlotte went through her points. Now it was like a block of cement had dropped into the space between my ribs. *What do you mean, "our Leah"*? it asked, but my actual voice interrupted.

"I need to be in New York for my birthday weekend instead," I said.

Charlotte did a cartoon blink. "What? Why?"

"David is giving a big talk Friday, and a Star Twin I want to meet is in town, too." I thought about inviting Charlotte to join, but the cement in my stomach would not let me.

"So this is about David? I've been worried about that . . . Leah, just no. He's divorced with a kid. He's not your husband."

This I could not stay silent about. "I didn't say he was, but, Charlotte, I haven't felt like this about anyone before. You always told me 'when you know you know,' and I think this may be it."

Charlotte reached out and placed her hand on top of mine, a move she'd learned from her mother. It made me feel like I was a little girl again, sitting for tea with Aunt Kath as she explained to me one more time how lucky I was to have such a saint of a father. "I think the David stuff is just another product of the upside-down time you're going through. Plus New York is not the chaos you need to finally recover," said, copying her mother's patronizing tone, too. "Trust me on this, Leah. I know you."

The cement inside of me had turned to fire. I pulled my hand back. "No you don't," I said. "Right now, I don't even think I know myself."

My icy tone shocked both of us. But Charlotte's face turned condescending, not concerned. "Oh, Leah, you do. And so do I. And we'll both get her back in Cape May. I promise." She'd flipped into her best surrogate big-sister voice. Today it hit my ear like the screech of gurney wheels down a hospital hall.

My palms hit the table in frustration, landing harder than I expected. Two teenagers a few seats over looked up. I recognized them, but that didn't stop me. "You're not listening to me," I said. "I'm sorry if this upsets you, but I need to go to New York. Charlotte, I feel myself figuring out things that seem really important, and maybe long overdue—about myself, my parents." She looked back at me like I was speaking a foreign language. *How can I speak hers?* "And it's really thanks to you," I said, brightening up. "You introduced me to Nova and helped me get the Star Twin Survey going."

"And you said Nova was a joke, and that the Star Twin thing was just something to kill time," Charlotte fired back.

"That changed," I argued, now on the edge of my chair. "People change, Charlotte. I think I am. And I have to see this through to the end. I really need you to understand."

My words hung in the air between us. It was quite possibly

the first time I'd asked my cousin for anything real in our entire lives together.

"Well, I don't," Charlotte said.

Her words landed in my chest with the same force I'd felt
with my dad not twenty-four hours earlier. She wasn't hearing
me, just like he hadn't. But with Charlotte there was an added,
chilling detail: the look on her face as she stared at me across
the table. I could not place it, but I knew exactly how it made
me feel: livid. I pushed my chair back from the table and
walked out the door.

Chapter
Twenty-Eight

THE SUN HIT Sandy Hook Bay, turning its deep-blue water into a layer of crackling glass. In the past two weeks, I'd been on the Venice canals and Bosporus strait, and this ranked right up there with them. The beauty of the view started as a helpful distraction, then it turned bittersweet: I was seeing it from a ferry I'd jogged past most days of my life. I'd made this forty-five-minute trip into Manhattan fewer than ten times. It was not lost on me, given all the thoughts unearthed these past weeks, that my beach-town mouse status was in part because of my mom's city-loving nature. She was constantly trying to get us there for a Broadway show, special meal, or museum visit. Dad was already more of a homebody, and it didn't help that Mom always took her excitement level to a twelve. Once she made plans to go in for an exhibit at the Metropolitan Museum of Art and then revealed she'd also booked lunch at some fancy spot in Central Park. *Imani would have loved her*, I thought. It did not occur to me until now that I might have loved that side of her, too. Seeing the silver-stepped outline of the Chrysler Building now, I remembered stomping down the street beside my mom in a pair of black patent-leather boots she'd bought me just for the occasion. When I'd looked down at them, I saw the building lights above painting glistening spots on their surface and thought it was pure magic. Where had that memory been? I glanced down at the white sneakers and denim shirtdress I had on today and felt somehow off. There was over an hour to kill before David's talk at Columbia, then meeting Heidi at the hotel where she—and now I—was staying on the Upper West Side. *Definitely enough time.*

I went straight from the ferry terminal to the closest department store. Every time something caught my eye, no matter how much the item surprised me—a silky fuchsia top with ruffles down the center, a citrus slip dress with a black lace hem—I tried it on. In the dressing room, I pretended I was a Burano local trying to match the *wow* of my surroundings, then I tested how the clothes felt performing those Turkish belly-dancing moves I'd learned on the yacht. I left with a shopping bag full of finds, wearing an oversized red linen blazer over a bright pink sundress, my white sneakers swapped for a just-as-comfy pair, but in gold. By the time I walked onto the subway to Columbia, I no longer had to pretend I was anyone else.

David was reviewing note cards in the front row of the large auditorium. I caught him mouthing the words of his talk, nervous in the most charming way.

"Hey," I said as I approached him. "You have perfect dimples. You can say anything up there and have the whole room in the palm of your hand."

David lit up at the sound of my voice, then gave my new outfit a welcome once-over. "And you look like you're ready to have a killer birthday weekend."

"I hope," I said, thrilled to be kicking it off in his presence. *These feelings are real*, I thought.

People were filing into the room now, a mix of put-together business school students and finance types in navy suits. "Break a leg up there," I said, then turned to take a seat in the front row.

Although I'd shown up, I had zero expectations of ending up totally captivated by the subject matter. In my world, doctors treated patients in practices, ideally their own. The system of business was the same as it had been when my grandad started LWM fifty-plus years ago. David, it seemed, was in the business of innovation. His passion was for serving communities with the greatest need and fewest resources. His approach was to bring together medical minds with the financially minded and expand what could be done with all parties working toward the same goal. I was rapt, and not just because he was my version of a hot boy with a guitar onstage. His ideas sent my mind in a million different directions. Our family's practice had remained one thing to one community for decades. What more could it be?

"Dimples or better than just dimples?" David asked once we found each other near the refreshments.

"Way better," I said. "You practically convinced me to go to business school."

"You should. Columbia's got a great program."

"I'm sure," I said, brushing that off. "Anyway, you were great."

"Thanks for coming. Have time for a pre-birthday drink? I've got about an hour until I need to be home."

"I'd love to, but I'm supposed to go meet my Star Twin Heidi."

"Ah, right," said David. "Well, sorry to say I'm tied up all day tomorrow, but I'll see you back in the Highlands for a session next week. Maybe we celebrate after? We're both owed half a milkshake."

Tied up with what? I wondered but did not ask. "Perfect. Maybe we'll celebrate by you fully curing my vertigo," I said. "I feel like we're close."

"Challenge accepted." A group of audience members had formed a line behind us, waiting to say hello to David. He kissed my cheek before heading in their direction. "Happy birthday, Leah."

On my way to check in at the hotel and change before dinner, I noticed a new voicemail.

Hey, Leah. Shitty news, but I'm pretty sick and need to get home. So sorry to miss meeting you in person, but I'd really love to say hello on our big day tomorrow. Let me know when you have a few minutes to connect. So sorry again.

My face fell, then my eyes narrowed. I'd canceled on a massive tradition; meanwhile, Heidi was treating our birthday weekend like brunch plans. *Flaky,* I thought. For a second I wondered if I should head home, too. Make up with Charlotte. Call off this city plan. Then I looked down at the shopping bag I'd filled earlier. Pops of color drew me in. *I came here for reasons beyond Heidi,* they seemed to confirm.

I deleted her message without replying and opened a text to David.

> My Star Twin canceled. Is it too late to say
> yes to that drink with you?

Those taunting reply dots started and stopped several times before his answer finally appeared on the screen.

> Too late for the drink, yes. But you are
> welcome to come to my place for dinner.
> Just FYI, I have a special guest in town.

Stella Remy stared daggers at me through the world's cutest red-rimmed glasses. She was wearing an oversized LSU T-shirt (maybe David's?) over a black-and-white gingham skirt with red sparkle sandals. Her curly hair (definitely David's) was in low pigtails she'd very obviously done herself. She looked like Dorothy as interpreted by a little girl who ran to her closet two seconds after finishing *The Wizard of Oz*.

"Hello!" I said. "You must be Stella. I'm your dad's friend Leah."

Stella sized me up, literally. Her eyes went from my toes to as far up my head as her little neck could crane. David swooped into the entryway, blushing.

"Hey, hey. Welcome," he said. "I see you've met our little FBI operative in training."

"CIA," Stella said, incensed. "Pop said the other one doesn't go outside America, and I have to get to France."

"Why France?" I asked, preparing for an answer way over my head.

"It's where Belle is from," she said with *duh* eyes.

Lost, I shot a look at David.

"Belle from *Beauty and the Beast*," he explained.

I'd lost points with Stella for that move, but her five-going-on-forty vibes could not have ranked her higher in my book.

"You guys get acquainted on the couch for a sec, okay? I'm just finishing dinner."

"He's finishing putting dinner on real plates," Stella said as we made our way into the living room. "It's take-out *Messican* food." That little speech slip eased my performance anxiety.

"Mmm," I said. "How do you feel about that?"

"It was my choice," she explained. "If I skipped the dog park we could cook, but the dog park is too important right now."

"Does your dad have a new dog?" I asked, quickly looking around.

"Not *yet*," she said, pointing a finger to make the timeline very clear. "We're exploring different breeds. Long-hair *Dassund* was in the lead for a long time, but today I saw a sheepa-doodle."

"And?"

"Going to be tough to beat . . ."

I cracked up. "I always wanted a husky. They talk a lot, and I didn't have any brothers or sisters, so I thought it would be fun."

Stella considered. "I don't either, but I think a husky would be hot in New Orleans."

Of course. Because that's where she lived. That's technically where her father lived, too.

"All right, you two," David called from the kitchen, saving my brain from going further down that path. "Dinner is served."

We dined on an impressive spread of chicken, shrimp, and steak tacos. Stella made me a version of her favorite combo: chicken, black beans, sour cream, shredded cheese, *no green stuffs*. Then she regaled us both with plans for the next phase of her dog investigation: a size grid of all the breeds. She was a child after my very own heart, but she was not my main focus in this dinner scene. David was an exceptional father. He was calm but firm. He suggested she try some cilantro and, when she refused, said, "Well, I love it, and maybe you will someday, too." And he was loving and affirming in a vocal way. He said, "Hey, I meant to tell you I was so proud of you for introducing yourself to so many dog owners at the park today." Yet he did not for one second forget that I was also in this room. "Leah just went on a trip somewhere really magical called Venice, Italy," he said. "Should we ask her some questions for when we take our big international trip?"

"Dad got me a piggy bank when I was born," Stella explained. "And when I'm ten we're going to crack it open and count all the money and go to France, *oviussly!*"

"I don't know . . . Leah was just in Italy. And you've got a long way to go before the piggy bank's full enough. What if you fall in love with Italy instead?"

She scrunched her sour-cream-lined lips to the side of her face. "What movie is there?"

"Um, I think *Pinocchio*," I said.

"France it is," Stella said, sending both David and me into stitches.

I finally learned I'd received her hard-won seal of approval over toaster-warmed churros.

"Can Leah stay to watch Pop's movies?" she whispered to David. "You said she's in them."

I turned to David, confused.

"My dad digitized all our old home videos," David explained. "I'll have to email you the links. There's some classic stuff in there." Then he checked his watch. "We'll do a screening next time, bug. It's already eight."

"I won't tell Mom," Stella whispered. I genuinely considered joining in on her begging, so curious to see evidence of little-girl me.

"You know we're not about that," David said, then his eyes went wide. "Stel! We forgot the most important part of the meal!" He leaned over for a secret in her ear. Her eyes lit up, too, then she scurried over to a kitchen drawer as he went for the fridge. Seconds later they were back with a giant birthday candle and a tiny ice cream cake. David must have run out to get it when I said I could join them for dinner.

"Daddy says this is a really special birthday for you," Stella said as David turned out the lights for singing.

My hand went to my chest; I was so touched, then so certain. "He's right."

They sang to me with dramatic flair, then David told me to make a wish. Every year in Cape May I'd repeated the same phrase in my mind: *Healthy patients. Healthy family.* Tonight I looked through the dancing flame into David's waiting gaze, holding it as I blew out the candle in one lucky breath.

Chapter
Twenty-Nine

I STAYED IN bed until nine on the morning of my birthday. I'd stirred around eight but it felt too cozy and relaxing in the giant hotel bed to get out and do what I would typically: throw on running clothes, shove a protein bar in my mouth, and go for a long jog. I had an ideal day to dream up, and that required extra rest. Then I decided it also required listening to David's meditation track, for purposes of both mental clarity and starting my day with the sound of his voice.

When the plan was exploring with Heidi, I'd envisioned long walk-and-talks about our similarities, differences, and whatever magical wisdom she'd promised to impart over a delish breakfast, lunch, and dinner. Now I was solo—déjà vu from Venice. But I did technically have a guide. I grabbed my phone and pulled up Nova's original email, rereading the last section without even a hint of an eye roll.

I was surprised by how many items were already in play, in general and today. The fact that I was even rereading this list was partial proof of a huge area I'd been skeptical of before: *I am guided by the pursuit of self-improvement and self-discovery.* I was alone by chance, but also by my own decision. A pink jumpsuit called from its hanger in the hotel room closet; my shopping spree had given me literal options for shining a little extra today. But shining while doing what?

My phone lit up on the nightstand. I grabbed it to find happy birthday messages from all the people I expected, then one I often forgot I'd see among the set: Mom. The last time I'd seen her name on this screen was when I'd considered whether or not to ask about her whirling dervish nickname. Now I could not resist replying with the question. Minutes later I received a very surprising answer.

> Of course I remember calling you that. It's because I'd always find you closing your eyes, to think. Then you'd open them and know exactly what you were going to do next. I only ever read about the dervishes but remembered them being connected to some kind of deep intuition or higher power, right? I thought that was little you, Leah.

I felt stunned. It wasn't that I'd never been sure of myself—I was, on the track field, in every med school class, and with my patients. But my mom was referring to a different kind of knowing, one connected to what I'd been experiencing these past few weeks. It felt like she was saying, *I watched you know yourself,* and that made me believe I could do so right now.

I closed my eyes in bed, trying to feel for at least one way I wanted to spend my day. Skipping in Burano was the first thought that landed. My mouth turned up immediately. Now *where*? I opened my eyes to find a *New York* magazine on top of the hotel desk. I grabbed it, flipping through it for intel on city neighborhoods, but just a few pages in was an image of dozens of people on roller skates, blissed-out adults doing the same activity I'd loved at many seven-year-old birthday parties. The caption below explained: *At the top of Central Park's Dead Road, skaters of all ages and skill levels gather for what they've termed Skate Circle. It's a party on wheels all day every day.* A jolt ran from my shoulders straight out my hands.

I found myself at a sporting goods shop thirty minutes later—post a mouthwatering croissant and cappuccino from a bakery near my hotel. The preppy coed in the Shoes Plus department did not have patience for my hemming and hawing over whether to go with pink skates and red laces or white skates and gold laces. But once I arrived at the Skate Circle, a small group of regulars made me certain I'd made the right choice.

"Oh *heeeey*, gold lace club!" an at-least-sixty-year-old man in denim cutoffs and a black mesh top shrieked as I sat on a bench just outside the "rink" wrangling the new skates onto my feet.

"Let me help you into that sweet, sweet set," a younger voice called out. My roller fairy godperson was G, who had gold tinsel in their long pink hair and wore a white denim romper covered in a rainbow of Jackson Pollock paint splatters.

"It's my birthday," I confessed as they helped me Bambi-skate around the circle for the first time in decades.

Mr. Cutoffs overheard. "Hey-yo! We've got a birthday in the rink!"

Two Taylor Swift look-alikes had arrived with a Bluetooth speaker. "Then you get to DJ!" one said.

"Shout out some faves, and we'll throw together a list," the other added.

I yelled an answer without a second thought. "One artist. Paula Abdul. Start with 'Cold Hearted.'"

The mini crowd went wild.

"Where have you been, birthday girl?" G asked as I managed my first turn around the circle with zero arm flailing.

"Long story," I said as my Paula picks started up through the speakers.

I pretended to be Kristi Yamaguchi performing her 1992 Winter Olympics long program if she'd gotten to do it to "Rush Rush." I wheeled my body around the concrete circle in bright pink, not giving a shit what anybody thought. I smiled so big and wide that my cheeks hurt, every inch of my body tingling. And when G tried to teach the Swifties made-up choreography to "Straight Up," I laughed so hard that I doubled over, risking a major vertigo incident. I recovered sans dizzy spell. I decided now was not the time to test that again, but I wouldn't have been surprised if two hours of roller-skating bliss was what finally landed my rogue ear crystals back in their correct spots.

"So . . . who are you? And what do you do?" the taller Taylor look-alike asked as I said my goodbyes and thank-yous. She'd become a full Paula convert after "Vibeology," a girl after my own heart.

I found myself not wanting to answer with the truth. "Who do I seem like?" I asked instead.

She considered me for a moment. "Like the kind of woman I want to be."

"What do you mean?" I asked, blushing.

The girl looked at me as if it were all very simple. "Like you know yourself, and like her."

I was shocked to feel the start of tears in my eyes. If you'd asked me what kind of woman I wanted to be when I was this girl's age, I would have said a mature, responsible, successful one. Someone like my med school professors. Someone like my dad. I would not ever have used the terms she had.

"Thank you," I said to the girl. "I'm trying."

"So what else do you have planned for your birthday?" G asked, grapevining by.

I wiped my face and then checked my watch. It was only noon. "I'd like to go do something that will make me cry really hard," I said, shocking myself and everyone else.

Cutoffs called out from across the concrete, "Broadway baby! I never make it out of a great show without a sob."

I chose *Funny Girl* because I'd never seen *Funny Girl* and when I told the former drama club president behind the TKTS counter that I'd never seen *Funny Girl*, she screamed, then sold me a ticket to the matinee at an extra 20 percent off.

There was something about the safety of a dark room filled with total strangers that left me with zero need to hold back a single tear. They streamed down my face from the first song to the last. But not just because of the moving show with its gut-punching songs (*my god*, the lyrics of "People" killed me . . .). I oddly felt emotional for the performers themselves: young, talented people who'd heard *That's a pretty impossible dream* and packed their bags anyway. What a badass life choice. *And what a gift to the rest of us*, I thought as my eyes darted between singers and dancers putting the absolute maximum effort into their every single move. My mind went to Sai's argument, and I understood it very differently. Their choice was the opposite of selfish. Watching this show was cathartic for me, healing even. But if all these performers had worried what their backyard neighbor thought about them moving to Manhattan to sing on Broadway, I'd be stuck taking some Circle Line cruise tour around the city instead.

I left the theater feeling like I'd had two Turkish coffees. It was almost five p.m. *Time for happy hour.* I closed my eyes and tapped my tongue to my lips, conjuring what would be the most delicious option. Instead, an entire scene came to mind: oysters and champagne under dim lights, some French singer in the background, wine-colored leather booths. It was a memory.

One of the times my parents and I had come to the city together was to meet an old friend from California. I barely remember the woman—just that she had dyed-red hair. But I suddenly remembered many details about what happened right before we met her. The plan was a quick meal at Grand Central Terminal. I think our original goal was to eat at some food stalls in the basement of the building, but I wanted to go to the place that caught my eye when we first walked in: the cavernous restaurant with the arched brick ceiling lined with hanging bulbs that illuminated checkered tablecloths below. I remember peering through the gold doors at the entrance to see towers of seafood, champagne bottles, and fancy-looking people. I begged to join them, which then led to a fight between my parents.

"We don't have to break the bank, Pete," my mom had argued. "We'll keep it reasonable, but come on, we're in *Manhattan*."

"She's eight years old, Celia," Dad had whispered, thinking I couldn't hear. "We don't need to be teaching her to be so indulgent."

"I was just joking," I said, jumping in. "I don't even like oysters."

It was not the first time they'd had that disagreement or that I'd rushed to be the one to end it.

The Grand Central Oyster Bar was miraculously still there after almost thirty years. I requested a booth under that same domed ceiling and then ordered a half-dozen oysters plus a glass of champagne.

I thought about my parents as I settled in. This was the day I came into their world. I imagined all their hopes for me, how thrilling and terrifying it must have been to feel singularly responsible for those dreams. I wondered how much of who I'd become was because of them—their very different cultures. What was mine, stripped of theirs? Was it even possible to know? Then I recalled the Nova list item I'd been most offended by on my first read: *I must learn to quiet the opinions of others.* I ordered another round of oysters and champagne, then sent my mind in another direction: brainstorming ideas for LWM based on all I'd learned at David's talk. What kind of legacy did I want to create as the next Lockhart at the helm, and the first woman? How did I want to feel going to work every day? With the question came a vision: the fellow Rutgers grad I'd seen on my jog through Turkey. She should have been overwhelmed preparing to manage that whole line of people in need, but I remembered thinking she looked the opposite. On a mission. Gratified. I wanted more of that in my life, challenges to tackle, diverse groups to serve, bigger problems to solve. I wanted to feel like I was doing the most I could with the privilege of my medical degree.

I filled a stack of cocktail napkins with more ideas over grilled Maine dayboat scallops and Old Bay–dusted French fries, getting more and more excited about my future building out the practice into more of a brand that could reach women with everything from free workshops to—dream of dreams— a book. By the time I was done, happy hour had turned into eight p.m.

I paid my check, which was, yes, large, but worth it in ways I couldn't describe and, better yet, did not have to. Then I passed through the main terminal of the train station. The space was quiet; it was too late in the evening for throngs of commuters to be darting through. I stopped in the very center of the room to take it in fully, looking up at the mural on the ceiling. *Right.* It was a map of the cosmos in glistening gold paint against a green sky, the Torre dell'Orologio in a different form. They could have painted absolutely anything on this ceiling: a map of the island of Manhattan, a collage of every flower present in Central Park, even gods and goddesses if they wanted an up-above connection. They chose astrology.

I let my eyes move left to right, calling out what I saw. Fish for Pisces. Swooping, swirling, and jumping. A ram seated comfortably as if lounging in a field; Aries. Then the rest in order until the crab for Cancer, my moon sign. But a few were missing, chief among them the lion.

I turned to a man standing to the left of me. He had wide-rimmed glasses and a very professional camera. I watched him crouch down for a shot of what had to be the entire ceiling, waiting until he got the shot to approach.

"Excuse me, do you know anything about the history of the ceiling?" I asked.

"Little bit," the man said from behind his lens.

"Why are some of the constellations missing?"

"It was designed to show the winter sky above New York, I think. That leaves a few of the signs out."

"Why?" I asked.

"Oh, I don't know. Why? Were you hoping to see one that isn't here?" He popped out from behind the camera, then gave me a once-over. "Let me guess: Leo?"

My eyes narrowed. "How did you know that?"

The man just shrugged.

For the first time in many, many years I did not mind being labeled a Leo. I maybe even liked it.

My phone pinged inside my tote. I grabbed it, delighted to find a text from David.

> Hi, birthday girl. Hope the day's been special. I'm sure you have plans but any chance you could fit me in for a quick walk near my office around 9 p.m.?

Heat rushed to my cheeks.

> Yes, in theory, but you're going to have to
> be way less vague than "a walk."

David took a second to reply.

> Fine. A walk to a birthday surprise.

Chapter
Thirty

I COULD NOT control the flutters running through me as I waited outside the meeting point David had texted, not that I was trying. Soon he was running toward me, forehead glistening.

"Sorry I'm late. My coworker came over to be with Stella, but she was running behind."

He'd arranged a very last-minute sitter. *Swoon.* "Follow me," he said, reaching out for my hand. I accepted, settling my fingers in the natural spaces between David's, but he shifted my thumb, tucking it inside his palm instead. Holding me.

Four blocks later we were standing in front of an old magazine stand with a chunk of shelving cut out. In its place was what looked like an ATM from a *Star Wars* movie. Silver lettering on the front said iStar.

"I found this on a walk one day," David said, practically twitching with excitement. "It's like Zoltar but with astrology. You ask it a question; it gives you your horoscope. We never made it to Coney Island for the real thing, but with your whole project, I thought maybe this was better. Not that I'm suggesting you believe a lick of this astrology bullshit," David teased.

I almost cried for the third time today. "It's the best," I said, rewinding to us sitting side by side in David's den watching the movie for the first of many times. I'd wanted so badly to be the Tom Hanks character, to grow up after one genie wish. Now I wished this machine could grant me the opposite. "You have to do it, too."

"Fair enough," said David as we stepped up to begin.

Up close the machine was more like a cross between a *Star Trek* prop and something from *Pee-wee's Playhouse*. Tacky gold buttons and knobs ran along the bottom of the fridge-sized structure, with rows of blinking lights surrounding the screen and stickers of the stars and planets stuck to the rest of the white metal surface. Jutting out from the top was a half-circle rod with a curtain slid to one side.

"Ready?" David asked, his hand on what I assumed was the curtain lever.

I nodded. The black velvet fabric swung around us, and a dim light turned on from the top of the machine. This was much, much more involved than Zoltar. And much more romantic.

David touched the screen. A vintage shooting-star graphic shot across it, then words in an equally old-school font: *Do you have a burning question for the stars?* An arrow pointed down to the center gold knob.

"You first," I said to David. "I'm sort of nervous."

David turned the wheel, prompting a list of options to cycle across the screen: *How do I get better at my job? Should I* move? *Should I start a cult? Why can't I get along with my brother?* One question finally stopped him: *Will my love life improve?* He pressed down, selecting that one.

"Ooh," I teased.

"Don't read into it," he deadpanned, but winked, making me laugh.

David entered his birth data. A countdown started from ten to one—on-screen and in an ominous robot voice coming from a speaker—then a slip of paper was spit out of a tiny slot. It looked more like a restaurant receipt than a destiny. David grabbed it.

"'Your sun in Pisces can create a rocky road if you're trying to swim with a partner that has differing views and emotions. But fish submerge deeply, so don't be afraid to set off for deeper waters. Just remember: home is where your heart is, Pisces.'"

"Wow . . . That's—" I said.

"Creepily accurate?" David's eyes turned from the paper to me as if the answer to another question was forming in his mind. "Your turn," he said.

I went for the dial. More random questions popped up as I turned. I almost went with *Will I find career success?* with my new work ideas in mind. Then I considered *How do I find meaning?*, given all Imani, Sai, and even Charlotte and Dad had made me wonder, then I contemplated the cheeky choice of *Will my love life improve?* to match David. But something eerie flashed up next: *Why have I been sick?*

I pressed down without a second thought and then filled in my info. David did a drumroll on the side of the machine as it counted down again. Seconds later, I was staring at my own paper horoscope, frozen. The first line read, *You may be suddenly sick because you are out of alignment with your destiny.*

"What?" David asked, seeing my stunned eyes.

"It says what Nova said. Down to the phrase 'out of alignment.'"

David tapped the machine. "What if this is some *Wizard of Oz* shit, and Nova's inside there spitting out answers?"

I laughed, but there was probably truth to that idea. There were only so many astrology resources in the world. Nova and the iStar people could have easily found their way to the exact same wording. Still, I took a breath and started to read the rest of my paragraph aloud.

"'Your sun and rising signs in Leo are strong placements with a significant pull over your deepest desires to be seen and heard. But with a moon in Cancer, you tend to hide. Your subconscious knows what's best, and it may be crying for help at this pivotal transit you've entered. Remember, Leo, your home is where your heart is.'"

I almost dropped the paper. David looked down at it, then to me, eyes double-sized. "Do you think it ends every horoscope that way?"

"There's only one way to find out," I said.

We picked three different questions using our same information. Not a single one matched or mentioned the identical phrase from our original answers.

"Wow," said David.

"I know," I replied.

We were frozen staring at each other until my paper receipt slipped from my hands, feathering down to the ground below. I bent down to grab it quickly, tipping my body fully to the left.

"Are you okay?" David asked when I was upright again.

"Yeah, why?" I said, and then it clicked. "Omigod, I am okay!" I tipped again, wondering if the first one had been a fluke. Not a whiff of dizziness.

"Want to try the right side?" David asked. "I'm here if it doesn't go as well."

I nodded, then more slowly angled my body over and down. A massive smile bloomed across my face as I stood straight once again. Before I knew it, I was in David's arms.

"I can't believe it! I can't believe it's finally over! And it's my birthday! And you're here, and—"

Before I could finish, David had grasped the back of my neck with his hands. Then he was kissing me, magnetic. *Finally.* Our whole bodies followed. Legs intertwined. Chests so close I didn't know which heartbeat was mine. I grabbed on to David's thick shoulders like they were the only thing keeping me from floating away. My lips moved from his mouth to his chin to his cheeks, then his jaw. His hands slipped slowly down me, stopping at my waist, then going lower to squeeze me in even closer. I'd waited twenty years for this moment, and it delivered. Until the sound of throat clearing pulled us apart. *Ugh.* I opened my eyes to a deeply annoyed teenage girl between the part of the privacy curtain. Her T-shirt said NOT WHILE MERCURY IS IN RETROGRADE. "Are you, um, all set in here?" she asked.

No, we are not, I wanted to say, but David answered. "Yeah. Sorry."

My mood sank for a second, then I felt David's hand on my wrist, whisking me out of the machine. In a second, we were tucked into an alley just beside the bodega. David leaned against the brick wall of the next-door building, pulling me into him for a kiss so deep my knees buckled.

"I want to bring you back to my place," he whispered once we parted. "But I don't think that's the best idea with Stella."

"I want to bring you back to my hotel," I said, "but I doubt your babysitter committed to an overnight."

"To be continued ASAP?" David asked. "Stella heads back Monday . . ."

I nodded, bringing my lips down to his neck. Then we proceeded to make out in that alley, like teenagers in the hidden corner of a prom dance floor, until David finally put me in a cab.

I rode with the windows down, eyes fixed on the little patches of sky I could see between the buildings. Maybe there was something up there writing the destinies of all of us down below. There was so much science still did not know about the human bodies we studied right here on Earth. Who was I to say that the planets and stars, which likely made us, didn't have something to do with the final products? The lights and sounds of the city pulled my gaze back down to street level, reminding me that only one thing mattered right now. I'd loved every second of this birthday: what I did, what I felt, and—I thought with a smile, remembering Imani's impression of that famous cartoon caterpillar—who I was. Now all I had to do was keep her with me as I finally got back to my life.

Chapter
Thirty-One

ON MY FIRST morning back to work, I somehow slept past my alarm, so much so that I couldn't even fit in a run. I rushed to grab a special breakfast for my team, forgetting that Atlantic Bagel always closes the first two weeks of August. Then I spent the morning completely discombobulated because my dad and Edie had rearranged the supply room. I was so exhausted by lunch that I took a power nap at my desk. That helped me through the afternoon of patients—all of whom asked more about my time off than their pregnancies. Of course, my Star Twin Survey and recent trip details had made their way around the rumor mill. No one said, *Must be nice*, but their tones and judgmental looks would have sent Sandy into a fit. *This will all blow over*, I told myself as I reviewed paperwork at the end of the day. I was so drained by six p.m. that I almost forgot my ritual glance at the ocean, then I overshot my chair-to-window push and slammed directly into the wall.

"Everything okay up there?" Edie shouted from reception.

"Yes," I said, but that did not feel true.

Dad had suggested a belated birthday dinner at One Willow, our special-occasions restaurant in town. I was originally excited to catch up on a new foot, eager to pitch him all the ideas I'd started to develop in New York, but now I just wanted to change out of my scrubs and into my pajamas.

He was waiting at a table set against the wall of windows overlooking the bay. *A little slice of Venice*, I thought, glad to be ending the tough day here.

"Doctor, you got all dressed up," Dad said, standing for our shake.

I'd thrown on a combo from my colorful new wardrobe to pep myself up, forgetting that everyone else in this room would be in business-casual muted tones. "I just picked up some new things in the city," I replied, brushing it off.

Dad nodded, then quickly moved on, launching into what turned out to be a detailed Dot-and-Cross from the weeks I'd missed at the office. He covered the new patients, the rising cost of landscaping for the office lawn, and the fact that he'd gotten in on my TOFC competition (he was now the reigning champ). I kept trying to find the right moment to segue into the brainstorming I'd done about the practice but couldn't find an opening. As he continued a sidebar on whether or not we needed a second full-time doctor, it dawned on me that this was how most of our conversations about work had gone over the years. I did the listening. In fact the biggest influence I could remember having on LWM was insisting that we offer paper gowns in a larger range of sizes.

After our mains, Charlotte's famous lemon tart arrived at the table. That meant she'd dropped one off at his house knowing we were having dinner tonight. It was a clear peace offering, but I found myself staring at it, unmoved. It felt so distant.

"I heard you and Charlotte had a little disagreement over your surprise New York trip," Dad said as I went to blow out the candle. His pivot distracted me from making a wish. "Hopefully that'll pass. Family first, right?"

I opened my mouth for an automatic yes, but just before the word crossed my lips, a thought arrived that closed it. My dad would have sided with Charlotte on every disagreement we'd had these past few weeks. I watched him serve slices of the tart for each of us, wearing the same blue-striped dress shirt he'd had since I was in high school. Confusion, not anger, filled me now. This was the man who'd given his entire life to that value of *family first*. I remembered once asking him why he never dated anyone after the divorce. There certainly would have been a line of local women waiting if he ever declared an interest.

"I don't need to change a thing about our family," he'd said. Was that wise? Or just avoiding the inherent risks of change?

"So, I wanted to wait until we cut the cake to give you your birthday gift," he said, putting his fork down. His face was relaxed, but my hands still went clammy. "I've been working closely with the team at the hospital for weeks, and they're prepared to close the investigation into what happened before your leave. They find no fault in your actions during the delivery. That patient can keep her lawsuit going, but you are officially out of the woods in terms of medical malpractice."

"Monica," I corrected him once again, startling us both by the forcefulness of my reply. And its focus. I should have been jumping up and down with relief and gratitude. This news meant I almost had my entire life back, and it was thanks to my dad. I smiled, finally but not fully.

"Right," he said, correctly confused. "Anyway, Jim thinks this news gives us an even better shot to get her to drop everything, but I've decided the best solution is for me to come back after my week off and stay until she hopefully lets it go. This way we don't give anyone a reason to question that Lockhart Women's is the place they should be coming to for the absolute best care."

Now my head was spinning. He'd spoken to my lawyer *again* without me? He was reinstating himself without even a conversation? And was it even appropriate that he'd been back-channeling with the hospital on my behalf this whole time? *All* without my knowledge? I doubted that was aboveboard from a legal standpoint; I knew it was absolutely unacceptable from a personal one.

"I have a different idea," I said, finally finding my words. I put my fork down and leaned forward, charged with the feeling that this was the moment to place myself back in the driver's seat. "It's a big pitch, but I think it could be the best way to resolve the whole situation. What if I close the practice and go on a sort of sabbatical? I've been learning more about what's possible for small medical firms with the right partnerships. Business schools like Columbia are even offering special MBAs for doctors, and I've been envisioning LWM serving a much bigger community—expanding into fertility, building out an educational arm. It's like you said in the hospital, going through a scary medical experience really helps clear your focus. I have a ton of ideas, but what better way to show our patients that I'm learning and growing as the head of this practice than by taking a pause now, regrouping fully, and then coming back more comprehensive than ever?"

I'd been too energized while I was talking to notice the total bewilderment on my dad's face. Or was that dismay? "No," he said, almost chuckling, as if I'd just asked for another slice of cake. "We're not closing the practice. And you're not running off again to get some newfangled degree. We have a good thing going, and it's your job to keep it that way."

That hit me like a cruel insult. I'd never heard him be so dismissive. "I'm not saying we don't, but I really believe I could grow it into so much more."

"Leah, enough," my dad said.

Now I felt five years old, and suddenly on the verge of a tantrum to match. "But what if this is what I want to do for the practice? How I want to run things?"

He shifted in his seat, cleared his throat, then put down his fork. "Now's the time for you to focus on keeping everything your grandfather and I built for you in the same excellent shape it's always been in. It's time for you to settle down. Find the right person. Start a family. That's how you can expand what our practice has to offer. Someday soon you'll be the first doctor in our family to understand what her patients are experiencing. An incredible gift in our field. That's how you'll put your mark on the Lockhart name."

My mouth all but dropped open. My dad had never once brought up the classic milestones I'd so far missed. Lockhart milestones. I'd always thought he was respecting my privacy and my time. Turns out he was just hiding how he really felt. *Family first.* That was my role. Follow the rules. Stay inside the lines.

I made a fist around the cloth napkin at my side, but it did nothing to quell my rage. "You retired and left me the practice," I said. "That was always the plan. Yes, I want to honor what you've built, but I also want to make it my own. Are you saying that I can't do that?"

"There's no need to get all riled up," Dad said, then he motioned for our waiter. I sat up straighter in my chair, far from done.

"I'm not *riled up*," I said. "I'm asking an incredibly important question about my future."

"Anything else, Doctors Lockhart?" I heard over my shoulder.

"We're all set, Max. Just the check, thanks," my dad said with a smile, then he turned to me. "Let's pick all this up after you get settled back at work. See how you feel then."

"I have feelings now," I said, "and I want to talk about them."

Dad nodded as if he'd been afraid I might say just that, then he leaned across the table for privacy. "You know what word I've heard you say more these past two months than ever before in your life? 'I.' *I* want. *I* need. *I* feel. *I* think. That's not how we live our lives. *We* have spent a century in this town as caregivers and community leaders. Lockhart is the name people think of when they need someone they can trust and count on and look up to. And *we*—you and me—fought to keep that our reputation. I don't know what the hell happened to you recently, but you seem to have forgotten that. And it concerns me deeply because we both know what happens when *me, me, me* thinking takes over."

I was devastated by everything he'd said but stung hardest

by that final point. I knew exactly what his coded language meant. "I'm not Mom," I said, mostly to myself.

"Then stop acting like her," was my dad's sharp reply. Then he signed the bill that had been silently dropped in front of him, pushed his chair from the table, and walked out of the dining room. I didn't know whether to cry or scream. Was he right? Had I become my mother, setting off a bomb in our family with the same selfish decisions? Sick as that idea made me feel, I could not bring myself to see a word I'd just said to him as anything but the truth. I slumped back in my chair, struggling to make sense of where we were now. Where I was. How could I move forward and still respect my father's wishes? I looked across the table to his empty chair as the answer swept through me with so much force I felt like it wiped out all my insides: *You can't.*

Chapter
Thirty-Two

I HEARD FOOTSTEPS in the living room, then the smell of bacon wafted through. David's head popped into the door frame seconds later.

"Oh, hey. You're up. An appointment canceled, so I ran out to grab you some breakfast," he said. "How are you doing?"

I shrugged. After dinner, David's apartment had felt like the only haven to escape my screaming brain. I'd told him that I had a fight with my dad and needed a place to cool off. I was passed out on his couch by ten thirty. I remembered him gently lifting me into the bed, tucking me in, and lying beside me, his hand holding mine with the thumb tucked in. It was not how our first night in a bed together should have gone.

David had already left for work when I finally woke up the next morning, fifteen minutes before I was supposed to arrive at my own office. I texted Edie with the lie that I woke up too sick to come in, then reached out to the three patients on the schedule, telling them to text me if they needed to speak before I could get them rescheduled. It was unacceptable, and I knew it, but I couldn't bring myself to do better.

"I can hang for an hour now, or I can just leave the food and let you get back to sleep," he said, dangling the take-out bag.

"I'm not hungry, but I'll sit with you while you eat," I said.

David unwrapped both bacon-egg-and-cheese sandwiches at his kitchen island, correctly assuming I was actually starving.

"You can stay here for as long as you need," he said. "And we can talk about what happened whenever you're ready."

"Thank you. But it'll just be for the day. I'm back at work now, and my dad's still out recovering."

He nodded, curious, but didn't push. "You need to do what's best for you."

I put down my food, appetite suddenly gone again. "That's a lot easier said than done. Right now my whole *Home is where the heart is* horoscope feels like some kind of sick taunt from the universe. If I follow my heart, it's going to destroy my home."

David nodded, this time with something behind his eyes.

"What?" I asked.

"Nothing," he said.

"David, I can't deal with any more tension with any more people right now. Please just tell me whatever it is."

He took a concerningly large breath. "I've been thinking about the iStar reading, too. I was supposed to be on sabbatical through this fall semester, but LSU asked me back to teach. And I said no originally but—"

"Teach now? Like this fall?"

"Like in two weeks. I'd finish out the rest of my work up here remotely. Maybe come back next summer but—"

"Maybe not." My mouth went dry.

"I don't know. I have to think about Stella, though. Months are like years in her life right now. And—you understand, but seriously, I didn't want to get into this now. Let's talk about it all after things with you calm down."

I laughed at that idea, or maybe some darker part of me was laughing at myself. I did understand. *I did this.* I knew it would end like this, and I had done it anyway. Charlotte had been right. It was my fucking *shoulder tingles* that were wrong—they were wrong about this and every other question that had blown up my life in the past weeks.

"There's nothing to talk about," I said. "I get it."

David's face fell. He rushed around to my side of the table. "No. I'm not saying this is over. It's the opposite. I wanted to talk about figuring something out. People make this work, Leah. We could date long-distance for a while, and then when the time is right, find some sort of compromise. Or, I don't know, maybe based on how you've been feeling, you could use a change of location? But this is it, Leah, I know it is. I think I've always known."

My chest tightened. David was inches from me, but I could not look him in the eyes. "I can't move to New Orleans, David," I said. "And this is not it. We were kids. And we've been reconnected for what? A summer? This is you falling for an idea and me falling for the person who helped cure my vertigo."

I heard my phone start to ring in my bag across the room. David shook his head. "You're wrong," he said, "and you know it. We shouldn't be talking about this now. Just get through what's going on with your dad, and we'll figure it out."

"Trust me," I said. Now I looked him dead in the eyes, having successfully turned my body to stone. "I'm doing us both a huge favor. I know exactly how this kind of story goes."

My phone rang again. This time I got up. The call had already gone to voicemail, but a name was still on the screen: Mikey Podcast. My eyes went to the date on the phone, then my stomach flipped.

"Omigod." I shoved my phone in my pocket and threw the tote over my arm. "I have to go. I completely forgot I'm booked to record my follow-up episode of *The Andi Hour* today."

I ran into the bedroom to grab the rest of my things.

"The podcast? Cancel," David called out. "You can't go do that right now."

"I made a commitment," I said as I rushed for the door. "And—you know what? I think I'm in a perfect place to do this right now."

⭐ ⭐ ⭐

I was completely numb for the whole cab ride to the podcast studios. I did not know what the fuck I was going to say. Maybe I'd just read through the stats from the Star Twin Survey, add some anecdotes, and zombie my way through the time? It honestly didn't matter to me one way or another so long as I got across the clear message that astrology could not be proven and certainly not trusted. I was living proof. *Things could not possibly get worse*, I thought as I raced through the studio doors to find Mikey hovering over Andi, who was seated close by. There was a figure sitting beside her; I did a double take, then stopped short, my head suddenly in flames.

"Oh dear," Nova said. "That face does not suggest you knew I was going to be here . . ."

Mikey perked up. "Hey, hey, birthday twin. You get the timing wrong or something?"

"What is Nova doing here?" I asked, steaming.

"What do you mean?"

"I mean who invited Nova to join without telling me?"

Mikey's eyes darted around the room. "Did someone forget to email Leah about this?"

No one looked up.

Nova was out of his chair. "This is not my style. If Leah even wants me here at all, we'll reschedule."

"Wow. Well done, team," Andi said, annoyed.

"Shit. Sorry, Leah," said Mikey, running over to me. "We just thought this would be a compelling add to the results episode, given how much attention the whole search got, so I had my girlfriend get me in touch with Nova. The focus is obviously on you. He'll just give some context, for fun."

I felt something snap in me. "*Fun*," I said with a bite. "Let's do it." Then I took my seat beside a clearly nervous Nova. I finally had a plan for what to say. Moments later, we were rolling.

"Okay, *bébés*," Andi said, kicking the episode off. "We're here with the guest who promised she'd return with results from a super-fascinating experiment. Remember Leah Lockhart and the Star Twins search? She's about to tell us how it all went down and—surprise, surprise—she's joined by the astrologer who helped her set up the whole thing. Welcome, Nova!"

"Thank you for having me, gorgeous," he said.

"All right, Leah. The floor is yours. Spill. The. Tea!"

I did not even stop to take a breath. "First, Andi, I'd love to go back to how this all started in the first place. Since we have Nova here. Cool if I provide a quickie recap?"

My voice dripped with sarcasm. Nova shot over a concerned look, which only fueled me more.

"Go for it," Andi said.

"Thanks. So I meet Nova at a party where he's giving quick birth chart readings, and after spending—what was it, forty-five seconds?—staring at my chart, he tells me my whole life is wrong. I'm not living according to my astrological chart and that is a big, big problem. Side note: he told my cousin not to have kids yet, to give you a sense of his boundaries." Nova's eyes fell. *Good*, I thought as I plowed ahead.

"After finding out I'd come down with a case of vertigo, he told me it was because of a big planet transit and that if I didn't believe in astrology, I should prove it wrong. A kind thing to say to a new client, right? But look, I took the bait. I set up the experiment. I found a hundred-plus Star Twins around the world, and turns out there was a statistical connection between what Nova predicted and what we lived. Sixty-two percent of respondents experienced the transits Nova outlined. So that's a win for Nova. I personally only connected to two out of the three, but it's fine. I'll give it to him. Maybe he was right. Maybe astrology is real. I did end up getting a pretty sweet vacation to Venice and Istanbul out of it. And my vertigo did go away. But what Nova failed to mention is that by following my astrological chart, I would ruin my entire life." Andi's eyes widened. Nova's closed. "Yep. Aligning with my stars probably destroyed my relationship with my father and cousin, made the one I barely had with my mother even more confusing, and left my heart more broken than it's ever been. All clear evidence of a premise I believed from the beginning and now know to be true: astrology is bullshit at best and dangerous at worst." I took a breath, finally feeling like I'd regained control of my life, no matter how destroyed it felt. I'd find a way to repair it, but at least up was up and down was down again.

The room was so silent you could hear the producers whispering to each other in the sound booth. Not even Andi knew how to recover. I saw Mikey waving to her through the glass. "Um. Okay. Wow," she finally said. "I feel like Nova should probably say something now . . ."

Nova turned toward me, then touched his hand to his chest. I refused to look at him.

"I'm so sorry this all happened, Leah. But it's not your fault. It's not mine. And it's not the stars'. Astrology is not about what happens *around* you once you finally align with yourself; it's about what happens *inside* you. You are more *you* now than you were before. I know you can feel that, and I believe that the best version of your life will unfold if you fight for that person."

Suddenly Nova and I were the only two people in the room. "You don't know that," I said, body clenched. He'd sliced through my certainty once again. "You can't promise me that." He reached for my hand, but I pulled it away.

"No, but I can promise you that you will find people in this world who want you exactly as you're meant to be," he said. "And that I'm one of them."

That cement block landed back in my center, freezing me. But this time I felt my shoulders turn on at the same time. It was like my insides were at war. What Nova said felt so right and so impossible, it made me wish for a vertigo spell to knock me out of this moment.

Out of the corner of my eye, I caught Mikey furiously motioning to Andi.

"Right," she said, snapping back. "*Super*-powerful stuff! Um, what's your take, fam? You know the drill. Drop it in the comments or email us at Andi Hour at Gmail dot com. We're going to take a quick break aanndd . . . maybe not come back."

I didn't wait a beat before pushing the microphone from my face and rushing out of the studio. There were footsteps behind me as I made my way toward the elevator bank—Mikey's, I assumed.

"Sorry," I said, jamming my finger against the DOWN button. "But you were wildly unprofessional not to tell me—"

"No, I'm sorry." It was Nova. I stayed facing forward. "Let me help you through this, Leah," he said. "You've come too far to go back now."

The elevator doors opened. I stepped inside, then turned to look Nova straight in the eyes, searching for just the right words to hurl at him so he'd understand that we were not the same. I wanted to go back. But the doors closed in front of me before I said anything at all.

Chapter
Thirty-Three

AT SIX THE next morning I pulled myself out of bed, ran my Hudson Trail loop, washed a protein bar down with a canned cold brew, and went to work. Edie asked me how I was feeling and ordered my favorite chicken Caesar wrap for lunch, but nobody else batted an eye. At four o'clock I got a text from my dad.

All good over there?

I gave it a thumbs-up. Everything was fine. Everything had to be fine. I would make everything fine again, starting with Charlotte. I dropped by her shop after work and told her I was sorry about canceling on Cape May. She wrapped me in a hug before I'd even finished the thoughts. But when she invited me over for dinner with her girls, I suggested we push it a week or so until I got readjusted at work. I left without her asking a thing about New York. Or about anything, really.

The next day, I signed up to run the Shore Points marathon. Training for a fall race would be the perfect place to focus my energy. That night I didn't fall asleep until two. I missed my first scheduled run the next morning. The next night's sleep was even worse. It made me blow past my alarm by an hour and race to work without breakfast or coffee. By midmorning I was dangerously close to nodding off during an appointment. It didn't help that long periods kept passing without me saying a thing in my own exam room. My patient was brainstorming a birth plan with her husband, mother, and doula present.

"Sound good, Dr. Lockhart?" they asked every so often.

"Yep," I said over and over again.

The Highlands had always been a place where patients had more support than most. Nowadays they came in with pregnancy apps and online classes as their guides. A sinking feeling crept through me as I met with a first-time mom-to-be the next day. She and her husband were walking me through their binder filled with resources and checklists for every stage of the coming nine months. They'd downloaded it off the Internet, they explained, thrilled. An OB-GYN with a huge online following had offered the materials free with her online course, they shared, impressed. I should check it out!

Feeling guilty for my bad attitude, even if I'd kept it internal, I sat down to do so on my lunch break that day. I could take a note from this doctor who had expanded online.

Edie poked her head through my door frame. "There's a woman here who says she needs to see you for an appointment, but I don't have her on our schedule," she said. "A Monica?"

I dropped the pen I hadn't realized I was holding. Edie noticed.

"I can tell her that—"

"No. I have a few minutes now. I'll squeeze her in," I jumped in before Edie connected the dots between my reaction and the name that had surely made its rounds through the office.

"Sure. I'll show her to a room," said Edie. "But don't you want a nurse to check vitals first?"

"We can do it after." I would have been wise to take a hint from Edie's skeptical look. This was a huge risk to my lawsuit, which still stood to define my entire future. But I couldn't stomach the thought of shutting Monica out. That wasn't the person or doctor I wanted to be.

She and bright-blue-eyed baby Skye were cooing at each other on the exam table.

"That is one happy-looking baby," I said. I'd caught their wide smiles.

"She is," said Monica, straightening. "Sorry I came here without an appointment. I think my incision is healing kind of weird, and I don't have a doctor. Or insurance, shocker. I figured if there was anyone I could convince to see me for free—" She stopped herself, realizing her brand of humor might not be welcome. She was wrong. I appreciated the levity and found myself proud of the way she was doing what she needed to take care of herself once again.

"Let me take a look," I said, feeling surprisingly relaxed.

Monica lowered herself onto the table, expertly repositioning Skye in her arms.

"It just hurts a lot when I bend in certain directions and if anything rubs against it. That's not normal, right?"

I examined the incision area, happy to see that everything

was fine. "It's healing slower than most, but correctly," I said. "When they quote recovery time at the hospital, they always forget to say that some people still experience discomfort three to four months after, especially if they're primary care-takers for the baby, doing all the lifting and holding."

Monica nodded to that. "Yeah. It's just me, for now."

That left me curious, but I needed to keep this interaction as neutral as possible. "You can gently massage the area to help increase blood flow a few times a day and try to avoid any clothing that's putting pressure on the scar. Also, the Internet will try to sell you expensive oils and creams, but the best remedy is running warm water over it when you shower and putting very light ice on the area if it's extra tender."

"Thanks," Monica said, sitting up. Skye was now sound asleep in her arms; the sight of her sweet, peaceful breathing left me with a rare pang of jealousy. I'd always managed to keep my own feelings about motherhood outside these rooms, but that felt much harder after my dad's comment at dinner.

"Happy to help," I said. "Any other questions I can answer while you're here?"

Monica considered for a second, then asked the very last thing I expected. "How are you?"

"Um, I'm good. Thank you. My vertigo is gone. If that's what you mean?"

She nodded. It was not. "I'm dropping the lawsuit," were the next words out of her mouth. I was so shocked I sat down on the rolling stool behind me, stumbling a little.

"Why?" I asked.

"Skye's dad got involved with it all, and I decided I can't have that." Monica's lips closed into a firm line. But the pink gloss covering them reminded me just how young she was, too young to be faced with these kinds of decisions.

"But you were the patient. You would legally receive any compensation if it came to that." *What am I doing?*

She shook her head. "It wouldn't work like that with him. We need a fresh start. I'm thinking of moving to be near some friends I have out in Colorado."

"Wow," I said. "That's a big change."

"I know. And with a baby I have no clue what I'm doing with, but—I don't know—I just have this feeling that if I take care of myself it will make everything better for her."

She shrugged at that statement, but her words landed on me with so much force I had to look away.

"I'm happy to be your OB-GYN if you stay in the area," I said, collecting myself. "We'll work out a payment structure that's comfortable for you."

"Thanks," said Monica as Skye's little eyes started to blink open. "I have to figure out where we're going to land, but I appreciate that. I also wanted to say thanks for what you said to me in the hospital when we met."

The memory flew to me. "About the body being resilient?" I said, shaking my head at the irony of having said that moments before vertigo took over mine.

"No," Monica said. "About how everything before today is in the past."

That I hadn't remembered saying. And now—after everything I'd been through—I didn't know if I agreed. But Skye did. She suddenly let out a dinosaur shriek three times her size. Monica and I both burst into laughter.

After, I went to my office and sat down to call my dad and

tell him that the lawsuit was officially over. Once I placed that call, everything would be back to normal. My future and the practice would finally be secure. But I couldn't bring myself to pick up the phone.

I organized my files. I straightened up my desk. I dusted off the tops of cabinets and swept the hard-to-reach corners of the room. When there was nothing left to do, I checked my email. The very first message was from a Nate Rosemont. It took a second for the name to register before I clicked to opened it.

> Hi Leah. I'm the husband of your Star Twin Heidi. I'm writing with the sad news that Heidi passed away earlier this week. I don't know how much she told you, but she'd been battling an illness since February. Two months ago it was finally diagnosed as pancreatic cancer. She thought she could make it through the New York trip to meet you but got too weak the second day. She was so sorry that you two never connected.
>
> But I'm really writing to thank you. Finding your whole project made a huge impact on her time remaining, and we're both forever grateful. We're doing a memorial this weekend that we'll stream for any friends and family who can't make it to LA. The info and link are below in case you'd like to learn more about your amazing twin.
>
> With thanks,
> Nate

I did not stop to wipe the tears from my eyes before I booked a round-trip flight to LA, and then texted my mother to let her know I was coming. My instinct was driving again, and I somehow knew that its singular goal was to help me do what Monica was doing—take care of myself.

Chapter
Thirty-Four

MY MOM TEXTED that she was a few minutes away from the arrivals terminal. She'd insisted on picking me up at the airport and driving me to the memorial an hour north. I didn't know whether to be hopeful or anxious about her enthusiasm or when to tell her I was only in Los Angeles for forty-eight hours and had booked myself a hotel near the airport. But I could not ignore everything leading me to this chance to be together—and in the city where I was born. Or, I would not ignore it. Seconds later a red Mustang convertible screeched up to the curb.

"There she is," Mom said, cat-eye sunglasses lowered down her nose. She'd let her hair go gray since the last time I saw her, and it was stunning—a thick bob of pure white against her tan skin. She saw my eyes dart around the car. "Oh, it's not mine. I borrowed it from a friend. We have to drive up the coast, and I thought a little style would make the whole day less painful. Who can't smile in a hot red sports car with the wind through their hair, right?"

She was exactly the same as I'd remembered, only it landed differently right now.

"Thank you," I said with a smile as I threw my luggage in the backseat and slid into the front.

"You doing okay?" she said.

No, I thought. I was surprised to find I'd said it, too.

"That's okay," my mom said with a reassuring smile before veering off into the airport traffic.

We were on the Pacific Coast Highway minutes later. The salted ocean air drifted straight into our open-topped ride, and I could see the glittery blue water for miles north, south, and west. It was expansive, and it made me feel like I could breathe for the first time in days.

Mom played tour guide as we snaked our way north on the coast highway, relieving me from worrying about what in the world we were going to talk about. I let her voice waft over me as I focused on how good it felt to have the sun on my face. Soon we were climbing into Topanga Canyon, walls of green surrounding both sides of the car. Boulders dotted the path, and every few hundred yards a cluster of lavender or yellow brush flowers popped up like a planted piece of art. At one point my mom slowed down and insisted I pick a bunch of them straight out of the car. Eventually, we pulled into a little town that looked more like a truck stop. Tucked off a side street was our destination: the Inn of the Seventh Ray restaurant.

"Do you want me to come in, or would you like some space?" my mom asked. She'd been talkative in the car, so much so that I'd forgotten to be anxious.

"I'm good," I said. "But you don't have to wait. I can get myself to your place after or—"

"I cleared the whole day for this," my mom said. "I'll keep myself busy. Call whenever you're ready."

My shoulders relaxed down my back. "Okay. Thank you for doing that," I said.

* * *

Old brick steps lined with wildflower arrangements curved down into a mysterious space below. There were little landings on the path with white, wrought iron café tables and chairs slipped in, like boxes in the Broadway theater I'd just visited. Above was a canopy of old-growth oak trees that had been taken over by sweet-smelling jasmine vines. I felt like I was walking into a very different type of secret garden. Thirty or so guests chatted quietly under a giant iron gazebo covered in screaming-fuchsia bougainvillea on a large, circular patio with the bricks laid out to look like an explosion of sun rays. Across that surface were dozens of large, colorful pillows for seating, like a little girl had arranged the coziest place to gather. It was incredibly welcoming.

My eyes went to a large lattice wall covered with framed photos of Heidi. She had been blond, tan, and athletic from playing tennis. People were standing around the display, hugging, crying, or laughing in that quiet way people do at events like these. I didn't know a single one of them. I didn't even know Heidi. What was I doing here? Just then a man stepped to the center of the circle under the gazebo.

"If everyone can find a seat, I'll just be sharing a few words."

The voice belonged to a surfer type now standing at a white podium. He had to be Heidi's husband, Nate. I looked around, finding an open purple pillow in the back corner as he cleared his throat at the mic.

"Thank you all for being here today," he said, then he looked down at his notes, shook his head, and took another breath, steeling himself, it seemed. "I am supposed to open by telling you that this is where Heidi wanted us to get married, but we picked the club to make it easier on everyone else because there aren't any hotels up here."

Many of the heads in front of me sort of cocked to the side, surprised by this odd start to a eulogy.

"To prepare you, this is not going to be a speech where I share stories about what Heidi meant to all of us and how much we all loved her," Nate continued. "You know that. Instead, she's asked me to share some things she came to realize over the past few months. But I'm sorry in advance because they're not easy things to hear."

Now people were whispering. Where exactly was this going?

"Heidi would also like you to know that she considered doing this as a video but only wants you to remember her looking fabulous because one of the things she learned about herself these past few months is that she's incredibly vain." That got a tension-relieving laugh. "And finally, these are entirely her words, so please do not shoot the messenger. But I would like to add that I agree with many of them, so, sorry. Okay. Jesus Christ . . . Here goes." He sucked in one more breath, then began. "'Dearest friends and family. It has come to my attention over the past few months that I didn't know myself as well as I should have and certainly would have liked to if I'd known I was going to die so young.'"

An older woman in the front gasped at that line. I feared it was Heidi's mother.

"'I have some theories as to how this happened, including but not limited to my personality, my upbringing, and the patriarchy.'" Three women my age in the middle laughed out loud. I noticed one had her phone up, recording. "'But they're not the point. The point is that I lived like I was living because I thought it was good. Appropriate. Nice. Pleasant. And certainly pleasing to all of you. Example: I drove to Sacramento every Thanksgiving to be with my husband's aunt and uncle because that's what good people do. They keep important holiday traditions with family.'" Nate sort of winced as he prepared for the next line. "'Even if that family is incredibly condescending—out loud— to your husband because he chose to be an artist, not a lawyer.'" The aunt and uncle revealed themselves with a gasp. "'If I had more Thanksgivings, I would not be so worried about being so nice. So appropriate. So thin. So successful. Or so pleasing to all of you. Even you, Nate; sorry.'" Nate smiled. He seemed to like that part, then his mouth turned down.

"'But I do not have more time. My life ended before I got the chance to fully live it. And I know that's hard to hear right now—just imagine how hard it is for me to be writing—but you all need to hear it.'" The same woman in the front stood up and walked out, tears streaming down her face. She had Heidi's long, thin frame. It was her mother. Pain shot through me as I considered how hard it must have been to learn that her daughter's life ended before she felt it had really begun. But that thought shifted as my heartache deepened. I wanted to walk out of the room, too. *In so many ways*, I realized, *I am Heidi*.

"'Please, please, please do not waste whatever short time you have on this earth living by someone else's rules,'" Nate continued. "'Please, please, please find out who you really are before it's too late. Do it for me. And when you do, I promise I'll try to send you some kind of applause from up above.'"

Nate stopped talking, to deafening silence. Then one person started clapping. Soon a few more people followed—mostly from the younger set. They were right to applaud, but I couldn't move. The longer I sat, the more furious I was that Heidi was gone. I wanted to ask her a thousand questions about how she'd become so sure of all this so quickly. I wanted to dig into the astrology, but even more so the life stuff—that upbringing comment Nate shared. A grim part of me even wanted to argue with her that it was easy to consider being yourself with just a few months left to live. You didn't have to live with the blowback from anyone or everyone. But I'd closed the door on that chance after judging her for canceling our birthday plans. I'd missed out. It was that very thought that compelled me up off my seat toward Nate. I had to at least meet him. That's when I saw a little girl with Heidi's blond hair and Nate's doe eyes run up and squeeze him. *Heidi had a daughter.* I stopped walking, the weight of her eulogy doubling. *Heidi died without her daughter knowing who she really was. Another mother and daughter disconnected.* It was too much for me to bear.

My mom found me in the parking lot thirty minutes later, head still between my hands.

"Oh, Leah. I'm sure that was hard. I can take you to my house," she said, concerned. "Make you some food, or whatever you need."

"I . . . don't know," I started. "I got a hotel . . ."

"Oh, that's no problem," she said. "I'll just take you there."

My head snapped straight. "That's it?! You're not even going to pretend to put up a fight for me to stay with you? After—what?—*wow*. I cannot even remember. I cannot even remember the last time I saw you in person." I'd filled with fire. "You're my fucking mother. How is that even possible?" I couldn't catch my breath. My mind raced with a thousand things that I wanted to spit out. "There's a little girl in there who doesn't even have a mother anymore! How *dare* you! How *dare*!" My rage didn't even make sense to me. She'd made one comment. But the dam was broken. I was crying, but it felt more like my eyes had just cracked open to find some new, terrifying shape.

Finally, I heard my mother's voice, gently breaking through my sobs.

"Shit. *Shit shit shit*. I knew I'd mess it up, and I did!" I looked up. Her head was in her hands now, fingers rubbing her temples as if they could rewind time. She looked up, eyes cloudy with her own tears. "I just . . . I've waited so long for this moment, but I don't know how to be with you, Leah. I don't know how to make it better. Does that make any sense?" I nodded, cooled down. My mom shook her head. "But that doesn't matter," she said. "What matters is that you're right. And I'm so sorry."

You're right. I'm so sorry. They moved through me like medicine. Like an antidote.

"Let's go to your house," I said.

Chapter
Thirty-Five

IT WAS BRIGHT out when I woke up the next morning. A scribbled note on my nightstand told me Mom had run to the market for fresh breakfast options.

I sat up and looked around the room where I'd slept the night before. The bed itself had been turned into a faux canopy with sheer, draped fabric hanging off a sort of beaded chandelier. The walls were covered in a floral wallpaper that looked straight out of an island resort. Across the room was an old wooden dresser with a dozen or so picture frames covering its top. I squinted to make out the images, then my heart swelled. *They're all me.* On the beach in the yellow polka-dot bikini Mom insisted we buy just so we could sing the song when I wore it. Riding my too-big bike, wearing my too-big helmet, in front of our house. Crossing the finish line at my very first track meet. "Would you just humor me and do a leap across the finish line one of these times?" I remembered Mom saying. She'd desperately wanted me to stick with dance. Finally, I made out the smallest one, dead center in the setup. It was my mom holding me in the hospital bed on the day I was born. Even from across the room, I was struck by how young she was, probably no older than Monica Shepard. She'd also made very big choices for her baby. *Me.*

On the nightstand, underneath my phone, was the program from Heidi's service. I'd left without talking to Nate. I wondered if it would be crazy to get in touch and ask if I could say hello while I was in town. There was so much I wanted to know. But that thought prompted another: I still had Heidi's Star Twin Survey responses. I grabbed my phone, logged in to the hub, and searched for her name. I now knew the eerie fact that she'd gotten sick in February of this year. I read on to learn that in 2011 she'd planned to spend a year backpacking, lost and burned out after getting a second master's. But she didn't go because her mother was still grieving the loss of her older sister, Heidi's aunt. She could not stomach leaving her in such pain. It was hard to imagine myself doing any different if my dad had lost Uncle Ted. Then I got to her entry for the earliest dates—the ones I still had not been able to connect any of my own memories around. Heidi had written the most about this transit.

In 1990, my family moved from this hippie community up north down to Orange County after my dad got a big new job. I don't remember much before the move or right after, but this survey inspired me to drive down to my parents' place and go through a bunch of old photo albums. I found several from before that move. In every shot I had wild hair, mismatched clothes, a silly pose, and a beaming smile. After the move, we got a camcorder, so I was able to watch home movies from all the years in our new town. Every clip looks like a scene from an old Sears catalog shoot. I have slicked hair in perfect pigtails and a ruffled dress that matches my sister's. Her take was that our parents were terrified of losing the security they'd found with this job and this life, so we played the part of a family that fit right in. She took to it like a fish to water because she'd always craved that life. I did not. I'd always felt like there was a sort of dark side of me stuck inside. But I think it only felt that way because I wanted to follow the same rule book as my family. Certainly, as my sister. But I was different from all of them. When I look at that evidence it is very, very clear to me. The before is me. The after is who I had to become.

I slumped back onto the bed pillows, even more devastated to have missed talking about all this with Heidi, sharing with her my *culture is contagious* lesson from a boatman in Burano. Then a lightbulb clicked on, launching me straight out of bed and over to the laptop in my luggage. There was a chance I had my own cache of evidence about little-girl me. I opened my email to the Remy home movie links David had sent after Stella mentioned them. They were labeled with numbers, not dates, so I clicked on volume three as a random place to start.

Little David opening Christmas gifts under the tree, dimples as prominent as ever. I couldn't stop myself from watching through a few scenes of him at the exact age he was when we met. David missing all three attempts of a T-ball at-bat, struggling to bring a tray of breakfast in bed to his mother, showing off his brand-new pet lizard to the camera. The twinkle behind his eyes was the same. I was jealous. Then I remembered our last conversation at the creek. Maybe the David I'd re-met was just newly back after choosing to leave his marriage.

The next video was of a crowded hotel ballroom. I knew it

immediately: the BeachWalk at Seabright, where Charlotte and Beau got married. The camera tracked around to a band playing, then I saw a CONGRATS SR. & JR. sign behind them. *This is the party my family threw to celebrate Grandad retiring and Dad taking over the practice.* I was only seven or eight. A thought hit me. *That means this happened between '89 and '91.*

The band finished playing a Bruce Springsteen cover. Then I saw my mom rush up to the mic in a Dolly Parton costume. She had on giant fake boobs and a sky-high blond wig. My chest clenched as memories flooded back. I knew exactly what I'd see next.

"Hello, hello," Mom said into the mic, full of energy. The camera panned around the crowd. I saw my grandparents, Uncle Ted and Aunt Kath, a very little Charlotte, and every other cousin, neighbor, family friend, and colleague in our lives. Finally, David and his mom. I wondered how many of the same people had been at the party we threw this past winter.

The camera refocused on my mom, beaming onstage. "Leah and I prepared a little something special to celebrate Pete taking over the practice. You might not know this, but he's a secret Dolly Parton fan."

Someone whistled in the crowd as the thumping beat of "9 to 5" started up. Mom waved her hands for someone to come onstage: *me.* I appeared in a similar Dolly costume, makeup and hair just as over-the-top as hers. Heels so high I kept almost falling over. The crowd did not go wild. I remember that now, too. At the time I thought, *Maybe they're surprised.* Now I knew: They did not think this was funny. They did not approve.

"Come on, y'all! Don't be so uptight!" Mom called in her put-on Southern accent. With adult eyes, I could see that she was anxious but trying to hide it.

We both started singing the words as we'd rewritten them to match's Dad life. *I head out for my run, then I rush into the office. Put on my white coat, double-check my files, then make sure every patient's more than fiiiine.*

I stepped back, shocked by how closely they now matched my life. Suddenly the sound cut out. The band was still playing, and we were still singing, but the power to all the instruments and speakers was off. I remembered this most.

"What's going on?" Mom yelled. The crowd was silent. "Sorry, folks. Maybe something got unplugged or something." She turned to the band. I could see her trying to get their help and receiving shrugs. I remembered thinking as a child that something was broken. But now I caught the very clear look in the band members' eyes: they knew what was wrong.

The camera refocused, catching my aunt Kath's face. My hand flew to my mouth. She was looking at Mom with the same expression I'd seen Charlotte give me the day of our big fight—the one I couldn't place. A devastating mix of pity and disgust, it said, *You are not like us*, and it hurt just as much watching it directed toward my mom as it had that day I felt the same from Charlotte. That's when Dad finally appeared on screen.

"Sorry, folks. Looks like we had a power outage onstage. We'll try to get this fixed. 'Til then, raw bar's still fully stocked!"

"We can just sing it without the speakers," Mom said, projecting to prove her point. Then she turned to me. "Right, Leah?"

Even knowing this moment was coming did not make it any easier to watch. Little me turned to Dad for the answer. He cocked his head half an inch. I looked back at Mom and said, "No."

Her whole body deflated. She knew then what I did now: he'd cut the power. He did not want us up there one second longer. This was not what his wife and daughter were supposed to do. And worst of all, he'd just gotten me to agree. That was the first of many, many times that followed. The power dynamic had shifted.

I squeezed my eyes shut, feeling like I'd just found the key to a thousand little doors that were all opening at once, a new scene flashing behind each. Mom absent for the rest of that party, then in bed the whole day after. Mom taking me places without inviting my aunt and cousins for the weeks following. Mom very obviously keeping to herself at every family function in all my memories from then on. It would be a few years before things boiled over into real fighting, but it all started then. I'd pushed those memories away, but they were crystal clear now.

My eyes flew open. *But I was the child. She was the parent. She still chose to leave me. Why?*

I heard the front door open and close. My mom was home. I considered for a moment, then jumped out of bed. I'd waited long enough for answers.

"Oh hello! Yay!" There was a woman in the entryway. She was in yoga clothes holding a bag of what looked like fruit.

"Leah, this is my dear friend Sue," my mom said.

"I was so hoping we'd get to meet. I brought over peaches from my tree. Your momma makes jam with them every year.

I keep telling her she should stop giving it away and sell it with me at the local farmers market, but you know how she is."

I did not. I couldn't even muster a fake smile.

Sue pressed on. "Anyway, it's really special to get to say hello to you. Celia is one of the most important women in my life. Really to this whole community. You're very lucky."

I was too raw to employ any kind of filter anymore. "*You're* very lucky," I said. "I barely know my mother."

Sue was not expecting that, but my mom wasn't surprised. She took the bag of fruit from her friend's hand and nodded a thanks.

"Come," my mom said once Sue left. "Let's go sit in the sun to talk."

* * *

There was a little porch off her tiny kitchen. Two large rocking chairs faced out to a lush yard beyond. The whole thing was the size of my bathroom, but every inch was covered in blooming flowers. One more secret garden.

"Do you mind if I say a few things I've been working on sharing with you?" Mom started.

"Go ahead," I replied, curious what she meant by *working on*.

"Leah, I was very young when your father and I married. My own mother struggled with issues I still don't understand. My father came and went. I moved to New Jersey as a brand-new parent myself, thinking I'd finally found the right people to keep me safe and happy. But it was never a fit. The more I found my way as a mom and woman, the further I was from being a Lockhart. So I assumed I was wrong." I put my foot down, stopping the rocking chair. That part surprised me. "Look at the life they'd built. Their way had to be right. So I told myself to change. Enjoy the stability. Let them have their say in raising you. But . . . I still can't really explain this, Leah. Eventually, it just broke me. I lost myself. I felt exhausted all the time. Depressed. Physically ill around your grandparents. Broken. I couldn't be the mother I wanted to be. I stayed as long as I possibly could—until I felt like you were mature enough. Then I had to go find myself again before it was too late."

Three months ago I would have looked at my mother like she was a weak woman with a thousand excuses. Right now I understood. I believed her. I even related, especially after Heidi's memorial, but I could not ignore the rage I still felt.

"But you could have come back and lived somewhere else!" I said. "You could have had the same independent life you have here, just not three thousand miles away from me! And, forget that even, you could have visited, called, written, anything! They may have pushed you out, but you chose to stay out. You chose to stay away from me. Why?"

Her eyes dipped, then quickly welled with tears. "I could deal with the Lockharts and your father hating me, Leah. But I could not handle when you looked at me and talked to me the same way they did. I didn't think you liked me. I didn't think you needed me. And it made me hate myself to a dangerous degree." Those words hit me so hard that my back straightened. I knew what it felt like to be on the receiving end of that look. "It took me years to even understand that, then more time to heal from it and try to forgive myself for not being strong enough to bear it all for you. It's not an excuse. It doesn't make how I handled things right. But it's the truth."

I sat back again, letting what she'd just confessed fuse with all the other thoughts racing through my mind. Her words didn't make it hurt any less. My hurt was burning so much I could barely breathe. But my mom had done what she did to save herself—and I could see it clearly from a place I never would have arrived at if not for everything that'd happened since I fell in Monica's delivery room. My mother had been through her version of the same journey. All these years I'd thought I was a Lockhart through and through, but I was my mother's daughter just as much. I covered my eyes with my hands, pressing down to stop the world from spinning for reasons that had nothing to do with vertigo.

"I know, sweetheart," I heard. "Now I'm going to tell you what it's taken me a lifetime to learn: you will hurt some people on the path to loving yourself. But if there's true love there, you'll find a way forward together." Then she reached over, grabbed on to my hand, and did not let go. There were many things I'd waited years for my mother to say. These would end up being the words I needed most.

We sat without moving for what felt like a very long time. At some point I closed my eyes, hopeful something inside me would know what to do next. The answer came as a vision.

"Let's go make your famous peach jam," I said.

Chapter
Thirty-Six

I CALLED MY dad in the morning to tell him I needed coverage for the next week because I would be staying in Los Angeles. He understandably had a lot of questions, chief among them "Are you with your mother?" I said yes, then answered the rest with one blanket statement: "I need to work through some important things. Thank you so much for handling the office for just a little more time." I'd drafted three versions, then practiced saying it a dozen times. It was perhaps the most uncomfortable sentence I'd uttered in my entire life, and I would never tell him the words came from a self-help book on boundaries that I found on my mom's guest room shelf. I knew he was confused, hurt, and angry, and *my god* was it painful not to jump to fix it—fly home, go back to work again, brush it all under the rug. But this, too, was an experiment.

Also new: I actually let my mom mother me. She carted me around to a sound bath, a forest walk, and this very weird breath-work session where you heave in and out so hard you start hallucinating. Then I watched hours of Remy family home videos. David and I were together in dozens of clips—running through a sprinkler in his backyard, showing off our collection of sea glass in mine, sitting side by side at every one of our birthday parties. I was a smiley kid at a young age, but in David's presence, my face went full wattage.

"Did you think I was in love with David Remy as a little girl?" I asked my mom over our last dinner together, her mother's famous tamales rancheros.

"Of course," she replied as if I'd just asked her to pass the salt.

"*Ugh!*" I slumped down in my chair like an exasperated teen. "But our lives don't work together. I'm setting myself up for disaster if I even try to date him."

My mom raised an eyebrow. "I think we've established that you do not know the future. You just have to do what's in your heart, even if it requires a lot of bravery. Especially *if.*" Then she smiled mischievously. "But you're a Leo. You were born for that."

Her classic line hit differently now. "Maybe you're right," I said. Then I thought about how much I desperately wanted to avoid a repeat of what had happened with my mother—years of silence because neither of us knew exactly what to say. An idea bolted through me. Minutes later I was curled up under the guest room canopy with my laptop and a very big smile.

Dear David,

Thanks for your last letter. Your new turtle sounds super cool, and I'm glad you made some friends

on the soccer team. I've never tried frying an egg
on the sidewalk and—no offense—don't think I
ever will. Gross.

Anyway, I'm sorry it's taken me so long to write
back. I was dealing with a lot of things in my family
when you wrote last. I've essentially been dealing
with those same things in one way or another
since. I'm going to work on all that now. I have no
idea where it's all going to lead, but I do know that
my answer to your question is yes. I would like to
see you again and I'd love to go out somewhere
together. Let me know when you're free.

My shoulders turned on after I typed that last line. I ran
out to my mom, who was cleaning up in the kitchen.

"Can you still take me to the airport if I fly tonight instead
of tomorrow morning?" I asked.

"Of course . . . ," she said, clearly trying not to pry.

"Good, because I'm considering doing the most romantic
thing I've ever done." My mom seemed to understand immediately, then she lunged for her cell phone on the table. "What
are you doing?" I asked.

"Calling my friend to see about borrowing the Mustang
again. I'm not about to drop my daughter off to do the most
romantic thing she's ever done in an old white Honda!"

She was dead serious. "I love you," I said through a head
shake and laugh.

"I love you, too," she said, then she put the phone down
and wrapped me in a big, long hug.

I stuck with the spirit of that Mustang decision when I landed off the red-eye to New Orleans, asking my airport ride to take me to the most charming street in the French Quarter. Once there, I identified the hotel with the brightest flowers hanging from its wrought iron porch boxes, booked it for the night, and begged my way into a very early check-in so I could freshen up. I'd texted David en route to tell him I would be in town and ask if he could meet for breakfast. When he said, Really? Sure. Where? I told him to pick somewhere beautiful near the center of town.

David was waiting under the green-and-white-striped awning of Café Beignet—a pink stucco building so charming I almost squealed. David did instead.

"Hi! Wow! You look—" His head shake finished the thought. I'd selected a dramatic gold-yellow sundress with a sweetheart neckline and tiered maxi skirt. The boldest purchase from my New York shopping spree.

"Thanks," I said.

"What are you doing here?" David asked.

"Turns out tapping into my savings account for spontaneous travel is a big feature of my newfound personality," I said, then I reached into my bag. "Also, I figured you'd waited long enough for this."

David knew what I was holding the second the envelope came into view. He snatched it from my hand, opened the letter, and read, dimples popping more with each passing second. Before I knew it, I was in his arms.

"Worth the wait," he whispered into me as our bodies melded again.

"Just so we're very clear, this breakfast doesn't count as the date," I said, breathing him in.

"Agreed," he said. "But I took the whole day off for you, so we'll get a proper one in before you go."

I pulled back. "You knew I was coming just for you?"

"No, just hoped," he said. I replied by leaning back into him for a very long kiss.

David spent the next ten hours touring me around his magical town, where everything from the street musicians to the fleur-de-lis flags seemed to move with a swagger. We covered the tourist basics right away—guzzling hurricanes from purple plastic tubes, eating crawfish from a cooler down an alley, and dancing in the street to "When the Saints Go Marching In." Then we went up to the Garden District for an over-the-top lunch at Commander's Palace, the only place worthy of my outfit, David claimed. The beauty of every ornate ironwork balcony, lush hidden courtyard, and massive moss-draped oak tree bowled me over—more evidence that travel was something I could no longer live without. But this was my first adventure with David as copilot. It could not be my last.

"So, am I allowed to ask what's next?" We were back at his airy loft in the Warehouse District after picking up fixings for his family gumbo recipe for dinner—the cherry on top of my intro to New Orleans. David was at work adding the final ingredients while I sipped a delightful mint julep at the kitchen island.

"Yes, but I'm trying out a new thing where I only answer for the next twenty-four to forty-eight hours," I said. "I'm going to go home tomorrow, unpack my luggage, and start thinking very long and hard about what I want to say to my cousin and my dad." I'd spent the day getting David up to speed on everything that had happened since I last saw him in New York.

"Fair enough," he said. I had not answered the question he was really asking.

"I don't know about the 'us' part yet," I said. "But this date was pretty convincing, so I'd like to at least go on one more." David had brought a spoonful of gumbo over for me to taste. It was so good I closed my eyes. "Fine. At least two more."

"I took to heart what you said about rushing into things," David said. "I don't want to do that with you."

I considered that for a long moment before responding. "I think I've been afraid of my instincts for a very long time. I don't want to be afraid anymore."

With that in mind, I stood up from my stool, crossed the room, and grabbed David for a long kiss. He lifted me up into his arms, lips still pressed against mine, then started walking me out of the kitchen. I considered protesting—he'd just made an amazing meal, the stove was maybe still on—but my body was screaming too loud to let any other part of me get a word in edgewise.

Three hours later David and I enjoyed a delicious late-night bowl of gumbo in bed.

★ ★ ★

"Hey, what happened with that podcast?" David asked as he drove me to the airport later the next day.

Mikey had emailed shortly after my train wreck recording

to say they couldn't use the episode, understandably. But David's question reminded me that I'd left a lot of people hanging as far as the Star Twin Survey was concerned. For the entire flight back to New Jersey, I thought about where I'd started and ended. It now seemed ridiculous to try to prove or disprove the legitimacy of astrology. But I had stumbled my way into a captive audience. What did I want to leave them with? That question suddenly unlocked an idea. I emailed Nate Rosemont as soon as I landed. By the time I was back home, he'd confirmed that, yes, his funeral speech of Heidi's had been recorded and, yes, I was welcome to explore making it public. Twenty-four hours later, I was sent a cut of an *Andi Hour* episode featuring my blowup and Nova's response, then a newly recorded section from me. In it, I said what I'd learned about how pieces of who we really are can be hidden by who we think we need to be, using the details of my own story as proof. But I gave the last words to Heidi. Nate texted as I was listening. I'd sent it to him for final approval.

It's perfect. Okay if I send it to her cousin who recorded the video?

My heart pinged as I replied yes. Then I sent the episode directly off to my own cousin for a listen, hoping it would help us start to find our way back.

Chapter
Thirty-Seven

CHARLOTTE HUGGED ME tight the second I was within arm's reach of her on the boardwalk.

"I'm so sorry for everything," she said. I felt her warm tears against the skin of my neck.

"Thank you," I said, giving her an extra squeeze. "Me too."

"Can we walk down by the waterline?" she asked, not bothering to wipe her eyes before grabbing my hand.

"Of course," I said.

We strolled for just a few minutes, enjoying the emptiness of early evening at the beach. Charlotte rambled about anything but what I imagined she'd brought me here to say. I held back sharing more, wanting to give her the floor.

"Was there something you wanted to tell me, Charlotte?" I finally asked, done sitting in the discomfort of pretending.

"There is," she said, dragging a toe through the sand, stalling. Finally, she turned to me, still silent but with an anxiety I knew all too well in her eyes.

"Omigod, really?" My hands clenched with joy.

Charlotte nodded, maybe happier that we were back to communicating telepathically than that she'd just "told" me she was pregnant.

I wrapped her into another massive hug. "Congrats! When are you due? How are you feeling?"

"I'm feeling . . . um, a lot," she said. "And I'm due in early April."

I knew that math like the back of my hand. "You've been pregnant since July," I said, face falling. "You didn't tell me."

She shook her head, guilty. "Even though I took your advice after our conversation back in May. But when it happened I just felt so far from you, Leah. And then—sorry—but you did a bunch of things that made me feel even further and—I don't know. I wanted everything to be like I'd always imagined it would be, and it wasn't."

"I can relate," I said, looking down the beach to one of the lifeguard stands we'd spent hours climbing around on as kids. "But I don't think trying to force that was going to work for either of us."

Charlotte shook her head, but I saw a familiar twinge of guilt across her face. "I still regret so many things I said to you, Leah."

"I know," I said. "I do, too. But we were both in very new territory. We weren't exactly raised to put ourselves first."

Charlotte cocked her head, unsure what I meant. I understood that reaction, too. "For another day," I said.

I looked up to see a figure walking toward us on the sand. Charlotte clocked him a second later.

"Have you two spoken since California?" she asked.

"Just about work," I said, nerves running up my arms.

"Are you ready to talk to him now?"

I nodded, then shook my head.

Dad had fishing rods in one hand and his dad's green canvas army bag full of supplies in the other, headed to the marina for his favorite evening unwind. His eyes narrowed, then he waved, finally recognizing us in the distance.

"I can wait up on the boardwalk, be there when you finish talking," Charlotte offered.

"Thank you," I said. "But I'll be okay. Call you tomorrow?"

She nodded, squeezed me tight, then started walking up the beach. I moved toward my dad, body tightening with every second closing the gap between us.

"Doctor. How are you?" he asked, shaking my hand. It felt so formal today.

"Not great right now," I said. "But I think I'll be better after I talk to you."

I couldn't tell whether or not he felt the same. We walked to the jetty, small-talking about which fish would be biting now that the sun was setting. By the time we sat down, I couldn't wait a second longer.

"I have to say some things that will be hard to hear, Dad," I started.

"I've been thinking you might," he said.

"I'm not sure I want to run the practice moving forward." I'd said it quickly, our rip–off–the–Band-Aid approach.

My dad's eyes darted. "Because of how I reacted to your ideas?"

"Not entirely," I said, shocked by how easily these words were coming.

"I don't understand. You want to hire someone else to run things so you can do more outside the practice?"

"No. And I don't want to stop working immediately. But I don't think that I'm meant to make our practice my legacy. There are different things I want to do with my life as a Dr. Lockhart."

"And you can't do them here?"

That had been the hardest question to answer for myself, but the more I'd thought about my future, the more I'd realized that I couldn't expand my life to meet the new scope of my dreams while running LWM.

"Not right now," I said. It wasn't black and white. That uncertainty still made my stomach churn a little, but I knew it would sit even more uncomfortably with my dad.

Panic landed on his face. "What are we going to do? Just . . . let the practice die? It's who we are." There was a time when hearing that would have brought me to the brink of my own panic. But what I was saying felt so simple and true to me that it was like I was wearing some kind of protective layer.

"It's part of who we are," I said. "But I need to go be who I am."

My dad fiddled with the worn edge of his fishing rod, leaving a tense silence between us. Then he finally asked the question I'd been anticipating most. "Did your mother convince you to do this?"

I took a breath. *No holding back.* "No, but she did help me finally take a look at our past. And I think that would be good for you to do, too."

His forehead wrinkled and flattened over and over. "So does all this mean you've been lying about what you wanted all these years?"

For this, I stole from one final exchange with Nova in which I'd asked a version of that same question. He'd answered in precisely my dad's and my language.

"Remember, there are three layers to the wall protecting the human heart," I repeated now.

I wasn't sure how that would land with my dad, but his face finally softened. "I thought it was my job to give it even more protection than that," he said. It stunned me to quick tears.

"I know," I said, letting them fall. "But I actually need your help breaking down what's already there."

That earned a classic Dr. Peter Lockhart nod of understanding, then he finally handed me one of the fishing rods. We caught three striped bass in an hour, lit by the same lanterns David and I had used down at the creek. Neither of us needed to do any more talking for now.

"Come over, and I'll grill these up," Dad said, packing the gear.

"How about tomorrow?" I asked. "I'd like to stay here for a bit longer tonight."

"Sure," he replied, dropping one lantern beside me to keep. After a moment, he leaned over and gave my shoulder a long, tight squeeze, his version of a very big hug. It warmed me from the inside out, but it was not the right mark on this moment. My arm reached out for our traditional shake, except when I opened my mouth it wasn't *Doctor* that came out.

"Dad," I said, offering my hand. He was as surprised as me at first. Then he nodded, certain.

"Leah," he said, shaking back as firmly as ever.

After, I walked out to the very end of the jetty. I sat down on a rock smoothed over by the hundreds of people who had done the same before me—many of them Lockharts, I'm sure. Then I lay back and stared up at the sky, and I did not look away until the stars finally started to glimmer at me from above.

Epilogue

March 2023

IT WAS ONLY my fourth time speaking, but data proved that if I sat at the edge of the stage after I finished, people were more inclined to ask questions. This group in Virginia was no exception. Over the next half hour, I answered everything from specific questions about prenatal vitamins and fertility windows to generic queries about irregular cycles and birth control. Nothing was off the table, as I'd explained in my kick-off speech about who I was and why I'd parked a fuchsia-painted van outside this building advertising free OB-GYN appointments. The fuchsia was part of my arrangement with the women's athleisure-wear brand sponsoring my East Coast tour. The van was a tricked-out mobile doctor's office built by my uncle, decorated by my cousin, and outfitted with supplies courtesy of my dad's practice. Or *former* practice. Dr. Eva Moreno had just taken over what would remain Lockhart

Women's Medical. I'd gotten her settled for two weeks, then left to prep for this adventure.

While I could not see more than six months down the road, some long-term dreams had started to materialize. One involved raising kids with David, maybe in New Orleans to start, then back up in the Highlands once Stella fully left the nest. Another included working abroad at some point. And I had a vision for cohosting a retreat for doctors with Imani, maybe at my mom's favorite yoga center in California. For now, though, I was focused on serving communities of women who needed care across a country that felt foreign to me given how seldom I'd left New Jersey. And I was equally intent on filling my hours outside that work with all the things that made me whole, chief among them time in my fabulous birthday roller skates.

"I think we have time for one last question," the councilwoman who'd helped coordinate my visit announced to the group. A hand raised tentatively in the back row.

"Hi. Yes. Go ahead," I said.

"I don't know if this is okay to ask about, but I read about that whole astrology project you did last year . . ."

I'd wondered if this was ever going to come up. "Sure. You can ask me anything," I said. "Unless it's about your sign, because, I'm sorry, I only know about mine. Leos are a little self-centered like that."

The group laughed. One among them extra loud. A fellow Leo. "No, I was just wondering if you believe in astrology now," the woman said.

It was a question I'd asked myself many times since all that had unfolded the year prior. Logically, no amount of research could ever prove that the movement of the planets and stars guided our lives down on Earth, but in the end, I'm not sure that was the point. At least for me.

"I don't think astrology is something you need to believe in," I finally said. "But I do think it offers a path to believe in yourself."

Acknowledgments

Completing this book was the most challenging and rewarding experience of my writing career. My village showed up for me in countless ways throughout and, maybe more importantly, helped me learn how to truly show up for myself.

Thank you first to the group of women that literally brought this book into existence—my Putnam, CAA, and Haven Entertainment families.

Kate Dresser, you are a writer's dream: an editor with equal parts enthusiasm and calm. Thank you for being my second (Leo!) brain in the true trenches of this project. I'd write books just to have calls about them with you. Thanks also to Tarini Sipahimalani for expertly keeping all trains on schedule with the most personal approach.

I wrote this manuscript while the rest of the incredible team at Putnam was launching my debut novel. Thank you, Nicole Biton, Alexis Welby, Ashley McCabe, Molly Pieper, and their expert crews for handling that with so much care and confidence. Alexis, I will never forget you gushing over PR ideas for *All the Signs* at the book launch for *The Heirloom!* And special thanks to Sanny Chiu, whose cover design is once again stunning.

Kathleen Carter turned publicity into the most fun and energizing part of my author experience. Her efficiency and expertise are bar none, but it's her honesty I've come to appreciate most—the best Jersey-girl quality.

I am so lucky to call Mollie Glick my agent, which in her rarest of cases means dear friend and biggest champion. Mollie, I feel your care through every call, and it trickles down into every writing session.

Thank you also to the CAA team guiding my career forward in so many categories: Sarah Harvey, Gabby Fetters, Berni Vann, Kate Childs, Via Romano, and all those who work among them.

For twelve years, Rachel Miller has been by my side from the first to last moment of every project. With this one she ping-ponged between manager, therapist, friend, life coach, nutritionist, and spiritual advisor. Rachel, every time you say, "You've got this," my confidence grows Grinch-heart style. Thank you to my fam with her at Haven Entertainment, especially Jesse Hara and Cole Friedman.

This book required a dizzying amount of research, but I loved every moment because it meant time with the brilliant minds of Joshua MacGuire, Mariel Schlesinger, Alexander Boxer, Liz Leiby, Mikey Land, and the one-and-only Paul Flanagan (where it all began). Thanks also to Chani Nicholas for her book *You Were Born for This* and very helpful app.

For story inspiration I want to thank the many Star Twins I met in my own version of Leah's journey. I also want to acknowledge the many dear friends that have been formative to this story: my Los Angeles writing sisters (plus Ally in New York!), my Boston College girls, Jenny Anderson, Melissa Cassera, Mike (Michael) Monroe, and Michael (Mike) Hundgen.

Life oddly imitated art on this project (I came down with everything but vertigo!), so thanks also to the people that took care of my mind and body: Rebecca Gendry, Noelle Mercer, Dina Amado, Majd Ali, and Jessica Walker.

Once again, my sister-cousin Geanna Barlaam held my hand through every draft, reading, and editing with the same eyes I've trusted since day one. Thank you for being the exact opposite of Charlotte.

This book is dedicated to my parents—Angie and Nat Rosen—with a cheeky nod to the fact that they're responsible for my astrological chart. But even a total devotee of astrology cannot deny the effects of nurture, and I received just what I needed to end up living out my dreams. Thank you. And thank you, also, for being the source of my home team support system: my sisters Dani, Sara, and Alex and their growing families. Also my aunts, Louisa Barlaam and Geanna Merola, and uncle Erik Landsberg. But especially my uncle Richard Barlaam, in whose loving memory this book is also dedicated. He was the original writer of the family.

Louie, thank you for the nap company, always. And last and most, Robby. I have never needed more support. You gave above and beyond it all, once again making my success your priority. Thank you for loving me exactly as I was meant to be.

About the Author

JESSIE ROSEN got her start with the award-winning blog *20-Nothings* and has sold original television projects to ABC, CBS, Warner Bros., and Netflix. Her live storytelling show *Sunday Night Sex Talks* was featured on *The Bachelorette*. She is also the author of *The Heirloom*, and lives in Los Angeles.

JessieRosen.com
@jessierosenwriter